I0670917

First edition August 2025

ISBN   979-8-9921513-2-9   (paperback)
ISBN   979-8-9921513-3-6   (ebook)

Ugly Beauty

by Sarah Zee

One

Bethany approached the brick building on North 13th Street. She'd just ended a call with Cam and looked up to see his tall skinny frame waiting at the entrance as promised, his out-of-control, dark, wiry hair standing out in all directions.

"It's early enough that you might not even see anyone else," he said as they entered the building.

Bethany followed him down a short hallway where he opened the door to a very small, florescent-lit, windowless room covered in white, fine fissured tiles.

"Thanks, Cam," Bethany said. "This is really helpful."

"No problem at all," Cam said. "I'm a rare breed of music major: the early riser. Only a few of us around. But now that you know how to get here, come by any morning you want. No one's gonna hassle you. Not like you aren't a student here anyway."

Bethany was a sophomore at Temple University, but a theater major. Fortunately, she'd recently become friends with Cam, a music major who was able to show her to the practice rooms. She was in dire need of private practice space.

"Well, I'll leave you to it," he said, offering a smile before shutting the door behind himself.

The closet-sized room felt stuffy. Bethany removed the plaid button-down shirt she'd been wearing over her navy blue tank top, and tied it over the waistband of her cutoffs. She adjusted the music stand to suit her 5'9" height and set her sheet music on it. She tightened and rosined her bow, attached her shoulder rest, and tuned her violin. Finally, she pulled her long dark curls back into an elastic, and warmed up with a few scales.

After rummaging through the sheet music, she selected her piece and began. She'd only played through the first sixteen measures when there was a knock at the door. Bethany froze.

"Shostakovich?" a male voice asked through the door.

"Yes," she answered, dropping her bow arm.

"Can I play second?"

"I'm just learning the *Prelude* now."

"It sounds great. I want in."

Annoyed, she set her violin in its case on the floor and opened the door to face the pushy violinist. Instantaneously, her irritation melted away. He stood only a few inches taller than Bethany, and had a slighter build than she typically liked in a man, but his bright sparkling blue eyes, boxy chin, and messy dirty blonde hair made up for it.

"Hi," she said.

"Hey," he responded, pushing past her into the tight practice room. He crouched down, setting his violin case beside hers, and began unpacking and preparing his instrument. "How ya doin'?" he asked, peeking up at her. "I'm Klaus Aufderheide."

"Sounds very German."

"Yeah," he said. "Well, my grandparents are anyway."

"I'm Bethany."

"Bethany..?"

"Bethany Schechter."

He turned, standing, and grinned at her.

"Sounds very Jewish."

"Yeah. Grandparents…"

Klaus quickly tuned up.

"Ya ready to go, Bethany Schechter?" he asked, moving to stand across from her.

"Okay."

"Let's take it slow, like uh, uh, uh, uh," he said, snapping his fingers.

"Okay," she repeated quietly, admiring his vibrant blue eyes again. "Do you need sheet music?"

"Nah, I'm good," he said transferring his bow to his right hand.

They lifted their violins, and Klaus counted off. Right away, Bethany was mesmerized by the sound they created together as she did her best to match his style. She wished she could watch him but had to keep her eyes on the page. His tone was strong and focused, dark and deep.

Forest green velvet.

She worked hard to evenly coat each of his notes in her own warm syrupy sound. Looking up, she caught a glimpse of his strong but slender hand creating a perfect vibrato, causing her face to flush. She fought to maintain focus, still striving to mimic his style. When they finally reached the end, she sat in the single chair in the corner of the tiny room, pulling her long hair from the elastic, hoping to hide her cheeks in case they appeared just as pink as they felt.

"Wow," he said quietly. "Your tone… It's like a crystalline golden amber. Warm honey."

She looked up to find him staring at her.

"Gorgeous," he said.

"Thanks," she said softly. "Yours is too."

"Let's go again," he said. "Little faster. Uh, uh, uh, uh."

Bethany stood, nodding. Klaus counted off. Again, she worked to match his style. The experience was much more intimate this time as she was able to anticipate his moves, fusing to each of his velvety notes. He had moved a bit off to one side in order to see around the music stand. She could feel him watching her and could feel her face growing even warmer. When they finished, she sat again, looking down to avoid his eyes.

"Damn, girl," Klaus said. "You're so pocket."

She smiled, looking up at him. He whistled.

"And that tone…" he said. "I think I'm in love."

She dropped her eyes downward again.

"One more time… a little faster. Uh, uh, uh, uh."

"Okay," she said, her voice coming out just above a whisper as she rose from the chair again.

He counted off, and again, they began. It was a much more beautiful, much more moving piece than Bethany had initially realized. She knew it was meant to include a piano, but they were making magic all on their own.

They were just reaching the ¾ section when there was a loud knock at the door. Abruptly, they both stopped. The door swung open. It was another student. He had long brown hair pulled into a ponytail and a bumpy red complexion. He looked upset.

"What's up, Lonnie?"

"Sorry, Klaus. There's been a… I don't know… a plane crash."

"What?"

"A plane… an airplane flew into the World Trade Center in New York."

"Huh," Klaus said. "That's… kinda crazy."

Still caught off guard by the disruption, Bethany hadn't yet made sense of the words.

"You from New York?" Klaus asked her.

"Uh-huh," she said.

Klaus's eyes widened at her response.

"Oh, shit," said Lonnie.

"Another plane crashed into the other tower!" a voice shouted from the hall.

"Oh, shit!" Lonnie repeated before disappearing into the hall, letting the door close behind him. Bethany sat in the chair again.

8

"Do you have people there?" Klaus asked.

"My grandmother, but she's in Brooklyn," Bethany said. "I'm sure she's fine."

"Okay," Klaus said. "Well… um… You wanna use my phone?"

He held a cell phone out to her.

"That's okay. I have one."

"Cool," Klaus said, returning the phone into the back pocket of his jeans. "I don't um…" he paused to shrug. "I don't know what to make of this."

"I guess a lot of people are dead," Bethany said.

"Yeah. Shit."

"Shit."

"Yeah."

They stood in silence a moment.

"So, um… You wanna just finish the *Prelude*?" she asked.

Klaus grinned at her, looking her up and down.

"You're not a music major. I'd definitely remember you. Where'd you come from?"

"I'm a theater major," Bethany said. "I just needed a place to practice."

"Sweet," Klaus said. "Will you be practicing here again?"

Bethany looked Klaus over. He raised an eyebrow. His lips curved into a slight smirk, his eye contact unwavering.

Confidence.

"Yes," she answered decidedly.

"From the top. Let's go. Uh, uh, uh, uh…"

Two

There'd been a small flurry of people outside on campus. Most students, professors, and staff seemed to gather in buildings near televisions. Bethany briefly stopped to watch the news with a crowd in the lobby of the Student Activity Center. They showed footage of the airplane crashing into the tower, then another into the second tower. They showed the towers smoking, people dropping to their deaths from the windows, mobs running down the city streets as the first tower came tumbling straight to the ground. They showed it all again and again and again. People stood around the lobby, staring in horror, sobbing, embracing, speaking in hushed voices.

"Bethany," someone said behind her.

She turned to see Jared Isaacs, a fellow theater major. She was regularly paired for scene work with Jared because of his height. Despite being the perfect tall, dark, and handsome type, and a talented actor to boot, Jared always managed to rub Bethany the wrong way. She wasn't able to pinpoint what it was about him that irritated her, but regularly found herself focusing on the stray wisps of his longish dark hair that were always falling into his eyes. His dark eyelashes were long enough to bat around the stray wisps, which Bethany found distracting.

"Hey, Jared."

"Shit, aren't you from New York?"

"Yeah, Brooklyn."

"Oh, my God," he said, sounding horrified. "Is your family safe?!"

"Yeah. Brooklyn, Jared. I'm from Brooklyn, not Manhattan."

"Still…" he said, resting a hand on her shoulder, "I'm really sorry."

"Heartfelt delivery," she said, grimacing at his touch.

Jared pulled his hand away, looking as though he'd been slapped. He often reacted that way, which only made Bethany want to continue being mean.

She turned to leave.

"Hey, wait" Jared said, touching her shoulder again, then quickly retracting his hand. "Can I walk you?"

"I'm just going to my car. I need to get home."

"You live off campus, right?" he asked, his eyelashes batting against his hair.

"Right, Jared," she said, "That's why I need my car."

"Right. Sorry," he said, pushing the hair from his eyes. "Can I walk you to your car?"

Bethany stood blinking at him, unable to think of a reason to say no.

"Sure," she responded tightly, turning again to leave.

It was sunny and clear outside. Bethany might have enjoyed the walk if not for Jared.

Just what does he want anyway?

"So, I was thinking—" Jared began. "Hey, is that a violin?"

"Good eye."

"Do you play?"

"No, but don't you think it makes me look talented?"

"Are you..? Do you..? Anyway…" he said with a slight shake of his head. "Are you free to rehearse later this week? I know you probably want to be with family for a while, but I was thinking maybe Friday for a cold reading and blocking, then rehearsal over the weekend?"

"Okay. I have Friday after Theater 100, and all day Saturday."

"Excellent. Basement of Tomlinson, Friday after Theater 100?"

"Sure."

"Um… Saturday, you could come to my place if you want."

"Sure," she said again.

"I'm in Northern Liberties now."

"Cool."

"Um… Have you looked over the scene?" he asked.

"Not yet."

"Oh. Um… There's a… Well… in the second act, there's a… there's a um…"

Bethany stopped walking and turned to look at Jared.

"What is it, Jared?" she asked impatiently.

Jared shuffled his feet around and looked at her through the wisps of hair.

"There's a kiss," he finally managed.

Bethany had already read the scene. She knew there was a kiss. She also knew Jared was going to make it awkward. She didn't really know why, but she almost enjoyed watching him squirm. It repulsed her, but she wanted to watch it anyway, much like the people standing around the televisions now, watching airplanes fly into buildings again and again and again, sickened, but unable to turn away.

"So, you want to rehearse that first?" she asked.

"Well, no, I just—"

"A lot? You wanna rehearse it a lot, Jared? Again and again and again?" she asked, stepping closer to him, staring up through his hair into his widening hazel green eyes.

"Bethany, I… Well, I just thought… I only wanted to…"

Bethany moved closer, backing Jared against the brick building. She leaned a hand on either side of him, lifted onto her toes, closed her eyes, and tilted her face back.

"Go ahead," she said. "Make it look real."

"Bethany…" he said just above a whisper.

She opened her eyes to catch Jared staring at her lips before raising his eyes to meet hers.

Fear.

"I have to get to my car," she said with an eye roll, turning to walk again.

"Okay," he said. "I um… I'll see you Friday!" he called after her.

Finally, Bethany reached her Dodge Neon. The yellow paint had peeled off nearly half the car, but the mileage was low for a 7-year-old car, and in the ten months she'd owned it, it had never given her any real trouble. Sitting in the driver's seat, she tried calling home, but the call wouldn't go through.

She drove out of the parking lot onto Diamond Street, then made a right onto Broad Street, and another right onto Dauphin to drive into her Kensington neighborhood. She lived on a quiet church block of East Cumberland Street just outside of Fishtown, but it was close enough to the roughness that she still came out to a smashed car window every once in a while.

Bethany opened the front door of 2155, the only two-story in a row of three-story homes. She stepped into the small alcove, then unlocked her apartment door and went upstairs.

"That you?" Killian called out.

"Yup," she called back, setting her violin on the living room floor.

She walked to the kitchen, pulled a bottle of Three Olives vodka out of the freezer, opened it, and took a swig.

"Holy shit," Killian said, coming into the kitchen. He swung Bethany around and held her, pressing his cheek to her forehead.

"Hey, Pretty," Bethany said.

"Where the hell have you been?" Killian asked.

"School."

"You don't have a Tuesday class."

"I was meeting a friend."

"On a Tuesday morning? I was worried. It's like the end of the world out there. The phones aren't even working."

He let her go. She offered him the bottle.

"It's like 11 AM," he said, making a face.

"It's the end of the world," Bethany said with a shrug.

Killian grabbed the bottle, took a sip, then replaced the cap, and put it back in the freezer. Bethany wandered into the living room and sat on the dark green recliner, closing her eyes, leaning her head back. Killian followed her, standing in front of the recliner.

"Did you hear about the Pentagon, and the plane shot down in Pennsylvania?"

"Yup," she said.

He stared down at Bethany. She looked up at him. He was still in his pajamas: a white t-shirt and a pair of gray sweatpants. Bethany enjoyed looking at Killian. He was tall and muscular with thick, wavy, shoulder-length golden blonde hair. His broad forehead topped a perfectly straight nose, a strong, square jawline, and the most beautifully cleft chin she'd ever seen. Bethany found his eyes to be his most mesmerizing feature though. They were a deep blue with tiny gold rings circling the pupils. She'd never seen another pair like them.

Strangers regularly approached Killian to encourage him to go into modeling. Having been his roommate for over a year now, Bethany knew Killian understood the effect he had on women, but she also knew he would much rather sit in his room, reading all day, or be locked in the chemistry lab at school than be out getting admired for his looks. He made rent tending bar in Old City, and there were those occasional nights when he wouldn't make it home, but he was always back before Bethany woke in the morning.

"You're not upset?" he asked.

She shrugged. "What good would it do?"

"I don't know," he said, hoisting Bethany out of the recliner in order to sit and pull her onto his lap. "None. I guess I just thought you might be upset."

"I'm kind of upset," she said, leaning back on him. "I have a kissing scene with Jared Isaacs."

"You wanna practice on me instead?"

She turned, giving him a half smile, then dropped her head back against his shoulder.

"I want to stop getting paired up with Jared Isaacs. I had three scenes with him last semester. Three out of five. He's not the only tall guy in class."

"I still don't get why you hate him so much. You said he's a talented actor."

"He is," she said. "And I don't hate him. I just—"

"Just?"

"I don't know," she shrugged. "He bothers me."

Bethany started to stand. Killian pulled her back to him.

"Sit with me a while."

He folded his arms over her. She rested her head back on his shoulder.

"Open the recliner then."

He tugged the lever on the side of the chair, opening the leg rest. Bethany snuggled into Killian, closing her eyes. They rested quietly for a few minutes.

"You brought your violin out with you this morning."

"Yeah," she said. "I had a friend show me the practice rooms in Presser Hall."

"Why?"

"To practice."

"You practice here."

"I know, but I like to practice in the morning."

"So? I like waking to it."

"I need to practice alone sometimes."

"Away from me?"

"Yes, away from you. Playing when someone else is listening is different from practicing alone. You get that, right?"

"Yeah, okay," he said. "I'll miss it though."

"I'll still play for you whenever you want. I'll just sound better when I do because I'll have actually practiced."

Killian turned Bethany's head toward him, puckering his lips at her. She gave his lips a quick peck.

"I should try to call Bubbie," she said. "I have reading to do for Physics too."

"Alright. I'm gonna check the news. I'll let you know if there's anyone left out there. Maybe they've all been killed off, and you and I are the only survivors."

"That wouldn't be so bad, would it?" she asked, standing.

"It would be a significant upgrade for me," said Killian.

Three

"Bubbie!"

"Oh, Bethany… I'm so glad you called!"

"I tried to call earlier, but the phones weren't working."

"Where are you, Bethala?"

"I'm at home, in Philly. Did you see?"

"Did I *see*?! Oy vey iz mir, I *heard* the first one. I was watching it smoke like a giant farkakte chimney, and then the second plane crashed. I watched it all from the balcony window. The sky is all brown and gray now. I'm staying inside. Your zayde died with the emphysema, you know. I'm glad he isn't alive to see this. We watched those towers go up before you were born. It took years. From this very same window, we watched."

"How are you feeling?" Bethany asked. "Do you think you're safe there?"

"Eh… Where else would I go?"

"You can come stay with Killian and me in Philadelphia."

"You want I should stay in a house with my granddaughter and her shegetz boyfriend?"

"I told you, he's just my roommate, Bubbie. And he's really nice. You'd like him."

"Sure, sure… Bethala, you're 20 years old…soon enough, 21. Find a nice boy, ye? Ease your bubbie's mind."

"I'll keep an eye out, Bubbie."

"That college campus must be crawling with nice boys. Don't you want nice children?"

"Of course, Bubbie," Bethany said. "You're sure you won't come stay with us?"

"Nah, nah… I'm staying put. I've got everything I need right here."

"Okay. I love you, Bubbie."

"I love you too, Bethala. You know I only want what's right for you. You marry a man who understands you, and you have children you'll know how to raise together. This is what's done. How's your weight?"

"Hundred and forty-two."

"Good, good. Stay mindful. Stay trim. Over one-fifty, you'll be too bosomy...zaftig, even for a tall girl like you. And you don't want to try to take it off after you have babies. Vos m'iz geveynt af der yugent, azoy tut men af der elter."

"I know, Bubbie. I'll stay mindful."

"Alright, bubeleh. Next time, call collect."

"Okay, Bubbie. B'bye."

"Dray zahkn shatn keyn mol nisht: shlof, bronfn, un a bod. Zay gezunt."

Bethany hung up the phone and climbed onto her bed with her physics textbook. She read through the first couple pages before Killian appeared in the doorway.

"Talk to Bubbie?" he asked.

"Yes. She's fine."

"Good," he said. "Maybe she should come here when she's able. The news is reporting poor air quality in Brooklyn."

"I offered. She won't."

He glanced down at the floor a moment. "Is that because of me?"

"No, of course not. She doesn't like to leave New York. It's all she knows."

He nodded then disappeared from the doorway. Bethany heard him enter the bathroom and turn on the shower. She knew if she kept watch, within the next 15 minutes or so, she'd be able to steal a glimpse of Killian passing by, wearing only a towel around his waist. She waited.

Four

Bethany got up early again on Wednesday morning, unable to decide if she hoped to find the practice rooms deserted or not. She showered, combed Infusium 23 Leave-In Treatment through her hair, then left it to air dry. She dressed in a pair of cutoffs and a white t-shirt, grabbed her backpack, and headed toward the living room.

Passing through the kitchen, she gasped, startled to see Killian sitting at the table.

"Sorry," he said, wincing. He set his spoon beside his bowl of cereal, "I didn't mean to spook you."

"You're up early," she said.

"Couldn't sleep."

"Oh," she said. "Are you okay? I should have asked you that yesterday."

"Yeah," he said. "Like you said, doesn't help to get upset. I guess it's just weird to think about."

"Yeah. Still, I'm sorry."

"For what?"

"You know… for… overlooking your feelings," she said. "I'm not as sensitive as I ought to be."

"You're exactly as you ought to be, Bethany. I wouldn't want you any other way.

Bethany smiled at him. He cleared his throat, picked up his bowl and spoon, and carried them to the sink.

"Leaving early again, huh?"

"Yeah."

He sighed. "Play for me soon, okay?"

"Of course."

"Today?"

"Sure. This evening after my physics class."

"I'll be looking forward to it then."

She went to the living room, slipped into her Keds, grabbed her violin, and headed down the stairs.

*** * * ***

As she approached Presser Hall, Bethany spotted Klaus sitting outside on a bench. He was dressed in a pale green t-shirt and jeans, his violin case on the ground in front of his feet. He stood up, smiling, as he watched her approach.

"Hey!"

"Hey."

"You need to warm up?"

"Uh, yeah."

"Alright. I'll go get breakfast and come back. Can I bring you a coffee?"

"No, thanks. I don't drink coffee."

"Muffin?"

"No, I'm fine."

"Alright. See ya soon."

Bethany hurried into a practice room and began practicing scales. She pulled out her Bach Double sheet music and began playing through the first movement, 1st violin. It felt so good to practice alone. She loved playing for Killian. He was a genuinely appreciative audience, and she was mostly comfortable with him hearing her make mistakes. But it wasn't the same as practicing just for herself. She needed this.

After the first movement, she went right into the second. She played through the second movement, repeating a small trouble spot a few times before finishing, then sat, waiting for Klaus.

After a moment, there was a knock and the door opened.

"You play any jazz?" Klaus asked, entering the small room.

"No. I like jazz, but I've never played any."

"Well, you're gonna start today," Klaus said, unpacking his violin.

Bethany looked up at him.

"Don't be scared. You'll love it."

"I'm not scared."

"Good," he said. "We're starting with the Mixolydian mode."

She stared blankly.

"It's just a flat 7. Intervals are whole, whole, half, whole, whole, half, whole," Klaus said.

He played a G Major scale with an F natural. Bethany played the scale back.

"Right," he said. "Give it to me in C."

Bethany played a C Major scale with a B flat.

"Give it to me in A."

Bethany played an A Major scale with a G natural.

"Perfect. Um… We need chords. Hold on," Klaus said, setting his violin in the case.

He opened the door, sticking his head out into the hall.

"Cam!"

"Yo."

"Guitar."

Soon, Cam entered the tiny room, carrying an acoustic guitar.

"Bethany, this is Cam," Klaus started.

"I know Bethany," Cam said.

"Cam's the one who brought me here," Bethany explained.

"Well done," Klaus said, patting Cam on the back. "Have you heard her play yet?"

"Uh… just a little now in the hall," Cam said. "Sounds good."

"Give us an E Dominant," Klaus said.

Cam played the chord.

"Groove on it," Klaus said.

Cam played rhythmically.

"Now, play the mode," Klaus instructed Bethany.

She did.

"Your guide tones are the third and seventh. Play around with the notes, emphasizing the third and seventh."

She sat, unsure of what to do. Klaus picked up his violin.

"Like this," he said.

He soloed over Cam, applying some interesting rhythms, then dropped his bow arm.

"You. Go."

Bethany lifted her bow and played, repeating exactly what Klaus had played.

"So pocket," he said, grinning. "Gimme a gliss."

He played through a similar melody, adding some glissandos here and there. Bethany again lifted her bow and parroted him.

"That's so fuckin' hot," he said, staring at her. "Alright, play your own thing now."

Bethany could feel her nerves setting in. She placed her bow on the strings, but didn't know how to begin.

"C'mon. Go for it."

She sat frozen, looking from Klaus to Cam, feeling her cheeks turn pink, unable to play a note. She dropped her bow arm.

"Do it," Klaus said, nodding encouragingly. "Play."

Bethany lifted her bow, but still found herself unable to move. Klaus stared a moment, then lifted his bow and began playing again. He stopped and waited for Bethany. Again, she echoed Klaus, then rested.

"Alright. Good," Klaus said. "Thanks, Cam. Gonna be around later?"

"I'm always around," Cam said, standing and leaving the practice room.

"I'm sorry," Bethany said, flustered.

"Sorry for what? Don't be sorry. Your tone is like sex. All the technique is already there. You just need to gain some solo confidence. You've got things to say; you just don't know it yet. I'm gonna have Cam record some stuff for you. We'll start with a basic 12-bar blues. You have a tape player at home?"

"Um… yeah."

"But I guess you're at the practice rooms because you can't practice at home?"

"Kind of."

"I'm gonna keep pushing you, but it seems to me like you need some space for this, just some time to fuck around by yourself," he said.

"It's not really that I can't practice at home. I just like to practice in the morning, but my roommate is home then."

"So, this'll be your night music. Practice whenever you can get alone time."

"Okay."

"Just stick with Mixolydian for now," he said. "I'll get the tape to you tomorrow morning. You'll be here?"

Bethany nodded, smiling. "I'll be here."

Five

Intro to Physics was taught by a small, balding Indian man with a thick accent, named Dr. Zameer Hasan. It was only the second day of his class, but Bethany had decided she liked this professor right away. He was funny and entertaining. She could tell he truly cared about what he was teaching and seemed to have a passion for teaching itself.

She liked the lively way he spoke about "*Copper-NEE-cus,*" and his physical demonstrations of concepts. One that he'd given during the first class on centrifugal force had him spinning round and round on a swivel stool atop the raised platform at the front of the classroom. He'd also mentioned that buying the textbook might be helpful but was not a requirement, and although he encouraged students to bring their friends for fun discussions of the properties of physics or just to listen in, attendance was not mandatory.

Bethany had opted to buy the text and follow along with the reading. She also planned to attend every class. The classroom was a huge, dimly lit lecture hall with tiered seating. She sat way up toward the back, in the dark, far away from all of the other students who clustered up front. She was grateful to have a place where she could listen, watch, and learn, without any obligation to participate.

Only a small number of students had shown up to class, and Bethany wondered if people were skipping simply because they'd learned attendance wasn't mandatory, or because of the towers falling.

"Bethany Schechter," she heard someone say.

Bethany turned her head to see Elias Bruland. At the start of her freshman year, Bethany had been assigned a dorm with Shayla Colreavy, a short, fat, purple-haired girl who loved to talk about rape. Shayla helped organize *Take Back the Night* rallies and had started a new organization for student campus safety called *SheSafe*.

Bethany soon realized Shayla seemed to define just about any sexual encounter between a male and female as rape and had personally shouldered the responsibility of preventing it from happening any chance she got. She'd been vocally outraged at Bethany for declining to join her organization and refusing to participate in *Take Back the Night*. Bethany had soon begun looking for a way out of the dorms. But before she'd found it, she met Elias.

Elias had long golden red hair and a matching mustache and goatee. He was fair skinned with dark blue eyes surrounded by golden white lashes. He was unusual looking, but Bethany thought he looked like a sexy Viking; plus he was tall with good arms. They'd met at "the wall of food," a series of storefronts behind a brick facade, selling ethnically diverse fast food to students.

That day, Bethany had gotten herself a honeydew bubble tea and sat, memorizing lines, at one of the outdoor picnic tables. Elias had approached her to ask what on Earth she was drinking before inviting himself to sit at her table. Bethany had been intrigued enough that she'd sat with him nearly an hour before agreeing to exchange phone numbers.

When he'd called only a few hours later, Bethany invited him to her dorm room. She wasn't entirely sure if she'd done it because she was attracted to Elias, or as an affront to Shayla, but either way, she'd enjoyed every bit of that night.

"You never took any of my calls," Elias said, taking a seat beside her in the back of the dark lecture hall. "Did I do something wrong that night?"

"No, of course not. I'm sorry," Bethany said. "I just got busy, and well... I guess I kinda stayed busy. School and stuff."

"Okay," Elias said with a shrug. "Cool if I sit here?"

"Of course."

"This guy's kind of amusing," he said. "Were you here on the first day?"

"Yeah. I like him. I'm surprised so few people made it back."

"Yeah. The World Trade Center thing, probably. We're part of the handful of suckers who came to class today."

Dr. Hasan began class by announcing that he understood people not making it to class today, and because he didn't want those students to miss a lecture, he'd be showing a video. Bethany decided to leave.

"Well, at least it's a chill day," Elias said, stretching his arm around her.

Now, of course, she couldn't leave; not without being horribly rude to Elias, whom she'd already sort of ditched once.

"So," Elias said, looking over at her. "You gonna let me take you out sometime?"

"Oh… Sure."

"Cool," he said, wrapping his hand around her shoulder. "Hey, is that a violin?" he asked, looking at her case placed on the floor beside her.

"Yeah."

"Do you play?"

"Just for fun."

"I'd love to hear it sometime."

Bethany smiled at Elias, then tried turning her attention to the video. Only a few minutes had passed before Bethany felt Elias's other hand cupping her knee. He began slowly working his way up her bare thigh. His hand was warm and weighty. In a more private setting, she might have enjoyed his assertiveness, but the back of a lecture hall during class felt uncomfortably public to Bethany.

"Stop," she whispered to Elias.

"Why?" he whispered back, pausing his hand.

"Because."

Elias cocked his head. "That's not a very compelling argument," he said in her ear, moving his hand up another inch.

"Stop," she whispered again, looking over at him.

He stared back at her intently, glancing down at her legs, over her chest, then back at her face. She noticed him briefly bite his bottom lip.

Lust.

Elias leaned in and kissed her. She kissed him back but quickly pulled away, worried that someone would turn and see. Elias continued kissing her, moving to her neck. Bethany could feel the prickly tingles of desire setting in. Nervously, she glanced around at the students sitting way up front in the first few rows, then at Dr. Hasan, aside at his desk.

Suddenly, Elias went for it, sliding his hand all the way up her inner thigh. Bethany gasped loudly, slapping her hand down over his, creating a loud *SMACK*. Dr. Hasan looked up from his desk and all the students turned in their seats to look back at them. Feeling her face grow warm, Bethany began tugging her curls closer around her face.

"Is everything okay back there, miss?" Dr. Hasan asked, standing, shielding his eyes to better see her.

"Yes!" Bethany called back. "Yes, I'm sorry, I… I thought I was going to sneeze."

"Ah," said Dr. Hasan. "GES-und-HEIT, as they say."

This prompted a few giggles from the students who turned back around. Elias had covered his mouth and was shaking with silent laughter. Bethany was embarrassed, but still turned on, and also struggling not to laugh.

"Where are you living now?" Elias asked.

"Off-campus, over in Kensington."

"Sweet. You wanna get outta here?"

"I can't."

"Why not?"

"I have a roommate."

"What, that same crazy bitch?"

"No, someone else."

"So?"

"I can't."

"Well, come to my dorm then. I can get us some alone time."

"Tomorrow." Bethany said. "I can't today."

"How do I know you'll answer your phone tomorrow?"

"I will," she said, looking over at Elias.

"You better," he said. "Otherwise, next Wednesday, I'm gonna make you… sneeze… right here in front of the whole class."

Bethany pressed her lips tightly together, nodding. "Tomorrow," she agreed.

Elias nodded back.

Six

Bethany noticed Killian's green Jeep Cherokee parked at the corner, on the cobblestone of Trenton Avenue alongside the old beautiful brick church. Bethany had learned early on that, although it offered ample parking, the church provided a blind spot for thieves and all sorts of mischief. To avoid break-ins and vandalism, she began parking a block or so down. But Killian had decided the amenity was worth the gamble.

Bethany carried her backpack and violin inside. She dropped them at the top of the stairs and kicked her Keds off beside the closet before walking to the green recliner and dropping into it.

"Hey, you," Killian said, entering the living room.

He was wearing jeans and a black t-shirt. Bethany gazed up at him.

"Hey, Pretty."

He walked over, hoisted Bethany out of the recliner, then sat, pulling her onto his lap.

"How was physics?" he asked, pulling the lever to the recliner.

Bethany snuggled into Killian, closing her eyes, resting her head back on his shoulder.

"Good. Did you go to class today?"

"Just the lab."

"How was that?"

"It was good."

"You want me to play for you?"

"Yes, but sit with me a while first."

"If I sit here too long, I'll end up falling asleep."

"I like when that happens."

Bethany woke to a darkening room with Killian's arms gently folded over her. She tilted her head back to see him gazing down at her.

"Hey, you," he said.

"What time is it? Don't you have work?" she asked.

"Shhhh… There's time. I can see the kitchen clock from here. It's not even 7."

"You need to eat before you go in."

"I will. I'm just gonna make eggs. Want some?"

"Sounds good."

Killian kissed the top of her head, giving her a light squeeze before lifting his arms away and pushing the leg rest down. Bethany stood and went to the kitchen. He followed her and got the eggs from the refrigerator. She sat at the table, still fighting off the sleep inertia as Killian scrambled. After a few minutes, he seasoned the eggs with salt and pepper.

"So, I'm sorry I'll have to eat and run."

"That's totally my fault. Sorry you got trapped, listening to me snore."

"You don't snore," he said. "Well, not really anyway. You talk a little sometimes."

Bethany's jaw dropped. "What do I say?"

"You tell me all your secrets," he said, turning back with a smile.

Bethany shielded her eyes with her hand. "I don't want to know anymore."

"Good, because I'm not saying anymore." He grinned playfully before turning his back. "It's nothing. Don't worry about it."

He divided the eggs into two dishes, setting a plate of scrambled eggs before her and one across the small round table for himself. He ate quickly in silence. Once finished, he carried his plate to the sink then carried the pan over.

"Leave the dishes," Bethany said. "I'll get them."

"Thanks. I better head out."

"Sorry I didn't get a chance to play for you."

"No worries. Tomorrow?"

"Um… maybe. I might have to be somewhere."

"Alright. We'll play it by ear," Killian said, pulling his sneakers on in the living room. "I'll see ya," he said with a smile.

"See ya, Pretty."

Seven

The nap had thrown Bethany off her schedule. She stayed up late enough to know that some lucky girl had gotten Killian to follow her home, and she ended up sleeping in until almost 10 AM. Lifting herself out of bed, she crept down the long hall to peak into Killian's room before getting into the shower. She smiled at the sight of him sleeping peacefully on his stomach in the center of his queen size bed.

Morning, Pretty.

It wasn't until a half hour before her American Theater class that she made it over to Presser. Klaus was exiting the building as she approached.

"There you are. I was about to send out a search party for the cute Jewish girl with the bewitching tone," he said, prompting Bethany to blush. She tugged her curls forward. "No violin today?"

"Sorry," Bethany said. "I have a class. Just came to see if you brought me a tape."

"Yup, I gotcha," Klaus said, pulling a cassette tape from his back pocket.

"Thanks, Klaus."

"Work on that," he said. "Come back to me ready to jam."

"I'll do my best."

"Hey!" he called after her.

Bethany turned back.

"Circle of Fifths," he said. "You know it?"

"Yeah?"

"Good. It's surprising how many classically trained musicians don't."

Bethany waited for him to continue.

"So, how well do you know it? Could you draw it?"

"Sure."

"Excellent. Do that."

"Draw the Circle of Fifths?"

"Draw it, and study it closely. You need to know the relationships between keys better than you know your own bad habits."

Bethany thought a moment. "Alright."

"Alright."

✻ ✻ ✻

American Theater was on the second floor of Barton Hall. Bethany enjoyed the walk, thinking about Klaus calling her cute all the way there. She arrived a bit early, sitting in the back row. A minute later, a pretty, petite blonde girl entered. She managed to make eye contact with Bethany before sitting directly in front of her. Bethany squirmed, staring ahead at the shiny, beautiful blonde locks of long, perfectly straight hair, and considered changing seats.

Bethany knew that God had endowed her with thick, silky, curly hair that had been the envy of other women for as long as she could remember. She also knew she had a good body with full breasts that were firm and round, and legs that were long, lean, and shapely. She regularly noticed men admiring her. It wasn't that she was ungrateful; it's just that her confidence was regularly undermined by her own imagination. She often found herself wondering what it must be like to be a man, to climb atop a woman, to enter her body and make love to her. She could imagine sex with a tall, attractive brunette such as herself could be quite satisfying, but also knew that, as a man, she'd much rather toss around a petite sundoll with golden cornsilk hair.

"I like your dress," the blonde said, turning in her seat.

Bethany was wearing a blue and white gingham sundress. She only owned a few dresses and seldom wore them, but it had felt like a sundress sort of day.

"Thanks."

"Do you think people will come to class today?" the blonde asked. "Almost no one showed up to any of my classes yesterday."

"I don't know," Bethany said, looking around at the mostly empty classroom. "Maybe. It's still a bit early."

"It's all so weird," the blonde said, staring at Bethany, waiting for confirmation.

"Yeah, it's weird."

"I mean, I guess we're safe here though, right?"

"I… I don't know."

Bethany watched the blonde's pretty cornflower blue eyes grow wide with fear, and thought about how nice it must be to have big blue eyes. Bethany's own eyes were deep set and dark brown. A high school boyfriend had once described them as "sexy and mysterious," which had made her appreciate them a bit more, but she still admired blue eyes whenever she noticed them.

"My parents think I should come home," the blonde continued. "You know, get away from the city."

Bethany nodded, unsure of how to respond.

"I'm from Idaho."

Again Bethany nodded.

"Where are you from?"

"New York."

"Oh, my God!" the blonde exclaimed, her pretty eyes filling with terror.

"Uh, no… Brooklyn."

"Is your family safe?"

"Uh-huh. It's just my grandmother there."

The blonde looked positively panicked.

"She's fine," Bethany said, trying to reassure her.

"Where are your parents?"

"Oh, um… Well, my mother died."

The blonde gasped, covering her mouth.

"No, not in New York," Bethany said, hoping the conversation would soon end. "I mean, she did die in New York, but a long time ago, while she was having me."

"Oh, my God, I'm so sorry," the blonde said, moving her hand to her chest.

Bethany had encountered this reaction several times since starting college. She'd mostly grown accustomed to it, but it still kind of irked her. She didn't even know this blonde, yet she was now somehow responsible for managing her emotions. It occurred to Bethany that maybe she ought to start telling people her mother lived in Idaho.

"Oh, it's fine. I was raised by my grandmother," Bethany said. The blonde still looked deeply saddened, so Bethany added, "She's great. It was great… ya know… my childhood and everything. Really great."

"Well, what about your father?"

"Oh, he's not dead. He lives in California. Works in the film industry."

The blonde seemed comforted by this. "Oh!" she said, tilting her head with a smile. "Well, that's fun. Have you been on actual film sets?"

"Uh… no. I don't actually know him," Bethany said outwardly smiling while bracing for the next outpouring of emotion. "It's cool though. He funds my entire life and has no say as to how I live it," she added quickly.

"Oh," the blonde said, sort of tilting her head one way then the other, then jutting out her chin.

Pity? Envy? Superiority?

Bethany couldn't decipher the response.

Pretty blondes speak an entirely different language.

"Well, that's… that's nice then," she added, offering a nod and a faint smile. "I'm Lisa, by the way. Lisa Apgar."

"Oh, like the—"

"The test for newborn babies! Yeah!" Lisa said gleefully, her big blue eyes twinkling.

"Bethany Schechter," Bethany said, extending her hand. "Schechter means ritual slaughterer."

She heard her cell phone vibrating in her backpack just as Lisa took her hand. Bethany reached for it and saw it was Elias calling.

"Sorry. I need to take this," Bethany said, carrying the phone out to the hall. "Hello?"

"You answered."

"I told you I would."

"I'm glad you did," Elias said. "Where are you?"

"American Theater. Barton Hall."

"When's class over?"

"2."

"I'll be there. Meet me outside on 13th."

"Okay."

"See ya soon."

Eight

Elias was standing just outside the building dressed in jeans and a charcoal gray t-shirt. His long, golden red hair was pulled back in a ponytail. Bethany smiled as she walked toward him.

"Look at you," he said, pulling her into a quick embrace. "You look crazy beautiful in that dress."

"Thanks. I wore it for you."

"Mmm… I like that. Can I take you for a late lunch?"

"No, thanks."

"Bubble tea?"

"Haha… No, let's go to your place."

He blew out a short whistle. "Alright. We can definitely do that."

He draped an arm over her, and they walked toward his dorm building.

The walls of the dorm were stark white just like her old dorm walls had been. There was a small open closet space and sitting area with the same orange industrial-style imitation leather sofa and chair set she'd had in her dorm. Then, further back, on either side of the room, there was a full size bed pressed against the wall, sitting unusually high off the ground in order to fit small shelving units and storage bins beneath. At the foot of each bed, there was a mini refrigerator, and some additional shelving holding condiments, snacks, and supplies. Behind each bed was a small computer desk.

"That's me, on the right," he said, gesturing.

His roommate's side was just a bit messy and heavily adorned with Kansas City Chiefs and Mavericks banners. Elias's was plain and neat. Bethany set her backpack and violin down, and walked over, sitting on his bed. Elias turned to his closet and pulled out a sock. He carried it to the door and hung it on the exterior doorknob before joining Bethany.

"You're a theater major, right?"

"Uh-huh," Bethany said, running her hand over his arm. "This is nice."

"My arm?"

"Yeah. Good arms."

"Oh. Thank you," he said with a smile. "I like yours too."

Bethany laughed.

"You laughing at me?" Elias asked, leaning into her.

He kissed her while gently pushing her back onto his bed. Bethany kicked off her Keds and relaxed back on his pillow. Elias leaned down, pulling off his boots, then climbed over her. She ran her hands through his long red ponytail, remembering the thick silkiness from when she'd last touched it. He reached a hand to the nape of her neck, kissing her more firmly while parting her legs with his other hand. He pressed himself between her thighs while bringing his hand up to cup her breast.

Bethany lifted up the back of Elias's t-shirt, running her hands over his back. He pulled away, kneeling to remove his shirt. Bethany took that moment to admire the full effect of his lean, muscular body with his sharp facial features, dark blue eyes, and shiny coppery hair. He was strong with a wild and fierce look about him.

Elias pushed Bethany's sundress up, then pulled her into a sitting position. Bethany raised her arms so he could remove her dress. He reached back, neatly draping the dress over the top of his mini fridge before turning back to remove her bra, releasing Bethany's breasts. He set her bra aside and stared at her a moment, taking a deep breath.

"I'm just gonna tell you this," Elias said. "I've thought about you a lot since that night last year... more than I probably should have. And you're even sexier than I remembered, but... I don't want this to be it."

He dropped his head, peering up at her through his golden white lashes.

Vulnerability.

"Take off your pants," Bethany said. "I need to feel you now."

Elias pressed his lips together. He climbed off the side of the bed, unbuckling his belt, then removed his jeans to expose a pair of black boxer briefs. Bethany reached for him, running her hand over the impressive bulge before tugging the underwear down. Elias finished taking them off before reaching for hers. Bethany lifted her backside to assist. He laid her underwear atop her bra then climbed back over her, kissing her.

Reaching a hand down to guide himself, he lifted his face to stare into her eyes while pressing into her body. Bethany released a soft groan as Elias began moving inside her. She took hold of his ponytail while kissing him, arching her back and thrusting her breasts upward against him. She remembered him, remembered his body, and worked to accompany his movement with precision. He was easy to follow, increasing a bit in tempo, but never straying from the rhythm.

Bold. Vigorous. Resolute.

Bethany moved with him, staring into his eyes. After a few minutes, she could feel a tension building inside her. She wrapped her hand tighter around his ponytail, pulling him closer to her face, then closed her eyes and clutched his arm as her body went rigid, cumming as Elias watched. He slowed, waiting for her to return eye contact before speeding up again, kissing her greedily. It wasn't long before he brought her to orgasm again just before pulling out to finish on her breasts.

"Stay right there," he panted, climbing off the bed and disappearing into the bathroom.

She heard the water running. Elias returned with a hand towel partially dampened with warm water. He used the dampened half to clean her breasts, then the other half to dry them before chucking it into the hamper near the bathroom door.

He climbed into the small bed beside her, draping an arm over her. Bethany stole a glance at his bedside alarm clock.

"You have somewhere to be?"

"Not this minute, but I should get going soon."

"Stay. I'll order a pizza," he said, propping himself on an elbow to look at her. "Or let me take you out somewhere. I have a car."

"I have homework to do for tomorrow."

"You're not gonna disappear on me again, are you?"

"No, of course not. I told you. I just got busy. Anyway, we have a class together."

"Mmm… That's right. I've got you for the entire semester," Elias said, giving her a squeeze.

Nine

Bethany kicked off her Keds at the top of the stairs and set her violin down.

"Hey," Killian said, walking through the kitchen toward her.

"Hey, Pretty."

"Dress, huh?"

"Oh. Yeah."

"Looks good."

"Thanks."

"Gonna play for me?"

"Sure. Any special requests?"

"You know what I like."

Bethany nodded, unpacking her violin, deciding to play her very favorite: Chopin's *Nocturne in C Sharp Minor*. She tuned up as Killian settled in the green recliner, then began. She wanted to play perfectly for him. She wanted to make him feel each note, each surge of hope, each swell of passion. She needed him to know the full spectrum of sentiment existing within the dreamlike melody which has no choice but to finally settle into quiet resignation.

She managed to play the piece almost flawlessly until her fingers stumbled over the long run toward the end. Refusing to allow the mistake to define her performance, she reigned in the nerves, held her focus, and ended strong.

Afterward, she packed up quietly, then stood before Killian. He held his arms out to her, and she lowered herself onto his lap. He folded his arms over her and nuzzled the side of her face with his before pulling the lever and lifting the leg rest, easing her back with him.

"Thank you, Bethany."

"You're welcome. Sorry I screwed up that run."

"It was perfect. You're perfect."

Killian reached a hand up and swept her hair back. He kissed her neck, then again, and again.

"I should start on my homework," Bethany said quietly, lifting herself from him.

Killian pulled her back, tightening his arms around her, speaking close to her ear. "Bethany, you know I—" he broke off, and she could hear him swallow hard. "I think about you."

Bethany turned sideways on his lap. "We have a special relationship, don't we?" she said softly, smiling at him. "You're my best friend, Killian."

Killian nodded and dropped his head, his wavy blonde locks falling over part of his face.

"You're my very best friend," she said just above a whisper.

"Yeah," he said, meeting her eyes again. "And you're mine."

"I should start on my homework," Bethany said again, touching his face and offering a gentle smile.

She began climbing out of the chair, but Killian pulled her back again, holding her against him. Slowly, he dragged his lips up and down the side of her face.

"You let me once," he said quietly next to her ear.

Bethany felt her face flush, prickly tingles rushing into the core of her body with the hazy memories of that night. It had been a couple months after they'd met and rented the apartment together. They'd already become close friends, and Bethany had known better. But they'd each found themselves alone on New Year's Eve, and she'd had far too much to drink.

The night remained mostly a blur, but she remembered Killian's bare, glistening shoulders moving above her, his body pressed down against hers on a blanket spread over the living room carpet. She remembered him moaning her name repeatedly. Bethany still thought of it sometimes, but neither of them had ever spoken of it.

Killian took hold of Bethany's hair, turning her head and kissing her lips, delicately at first, then growing more intense. His tongue swept through her mouth. Bethany tried pulling away, but he held her tightly and continued the kiss. When he finally released her, she felt a bit dizzy. She kissed his cheek and climbed out of the chair.

"I should start on my homework," she said again, walking back to her room. Once in her room, she lay on her bed, closed her eyes, and thought about Killian.

Ten

Bethany rose early the next morning, realizing she'd fallen asleep without ever even listening to the tape Klaus had recorded for her. She wouldn't be able to practice this morning, and didn't want to go to Presser without at least having tried to play along with the tape. She'd have to go without violin until Killian went to work that night. She hated days without violin.

Bethany showered and dressed in jeans and a purple tank top. Theater 100 didn't start until 12:30, but she didn't want to be sitting around at home, so she drove to campus, parked, and made her way over to the cafeteria for breakfast.

Sitting with her plate of scrambled eggs, toast, and orange juice, she began looking over the printout of her new scene.

"Hey, Bethany."

Bethany looked up to see Jared holding a tray of food, staring down at her.

"Hey."

"Mind if I sit with you?"

Bethany gestured toward the chair across from her.

"Thanks," he said, setting his tray across from hers. Bethany noticed that he had the exact same breakfast she had. Then she noticed the long wisps of hair hanging into his eyes, his eyelashes batting them around.

"Are you memorizing?"

"I just opened it, Jared," she said.

"We can do a cold reading now if you want. Then we'll only need to block it after Theater 100."

"Can I eat first?"

"Sure. Let's eat," Jared said, starting on his eggs.

The two of them ate in silence as she continued reading. When she finished eating, Bethany picked up her orange juice and pushed her tray aside. Jared stood, stacked his tray onto hers and carried them both to the garbage, returning with only his juice.

"I don't ask to get paired up with you, ya know," he said, sitting again.

"I know," Bethany said, waiting for him to continue. He didn't. "Is there a problem, Jared?"

"No… No. I'm sorry. I just know we get paired up a lot, and I didn't want you to think I had asked Lawrence to pair us up. It's probably just the physicality thing."

"Does Lawrence accept scene partner requests from students?"

"Probably not. Maybe. I don't know, because I've never submitted one."

"It never occurred to me that you would have, Jared."

"Okay," he said, pushing the hair from his eyes.

"Are we good?" Bethany asked, gesturing toward her script.

"Yeah," Jared said, digging into his backpack and pulling out his copy. "No," he said, slapping his hand against the table. "I really hate the way you say my name."

"What?"

"I'm proud of my name, but the way you say it makes it sound like an insult. You say 'Jared' like it's a synonym for jackass," he said. "And I don't know, maybe I've offended you somehow. Sometimes I offend people without meaning to. Have I offended you? Is that why you keep saying my name like that?"

Bethany sat blinking a moment. "I wasn't aware that I was saying your name any differently from the way you say it, Jared."

Jared's eyes narrowed.

"Would you like me to call you something else?" she asked pointedly.

He pursed his lips, staring at her silently.

"Are you ready to start?" she asked impatiently.

"Yeah," he said glumly, his hair falling into his eyes. "Your line."

Eleven

She and Jared had completed a cold reading. Afterward, Bethany left him in the cafeteria in order to wander aimlessly before Theater 100. She walked down West Montgomery Avenue to 12th Street. Just as she was passing the wall of food, her phone began to buzz. She stopped and pulled it from her backpack, seeing it was Elias calling.

"Hello?"

"Hey. Where are you?"

"I'm walking past the place where we met actually."

"Great. I'll come meet you."

"I have Theater 100 in less than an hour."

"Well, I'll keep you company until then."

"Okay."

"See you soon."

Bethany sat at a table. Only a few minutes passed before she saw Elias walking up, dressed in gray jeans and a hunter green t-shirt. Looking him over, Bethany suddenly wished she had more time to kill before class. She stood and they embraced.

"Hey, beautiful girl," he said with a smile. "Can I buy you an early lunch?"

"I had a late breakfast," she said. "Take a walk?"

"Sure," he said, taking her hand and lifting it to kiss it before letting it go.

They began walking, turning toward the bell tower.

"I'm really enjoying this, by the way," he said.

"Enjoying what?"

"This thing where I call you, and you...ya know, answer your phone."

Bethany smiled, rolling her eyes.

"Don't you roll your eyes at me," he scolded.

He pulled her against him. Bethany reached a hand beneath his hair to rest over the nape of his neck. As she kissed Elias, she became aware of an amplified voice somewhere in the background. The voice was shouting when it unexpectedly addressed her.

"Bethany Schechter!"

Bethany dropped her hand from Elias, and looked around for the source. Standing a few feet off the ground on the platform of the bell tower was Shayla Colreavey, whose hair was now short, spiky, and a bright shade of blue. She had a bunch of new face piercings: two eyebrow hoops, a bridge piercing, septum piercing, and a labret. She also looked a good twenty pounds heavier, dressed in very tight cut-off shorts and an ill-fitting black tank top, displaying an upper arm tattoo of a cat holding a sushi roll. It almost seemed as though she were aiming to assault people with her appearance. She was holding a megaphone above a small crowd of maybe two dozen female students on the ground.

"Everyone, look over there to see what a rape apologist looks like!" Shayla shouted, pointing at Bethany. "That's Bethany Schechter. She thinks it's totally fine for frat bros to take advantage of female college students."

Bethany took a deep breath. Unsure of what to do, she waved at the crowd of gawking girls. Looking over at Elias, she saw he was frowning, his shoulders back very straight.

"I'm really sorry for this," she said.

"Isn't that your old roommate?"

"Yeah."

"Wow, she really is nuts."

"Yeah."

"Who are all those other chicks?"

Bethany shrugged.

Elias continued frowning at the crowd of girls.

"Yup, that's right, ladies," Shayla continued. "Bethany Schechter doesn't believe in date rape. She thinks if a female student agrees to go to a party, or to a male student's apartment or dorm, or even just gets into his car, she's already consented to whatever he might have in mind, to whatever he decides for her."

Bethany looked over the crowd of now booing girls, noticing there was one girl not booing, and instead standing perfectly still, her mouth slightly agape. It was Lisa Apgar, the pretty blonde from Idaho. She'd added a single bright blue streak to her pretty blonde hair.

"She thinks if we have a couple drinks, or dress in sexy clothing, it's an open invitation!" Shayla continued. "She thinks we're asking for it! She believes in a man's right to dominate us, to oppress us, to use us as his play things!"

"What the fuck is she talking about?" Elias asked.

Again, Bethany shrugged.

"You wanna get outta here?" he asked.

Quietly, she nodded.

Shayla climbed down from the platform of the bell tower, approaching Bethany as she was trying to pass by. She stood just a few feet in front of her.

"Tell us about your boyfriend here, Bethany!" she said into the megaphone. Instinctively, Bethany stepped in front of Elias. "He looks exactly like the kind of guy who goes for a female suffering with internalized misogyny, doesn't he, ladies?"

The girls began cheering and shouting.

"That's enough, Shayla," Bethany warned.

Elias placed a hand over Bethany's shoulder.

"That's right!" Shayla continued, louder. "Bethany acts tough. But we know the only women who hate other women are what, ladies?"

"VICTIMS!" the girls shouted.

"Let's go," Elias said, taking her hand and pulling her the other direction. Bethany turned and walked with him.

"Don't leave, Bethany! Name your attacker! What's this rapist's name?"

Bethany yanked her hand from Elias, pivoted, and made a run at Shayla. Elias grabbed her around her waist, and swung her back around. The crowd of girls were shouting and booing.

"Come on!" Elias shouted, pulling her back toward 12th Street. "Ignore that bullshit."

Bethany nodded, walking with him as Shayla continued shouting and the girls continued cheering. He took her arm, and they made their way down 12th, away from the noise.

"I'm so sorry you got dragged into that, Elias," Bethany said. "I'm so sorry."

"Hey," he said, stopping and turning Bethany toward him. "Don't be sorry. I don't give a shit about any of... whatever that was, okay? I'm sorry I had to grab you like that. Can't have you making a mess of your life over some nothing bitch though."

Bethany reached her hand up to the nape of his neck and pulled him in for a kiss.

"Thanks for lookin' out," she said. "I don't usually let things get to me like that."

"Well, you were fighting to defend my honor," he said with a grin. "It was actually kinda hot."

He gave her shoulder a squeeze then draped his arm over her as they continued walking.

Twelve

Tomlinson was a large proscenium theater. Theater 100 packed the entire School of Communications and Theater student body into the seats each Friday of every semester for a scheduled speaker or performance of some kind. Usually, the presentation was fairly interesting.

Quentin Baines, the dialect coach and stage combat director climbed onto the stage and began talking about the attacks on the World Trade Center, and the importance of not responding to violence with more violence. Quentin was a thick-set man with a big, round belly, heavily hooded hazel eyes, and short, sand-colored, curly hair. Bethany supposed Quentin had been quite attractive maybe a decade or so ago.

She had taken Quentin's acting class her first semester. He was an easy-going professor who dressed sloppily in cargo shorts and faded, tight-fitting t-shirts. At times, he looked and even smelled like he hadn't bothered to bathe. But he seemed fairly passionate about his work, and had taken a special interest in Bethany.

One night, Bethany had accepted an invitation to see him in a play at the Forrest Theater in exchange for extra credit, although she certainly hadn't needed the extra credit. She'd noticed Quentin had something of a crush on her, and had gone to his play simply for the thrill of discovering what would happen next.

After sitting through the poorly executed production, she agreed to go to dinner with him where she managed to get served two double shots of vodka. After dinner, she agreed to go back to his apartment. And after a night filled with dull conversation and unpleasant sex, Bethany decided to chalk the whole thing up to a learning experience. She'd had a rotten time and had inadvertently hurt Quentin's ego by declining to see him again, but she now knew there was nothing especially interesting about going home with an old theater professor. Fortunately, Quentin didn't seem to hold any serious grudge, and they'd gotten through the remainder of the semester without issue.

"Hostility toward Muslims or any other group of people must not be tolerated!" he was announcing to the house of cheering, applauding students and staff. "We ask that you report racism or bigotry of any kind, in any form, to the head of the department. David Melemed's mailbox is right upstairs. Feel free to report anonymously. And my office is right up there too, guys. Okay? I'm always happy to talk to any of you. If you witness or experience something that feels unsafe or unfair or makes you uncomfortable, please know you can come to me." The cheering and clapping continued.

Quentin talked long past the time he usually took to introduce the speaker or performer of the day. Eventually, it became evident that no theater-related talk or activity would be taking place in Theater 100. So, Bethany got out her script and began the memorization process.

After class, she made her way downstairs to the basement. It was a wide open space covered in the same dark red carpeting as the house of the theater. She sat on the floor and continued reading her lines. Jared appeared a few minutes later. He sat a few feet away from her on the floor, his mere presence bringing Bethany mild irritation.

"Hey, Bethany?"

"Yes?"

"Hey, um... did you um... Did you pass the bell tower on your way over here?"

"Yup."

"Didn't that girl with the blue hair used to be your roommate?"

"Yup."

"Is she..? I mean, do you think she's..?"

"Just steer clear of those girls, Jared."

"Well, all I did was walk by, and she started yelling at me, claiming I was trespassing. And when I told her I wasn't, that I'm a student here, all those other girls started shouting with her. She said… other things too."

"Called you a rapist?"

"Oh, my God, you were there," he said, his eyebrows knitting together. Bethany watched as his face darkened, his eyes cast downward.

Humiliation.

"But Bethany, I swear—"

"Ignore her. Ignore all those girls," Bethany said, imagining what it would have felt like to pummel that blue-haired cow with her own megaphone.

"But Bethany, I've never… I mean, I wouldn't—"

"Shhh… Seriously, Jared," Bethany said, moving close to sit directly in front of him. She placed her hand firmly over his arm, making eye contact. "Don't give those nasty bitches another thought. They are unwell. Don't waste another minute of your time thinking about them."

"Oh," he said, blinking, his eyelashes batting against his hair. "Okay. Um… Thanks."

"So, ya ready?" Bethany asked, lifting her hand away.

"Uh… Yeah," Jared said, clearing his throat and pushing the hair out of his eyes. "Well, um… I was thinking most of Act I could take place like stage left, at a table… if that seems okay to you."

"Works for me."

"And then, when they walk to the atrium, I was thinking we could move a little farther downstage, center, with the gardens being out past the fourth wall."

"Sounds good," Bethany said, scribbling Jared's blocking into her script.

"And then, Act II is um… Well, it's… it's got the um…"

"Yes," Bethany said. "Why don't we get that out of the way right now? I think it'll be easier if we break the ice."

"What um..? What exactly do you mean?"

"I'm asking you to kiss me."

"Um… Right now, you mean?"

"If you wouldn't mind."

"Oh… Okay."

Timidly, Jared leaned forward and pecked her on the lips. Bethany looked up at him.

"Again?" she asked patiently.

Jared took a deep breath, closed his eyes, and leaned in again, kissing her softly, gently. He reached a hand to press against the base of her head, kissing her more firmly. Then, very suddenly, he pulled back, staring at her through the dangling wisps of hair.

"That was perfect, Jared," Bethany said. "You're really good at that."

Jared smiled.

✶ ✶ ✶

"Hey, warm honey! Get over here!"

Bethany turned and looked across the street from the exit of Tomlinson Theater to see Klaus standing outside of Presser Hall, shielding his eyes. She crossed the street to him.

"Hey," she said.

"Where's your ax?"

"Home."

"Why?"

"I haven't gotten a chance to practice with the tape."

"So? I still wanna jam with you. How close do you live?"

"Off-campus. Kensington."

"Let's go."

"I can't. I have a roommate."

"A music-intolerant roommate?"

"No. It's just that… we don't have guests."

"Hm. Well, I won't make you drive home and come all the way back. Whatcha doin' tomorrow? You can come to my dorm."

"I have a rehearsal tomorrow. I'll bring my violin Monday morning."

"Well, I guess that'll have to do," Klaus said. "Alright. I'll see you Monday morning. No excuses."

Thirteen

Bethany quietly entered her apartment, careful not to let her keys jingle, then began creeping up the stairs. Before reaching the top, she could hear the thrash metal music, which meant Killian was lifting weights back in his room. Moving through the kitchen and into the hall, she could make out the familiar lyrics:

> *Just like the pied piper*
> *Led rats through the streets*
> *We dance like marionettes*
> *Swaying to the symphony of destruction*

Usually, Bethany would think up an excuse to go talk to Killian when she knew he was lifting, but today, she felt it best to keep her distance. She slipped into her bedroom and closed the door, then got out her script, sat at her desk, and continued memorizing. After just a couple minutes, the music stopped. A few seconds later, there was a knock at her door.

"Come in."

The door opened, and Killian stood in her doorway dressed in his gray sweatpants and a white tank top, his body and hair damp with perspiration. Bethany felt her pulse increase.

"Hey."

"Hey, Pretty," Bethany said softly.

"I'm sorry if I made things weird," Killian said. "I don't want things to be weird between us."

"We won't let that happen," Bethany said. "No weirdness."

"You closed your door."

"What?"

"You closed your door. You never close your door."

"Oh," Bethany said, lifting her script to show him. "I wasn't shutting you out; just Megadeath."

"Right. Sorry."

"No, it's fine."

Killian nodded, turning toward the bathroom. Bethany stood and rushed to her door.

"Killian!"

Killian turned back. "Yeah?"

"No weirdness, okay?"

He walked back to her and puckered his lips out. She gave them a peck kiss.

"No weirdness," he said, turning back toward the bathroom.

✳ ✳ ✳

After Killian left for work, Bethany again sat at her desk to draw out the Circle of Fifths as neatly as she could and examined it for a while. Then, she popped in the tape from Klaus.

"Hey, warm honey."

Bethany was surprised to hear Klaus's voice on the recording.

"This'll be Cam playing through a 12-bar blues in three different keys. Remember your guide tones are the 3rd and 7th of each chord. I trust you're alone, so play with it. Don't be afraid to get sloppy. Be wild. Let it all out. Looking forward to hearing you... and seeing you, soon."

The recording clicked off then back on. She heard Klaus counting off, snapping his fingers, then Cam began playing. Bethany rewound the tape to listen to Klaus again, and then once more before getting her violin.

She played over each chord, first just the guide tones, then 1-3-5-b7, through each of the 12-bar blues. She thought about Klaus effortlessly soloing. She wanted to be able to do that, but found herself dutifully swinging 1-3-5-b7 quarter notes again and again.

Why couldn't she break free? Why couldn't she solo? She couldn't even bring herself to try. She started to dread facing Klaus on Monday.

Still, when she got into bed, she played the tape through Klaus's spoken intro, then again and again in her mind as she thought of Klaus's piercing blue eyes, his beautiful bow grip, and his strong, slender left hand creating the perfect vibrato.

I trust you're alone, so play with it. Don't be afraid to get sloppy. Be wild. Let it all out.

Fourteen

The door to the first floor Northern Liberties apartment opened before Bethany had the chance to knock. Jared stood barefoot in the doorway, dressed in jeans and a navy blue t-shirt, which was precisely what Bethany was wearing.

"Hey, Bethany. Come on in."

"Hey, Jared."

Jared's apartment was neat and fairly stark, much like her own. There was a small blue loveseat and a mismatched yellow floral print wingback chair. The living room had the same ugly beige wall-to-wall carpeting as she had in hers.

"Sit down. Can I get you a coffee?"

"Oh, I'm fine, Jared. I don't drink coffee. Thank you."

Bethany could tell right away from Jared's demeanor that he'd fully memorized his lines. As much as he irritated Bethany, Jared was an excellent scene partner, and she knew she was lucky to have him. He'd never let her down. Plus, once he was off-book, his entire manner shifted to that of the strong, gifted actor he was. He was confident, ready to shine. Bethany was relieved and suddenly looking forward to the work ahead. Jared was actually a lot of fun once he was able to move past his self-doubt and self-tormenting, over-intellectualizing neurosis.

As expected, they moved quickly through the scene. Jared didn't even hesitate at the kiss. He held Bethany firmly against him and kissed her like he meant it, as though he'd done it hundreds of times… smooth and sexy.

They'd run through the scene, top to bottom three times, discussed a few notes, and were about to start it a fourth time when someone unlocked and opened the front door. It was an attractive medium height girl with dark eyes and dark curly hair just like Bethany's. She smiled nervously as she entered.

"Hey, Rachel," Jared said, his hair falling into his eyes.

Bethany watched as Jared shuffled his feet around, shoving his hands into his pockets, dropping his head to watch the girl. He transformed from the smooth, sexy actor back to a self-conscious bag of nerves right before her eyes.

"Hi, Jared," Rachel said. "Sorry, I didn't know you had company."

"Oh, um… This is Bethany. She's my scene partner. We're just rehearsing for Monday," Jared said. "Bethany, this is my roommate, Rachel. She's an Education major."

"Hi," Bethany said. "Nice to meet you."

"Hi. Same," Rachel said, looking over at Jared, then quickly back to Bethany. "Well, I'll um… I'll leave you guys to it. I can just um… Well, I'll just stay in my room until you're done."

"Actually," Bethany interjected. "If you wouldn't mind, we could really use a fresh pair of eyes. Are you able to stay and watch us run it through once?"

Jared's eyes bulged a bit as he stared down at his feet.

"Oh," Rachel said, looking to Jared. "I… I would love to… I mean, if it's okay with you, Jared."

"Oh, um… sure, Rachel… if you don't mind."

"I just have to call my mom quickly to let her know I got back home. I'll be right out, okay?" she said, hurrying from the room.

"Bethany, what are you doing?" Jared hissed.

"I can tell you like her, Jared," Bethany whispered.

"What?!" he asked, his eyes darting around in a panic. "Okay… So?!"

"So, run the scene exactly like you did the last three times. Let her see what you're made of so she can fall in love with you."

"What?!" he asked again, then quickly lowered his voice. "Wait. Really? Like you really think..?"

"Yes, Jared. I really think. Play it exactly the same as you just did it. You're a total stud!"

Jared beamed at her then quickly composed himself as Rachel re-entered.

"Okay. All set," she said, sitting in the yellow floral print wingback chair.

"Great!" Jared said. "Uh… You ready, Bethany?"

"Ready."

Jared played through the scene perfectly, transforming back into a star. He was confident, charismatic, and dripping with sex appeal. At the end, Bethany turned to Rachel, who sat wide-eyed, her gaze shyly darting back and forth from Bethany to Jared.

"Wow, that was… really good. Jared, you're so… I mean… you're so… different."

"Well, sorry to do this," Bethany said quickly, "But I've gotta run. Dinner plans with my boyfriend," she explained to Rachel.

"Oh!" Rachel said. "Thank you! I mean, that was really wonderful, you guys. I really enjoyed that. Definitely an *A plus* if I were grading."

"Thanks! Thanks for watching. I'll see you Monday, Jared, okay? Pretty sure this is in the bag."

"Right. Monday. Yeah. See ya, Bethany! Thanks."

✶ ✶ ✶

As Bethany walked down North 3rd Street to her car, she took her phone out of her back pocket and saw that she had two missed calls, both from Elias. She was about to dial him back when her phone began buzzing. It was Elias.

"Hello?"

"I got you!"

"You got me."

"Where are you?"

"Northern Liberties."

"Oh, right. Rehearsal. Are you done?"

"Yup. Just left."

"Well, let me take you out. We'll get dinner."

"Let's order in. Your place."

"My dormmate is there. How about your place?"

"I can't. Sorry. House rules."

"Huh. Well… Dinner first? It's Saturday night. My dormmate'll be gone by like 7 and he'll be out until after the bars close."

"Okay. Do you know Silk City on Spring Garden?"

"Sure. You on your way now?"

"Yep."

"See ya soon."

It was only a few blocks to Silk City, so Bethany decided to leave her car and walk. When she arrived, she saw Elias dressed in jeans and a rust-colored t-shirt. She was excited to see him and jogged up to wrap her arms around his neck. He gave her a tight squeeze, lifting her off the ground a bit before kissing her.

"Hey, beautiful girl."

"Hey, sexy Viking."

"Is that what I am?"

"That's what you are to me."

"Good to know. I'm not expected to wear a costume or use props or anything, am I?"

"Definitely not," she answered with a laugh.

"Alright. Just checking," he said with a smile.

They entered Silk City and sat in a booth. A waitress came by and gave them menus. They both ordered water and began looking over the menu.

"It's good to see you," Elias said, stretching his hand across the table.

Bethany took his hand.

"Good to see you too."

"How was rehearsal?"

"Great!"

"Oh, yeah? Tell me about it."

"Well, my scene partner, Jared and I work together a lot. He's easy to work with once we get rolling. Very predictable… in a good way."

"Nice guy?"

"Very nice. I guess I'm not always so nice to him. But I'm working on it."

"In what ways are you not nice?"

"Oh, I dunno… I guess I tend to be somewhat intolerant of certain… personality types."

"Really? What types?"

"Um… overly sensitive, timid types, I guess."

"Hm. I'll have to remember not to be overly sensitive or timid, I guess."

"I can't even imagine it," she said.

✳ ✳ ✳

Elias drove Bethany back to her car so she could follow him back to campus. As Bethany was just about to get into her car, she heard Jared call out from his door half a block down. She looked back to find him rushing down the street barefoot.

When he reached her, he hugged her, lifting her off the ground and kissing her cheek before setting her back down.

"Thank you, thank you, thank you!" Jared said in a hushed voice.

"Wow. I guess your roommate really enjoyed our scene?"

"My roommate? Oh. You mean Rachel… my girlfriend?!" he said ecstatically.

"Really? Well you certainly managed to hurry things along."

"Not exactly. I've been trying to work up the nerve for weeks."

"Awww… Well good for you, Jared. I'm very happy for you."

"You did this, Bethany. I'm so grateful."

"Silly, I didn't do anything. You're the heartthrob actor. You always have been. Get back inside before she comes looking for you."

"Okay. Okay. Thank you, Bethany," Jared said again, kissing her cheek again before rushing back to his door. "See you Monday!" he called back.

"Monday!"

Bethany got into her car, smiling to herself as she followed Elias to campus.

They parked side by side in a student lot. Elias was quiet as they began walking together. Bethany took his hand which he acknowledged with a faint smile.

"You okay?" she asked.

"Any reason I shouldn't be?"

Bethany was quiet a moment. "No, I don't think so."

"You don't think so?" he asked, stopping to turn toward her. "So then, it wouldn't bother you to see me with another girl, I guess. Not at all?"

Bethany stared back blankly a moment before blinking. "Oh. Jared? You're getting weird about Jared?"

"Well, I wouldn't want to come off as overly sensitive."

"Good," Bethany said. "And you certainly shouldn't be bothered by Jared. Remember? He's not my type."

"Really? That guy looks like he's every woman's type."

"Well, I guess looks can be deceiving."

"So, he just came running out of his house barefoot to kiss you and there's nothing at all between you? He didn't seem very timid to me by the way."

Bethany pulled her hand from his.

"Elias, I don't want to do this, okay? Jared is my scene partner and nothing more. I came here for some time with the sexy Viking. If you're planning to pick a fight instead, tell me now so we can have it over the phone while I'm driving myself home."

Elias pursed his lips and stood quietly a moment before wrapping his arms tightly around her. "I'm sorry. I'll drop the interrogation. I don't even know where that came from. C'mon, let's go."

"Alright," Bethany said walking along again.

"Smile, will ya?" he said draping an arm around her. "You've got a date with the sexy Viking."

Bethany smiled.

✳ ✳ ✳

It was late when she got home. Her block was quiet. It was beginning to feel like autumn. She took a long, hot shower, then wrapped herself in a towel, and combed Infusium through her hair. Opening the bathroom door, she shrieked, unexpectedly finding Killian on the other side of it.

"Sorry!" he said with a wince. "There's not usually a line for the bathroom at this hour."

"Oh. I'm sorry. It's early for you to be home on a Saturday, isn't it?"

"No, normal time. You were singing in there. You always lose track of time when you sing in the shower."

"Do I?"

"Uh-huh."

"You should have knocked to let me know you were waiting."

"And interrupt the concert? Never."

As Killian's eyes began drifting over her, she suddenly became very aware that she was standing in only a towel.

"Well, I'm headed to bed."

"Right," he said, stepping aside for her to pass.

Bethany finished drying, stepped into her closet to slip into an oversized t-shirt, then got into bed. She watched as Killian passed by her bedroom door to go to his room, then closed her eyes, trying to think of anything other than Killian who was in his bed in the room at the end of the hall.

Fifteen

"Hi, Bubbie."

"Bethala! I wasn't sure I'd hear from you today!"

"I always call on Sunday."

"Well, I just heard from you Tuesday, so I wasn't sure."

"How are things?"

"Quieter, but you know this place. Always some reason to hegdish. There's a sadness though."

"You can still come here, Bubbie."

"Ech. We sometimes need a reminder to keep from becoming overly joyous. Anyway, azoy geyt es! How are you? How's your weight?"

"Hundred and thirty-eight-and-a-half today."

"You're not eating?"

"I'm eating. Just some fluctuation."

"Have you met a nice boy?"

"Not yet."

"You know, Ruth has a nephew at Penn. He's a med student, Bethala!" Bubbie sang.

Ruth Finklestein was Bubbie's upstairs neighbor and dearest friend. Ruth's husband had died when Bethany was very young, and Ruth had practically become a second grandmother to her.

"I'll meet someone, Bubbie."

"Okay. I'll see about Ruth's nephew in the meantime. You want I should give him your phone number?"

"No! No, Bubbie."

"What 'no'?! He's a med student… a nice boy. His parents live on the Upper West Side. They're nice people. You don't want to marry a nice boy from a nice family?"

"Of course, Bubbie, but I need to find him myself."

"I only want what's right for you, bubeleh. You're such a pretty one. This is what's done. You don't want to end up the alteh moid."

"I won't."

"You've had your fun, Bethala. Ach… goy crazy since before puberty hit. It's time to think of your future, of family."

"Bubbie, please don't give my phone number out."

"Oy… Es vet helfn vi a toytn bankes!"

"I have to go. I love you, Bubbie."

"I love you too, bubeleh. Next time call collect."

"Okay, Bubbie. B'bye."

"Tsu gezunt, tsum lebn, tsum vaksn, tsum kveln."

As soon as Bethany hung up, her phone began buzzing. The call was from an unknown number.

"Hello?"

"That you, warm honey?"

"Klaus!"

"Got your number from Cam. Whatcha doin right now?"

"Um… nothing really."

"Bring your violin over."

"Over where?"

"I live in the dorms. 1940. Music-friendly floor."

Elias's building.

"Uh… No, sorry, I can't."

"Why not?"

"I have to study my lines."

"Alright. Still on for tomorrow morning though, right?"

"Right. Tomorrow at Presser."

"What time is your first class?"

"1 o'clock."

"Alright. Get there bright and early."

After hanging up with Klaus, Bethany began to worry. She wished she could practice, but didn't want to try anything new with Killian home. Still, she decided, she should practice something. She went to the living room and opened her violin case. As she rosined her bow, she thought about Klaus, wondering what would have happened if she'd gone to his dorm. She liked Klaus. She found him very sexy, but not sexy enough to trade in Elias.

Bethany stood and played a few scales before beginning the first piece that came to mind: Bach's *Sonata for Violin No. 3 in C Major*. It was Bubbie's favorite. It was the one she'd always had Bethany play for company.

"Pretty, but not so showy like the others," she'd always said.

The Sonata was actually a very complicated piece that included a movement full of contrapuntal tricks, but Bethany understood what Bubbie meant, and also why she liked it so much. It was a deeply intellectual piece, and also managed to cover a full range of emotion in its four movements: *Adagio* was slow and full of serene arpeggiated chords. *Fugue* was stimulating and intricate. *Largo* was deeper, introspective, and somewhat sad. *Allegro Assai* was energetic and joyful.

Of course, Bubbie loved Chopin too, but Chopin felt somehow inappropriate for the moment. As she began the *Adagio*, Bethany thought of Bubbie… her lifelong steadfast love and support. Zayde had been a strong father figure, but he'd died shortly after Bethany's 14th birthday, leaving her with only Bubbie. After Bubbie, there would be no one left.

But because of Bubbie's strength, guidance, and undying determination, Bethany knew she would never be alone. Although she liked to indulge in reveries of sweet liberation, Bethany knew she was destined to maintain the foundation of familial values. She would always have the comfort and sense of belonging that came with it. And like Bubbie, she knew she would someday fight for its preservation.

When she finished the Bach, she looked up to find Killian watching from the kitchen, startling her.

"Sorry," he said shyly. "Okay if I listen a while longer?"

"Of course," Bethany said, smiling at him.

"I can just sit here," he said, taking a seat at the kitchen table. "That was Bubbie's favorite, right? The Bach Sonata?"

"Yes."

"Did you have your Sunday call?"

"We did. She seems well."

"Glad to hear it."

"Is there something you'd like me to play for you?"

"No, I don't want to intrude any more than I already have. Play whatever you're feeling."

With Killian listening, Bethany could only think to play Chopin. She began playing the *Nocturne Op. 9 No. 2*.

Closing her eyes as she played, she focused her energy in order to present him with a perfect piece, an uncomplicated, untouched, unreachable part of herself that was only for Killian, that would only ever be for Killian. She was desperate to make him feel the sweetness, the intense yearning. She needed him to know the depths of her admiration, her passion, her sorrow. With each note, each stroke of her bow, she made love to Killian, wanting him to taste the warm honey.

When she finished, she quietly packed up, then stood to see Killian sitting very still in the kitchen, his head tipped back against the wall. She watched him take a deep breath, his chest slowly rising then falling. Finally, he lifted his head to face her. She stood still, awkwardly staring back, too afraid to move any closer to him. Killian offered a gentle smile, then stood and blew a kiss before turning and walking back to his room.

Sixteen

Bethany showered and dressed in jeans and a black t-shirt. She made it to Presser by 7:30 AM, hoping for a little practice time to herself. But Klaus was already there, waiting outside. His sparkly blue eyes looked even bluer against his light blue t-shirt.

"How'd you do with the tape?" he asked, standing to greet her.

Bethany shook her head.

"No? Damn. What's going on?" he asked as they entered the building together.

"I don't know," Bethany answered honestly. "I just don't hear anything. Well… I do, but I can't play it. As soon as I try, it vanishes."

"Okay," Klaus said, nodding. "We'll get there."

Klaus opened a practice room door for her and followed her in. He began unpacking his violin. She did the same.

"It's interesting," he said, rosining his bow, "because you're able to hear exactly what I play and quote it back so precisely. You have a great ear. You've got all the technique. You can swing. I wonder what's happening."

"I don't know. Maybe I'm just not creative."

"Heh."

"No, really. I mean, maybe I don't have anything original to contribute."

"Bullshit," Klaus said, looking at her with an odd, sudden intensity. He moved in close to her, gazing into her eyes, a slight grin spreading over his face. "Wild currents lie beneath that placid surface," he said softly. He was standing close enough for her to feel his breath on her face. For a moment, she thought he was going to kiss her, but he only continued staring into her eyes. "I can read you like a book," he said.

Bethany's breath caught. She felt her face flush.

"There's a disconnect somewhere," he said, stepping back, returning his bow to his case. "It happens. Just need to find it and restore continuity."

"Of course," she said, unsure of what Klaus meant or how to respond.

"Excellent. I'm gonna give you some space to warm up. I'll be back in like 20 minutes. Get ready cause I'm gonna ride you hard."

"Okay," Bethany said, her voice coming out just above a whisper.

"You want anything? Breakfast on me."

"No, thanks."

"Alright. Make good use of your time."

Bethany tuned up, played a few scales, then played Paganini's *La Campanella* in order to give her arms and fingers a workout. Afterward, she sat and waited. Klaus soon returned with Cam who carried in an upright bass, and Lonnie, who Bethany remembered from Tuesday, carrying a guitar. The already stuffy room suddenly felt much warmer and tighter.

"Alright. Cam's on bass today. We've got Lonnie to comp. 12-bar blues. We'll just screw around."

"Klaus, I can't—"

"Cam and Lonnie and I are gonna play twice through the head," he interrupted, turning to face her. "I'm gonna solo through it, then you and I are gonna solo through it. You're gonna repeat every phrase I play."

"Oh."

"I want a perfect echo... note for note, okay?"

"Okay."

Cam started walking a bassline. Lonnie came in on rhythm guitar. Klaus played twice through a melody unfamiliar to Bethany, then soloed through a few times. Afterward, he looked directly into Bethany's eyes and played a short lick. Bethany repeated it. He played a more rhythmically complicated one. Bethany repeated. He played a longer, glissy one. Again, Bethany repeated. They continued on and on that way many times through before Klaus finally let up, and he, Cam, and Lonnie played twice through the head again.

"Goddamn, that's fuckin' sexy," Klaus said, sucking his bottom lip. "Mmm… I could stand here, making you do that all day long."

Bethany felt herself blush. Repositioning her bow, she reached up to tug her curls forward.

"Let's try another one," Cam said.

"Cam's diggin' it," Klaus said with a smile.

"Yeah, man. It's kinda wild."

Lonnie nodded.

"Call a tune," said Klaus.

"*Equinox* in C Minor," Lonnie quickly replied.

"Another 12-bar blues," Klaus told her. "14-bar intro. We'll play twice through the head."

Klaus counted off, and they began. Again, they played through the melody. Bethany knew *Equinox*. Zayde had been a John Coltrane fan. She listened in awe as Klaus soloed through a few times. Finally, he looked at her again and began playing short phrases for her to parrot. They played on and on that way many times through.

"Cam, keep going," Klaus called out. He looked over to Bethany, making eye contact. "Alright," he said, "we're gonna keep going too, but this time, don't repeat me. I want you to answer me. I'm gonna tell you something. You tell me something back."

Bethany felt her body stiffen as Klaus began. He played a lick, and she stood frozen.

"Answer me."

He played another. She was silent.

"Let me hear it, girl."

He played another. She remained still.

"C'mon, give it to me!" he yelled.

He played again. Bethany raised her bow, but hesitated, then dropped her arm.

"I know you hear what I'm saying to you," Klaus said, again looking directly into her eyes. "Don't leave me hangin'. Don't. You know what I need to hear. Tell me what I need to hear."

He played another quick phrase. Bethany played a quick one back.

"WHOA!" Cam and Lonnie cheered in unison.

"She told you, bro!" Cam shouted.

Klaus grinned, playing another phrase. Bethany answered him. He played more. Bethany followed up.

"Alright, warm honey. I'm gonna tell you the rest now. Let me get through it, and then I want you to respond. I'm gonna tell you everything I need you to hear. You tell me everything I need to hear back."

Klaus played through the 12 bars a few times, then looked to her and waited as Bethany played back to him.

"Holy shit!" she heard Cam say at some point.

"Keep going," Klaus said at the end of the 12 bars.

Bethany continued, finding she had more and more to add, building her solo over the 12 bars a total of three times through before she began to feel self-conscious and abruptly dropped her arm. It was only then she realized she had tears running down her cheeks.

Klaus looked away from Bethany, lifting his eyes toward Cam and Lonnie who began accompanying him through the melody. Bethany used the opportunity to wipe her face with the back of her hand, composing herself as best she could. She sat in the chair, resting her violin in its case. Feeling completely exposed, she pulled her hair forward. Once finished, the three guys stared over at her, Cam still looking stunned, Klaus and Lonnie both grinning. She smiled up at them, feeling a strange mix of pride and embarrassment.

"Turns out you have plenty to contribute, huh?" Klaus said, sucking his bottom lip. "That was some wild and sexy stuff you just said to me. We should probably be making out right now."

Bethany blushed even more, casting her eyes to the floor.

"Easy," Cam scolded quietly.

"Alright," Klaus said. "I can let you head out for now, but I want you to start playing around with the other modes. Here."

He pulled a folded piece of lined paper from his back pocket and handed it to her. Bethany took it and unfolded it, reading it over:

Ionian: 1-2-3-4-5-6-7-1
Mixolydian: 1-2-3-4-5-6-b7-1
Lydian: 1-2-3-#4-5-6-7-1
Aeolian: 1-2-b3-4-5-b6-b7-1
Dorian: 1-2-b3-4-5-6-b7-1
Phrygian: 1-b2-b3-4-5-b6-b7-1
Locrian: 1-b2-b3-4-b5-b6-b7-1

"And listen," Klaus continued as Bethany studied the paper. "Are you listening?"

"Yes," Bethany said, looking up at him.

"You'll realize modes are just scales starting on different degrees. And they're often taught that way, but I don't want you learning them that way. I don't want you thinking about them that way."

He raised his eyebrows, waiting for a response.

"Okay," she said simply, not fully understanding.

"Dorian has a unique sound, a distinct feel. Identify it. Memorize it. Phrygian has a unique sound, a distinct feel. Identify it. Memorize it. Learn to recognize the distinct sound and feel of each mode the same way you recognize colors or flavors. Get me?"

Bethany nodded.

"I know you do," he said with a grin. "And I want you to come to my dorm tonight. We need to explore this new development."

There was a knock at the door.

"Thought I heard violin," a voice called. "That you, Klaus?"

Klaus opened the door to a small Asian guy with glasses, greasy looking hair, and a mild case of acne.

"Hey, man," the Asian guy said. "Can I get you to play through my new composition? It'll only take a few minutes. I just need to hear it in the right voices," he explained, swishing his fingers around his ear.

"Yeah, man, let's go," Klaus said. "Tonight, warm honey. I'm gonna call you later."

"Nice jammin' with you," Lonnie said to her with a nod before following Klaus out.

Bethany began loosening her bow, dropping down to the floor to pack up.

"That was insanely fucking awesome," Cam said.

"Thank you," Bethany said. "It felt insanely fucking awesome."

"Right on," Cam said, holding up a hand. Bethany high-fived it then continued packing up. "Um... Look," Cam continued, "I know he comes on strong, but just so you know, you don't have to worry about Klaus. I mean... It'll just be music in his dorm."

"Oh. I um—"

"Like, he's a hundred percent into you, but it's just the whiff he's after."

"The what?"

"The sexual tension. Klaus guards it like it's a priceless resource… which in music, it basically is. But Klaus is… I dunno, he's weird. Diligent. He never gives into temptation," Cam said. "I mean, he gets with girls and all. He just won't touch a talented musician… not even vocalists, and they're a dime a dozen. So, I'm just sayin'… if you wanna jam tonight, you should come out. It'll just be music, plus ya know, all his extreme flirting," Cam added with a small laugh. "Probably better if you don't tell him I said anything."

"Huh," Bethany said. "No, I won't."

"Cool. Well… Awesome playing with you today. Hopefully we'll see you tonight."

Seventeen

Because Jared always memorized his lines early, Bethany made sure she memorized hers early too. The two of them always went off-book for their first classroom performance. During her first semester, she'd realized having her script memorized early was something other students, notably other female students, seemed to resent her for. For some reason, they'd always assumed it was something Bethany had pressured Jared into. But memorizing early had never been Bethany's idea. Jared had always prepared early, and Bethany simply wanted to keep up, especially since working off-book magically transformed her partner from wuss to stud.

Bethany wondered if the other girls were jealous because she was so frequently paired with Jared. She couldn't ever be too sure what they were thinking, but it seemed to Bethany that other girls often looked for reasons to be angry or to get upset. Her decision to major in theater instead of music had come out of a desire to better understand people. Studying subtext, motivation, vocal inflection, facial expression, and body language had proven useful to Bethany, but she still found it difficult to relate to other women. She supposed that was mostly because she'd been raised by Bubbie, a rare sort of woman who'd always spoken her mind very plainly.

Other women often didn't seem to say what they meant or to mean what they said. There seemed to be reasons for getting angry and upset, or perhaps just acting angry and upset, that Bethany couldn't quite understand. She wasn't sure she'd ever truly understand. But since she certainly understood men better than most other women seemed to, she figured she was in a winning position despite her handicap.

"I can't say enough good things about this scene!"

Lawrence was a small-boned middle-aged man who wore lots of fitted turtlenecks and used lots of dramatic hand gestures. His wide-set green eyes made him resemble some sort of peculiar insect, but many female theater major seemed to fawn over him anyway.

"The two of you work beautifully together. Magnificent!"

Bethany was new to working under Lawrence's direction, but she could tell from the critiques given to other students that she and Jared had received high praise from quite a stickler. She guessed the other girls would hate her for it, but she couldn't really find a reason for being too concerned with that. After their scene, she and Jared sat side by side in the half-circle of students.

"You're the best," he whispered, bumping Bethany with his elbow.

"*You* are," Bethany said with a smile. "How's Rachel?"

"Great," he said, beaming. "She's great.

After class, Bethany decided to make her way over to the food trucks. On the walk there, she checked her phone and saw she had two missed calls from Elias. She was just about to call him back when her phone buzzed. It was Elias calling.

"Hey!"

"Hey. What are you doing?"

"On my way to get lunch."

"I'll treat. Where ya headed?"

"Teppanyaki."

"See you in about three minutes."

Three minutes later, Bethany saw Elias approaching the teppanyaki truck from the other direction. He was dressed in jeans and a burgundy t-shirt. She wondered if his dorm was vacant.

"Hey, beautiful," he said, wrapping an arm around her.

"Hi."

He pulled her close and kissed her before stepping back to look over the menu.

"Know what you want?"

"Uh-huh," she replied, looking him up and down.

He smiled at her. "Let's eat, then we'll head back to my place."

"Sounds good."

"Got your violin with you again. You gonna play for me?"

"Uh… maybe."

"C'mon, I wanna hear that thing."

"Maybe."

They carried their containers of teppanyaki to the tables in front of the wall of food and sat. Elias used his fork to drizzle the thimble-sized cup of sauce that always came inside the container of teppanyaki. Bethany took a bite of her meal.

"Whoa, whoa, whoa…" he said.

"What?"

"That's not even worth eating without the sauce."

"Really? I never tried it."

"Well, you need to remedy that immediately," he said.

Elias removed the lid of the tiny sauce container that had come with her lunch and dabbed a bit onto a small portion.

"There. Hoy Fong chili garlic sauce. Dig in."

Bethany took a bite. The flavor lit up her taste buds. She could feel her eyes widening with delight.

"Oh, my goodness… This is an entirely different meal."

"Uh-huh," he said, using his fork to drizzle the rest of the sauce over her teppanyaki.

"I'm gonna get myself a water. Can I buy you a bubble tea?" he asked.

"No thanks. I'll take a water too though."

"You got it."

After a couple minutes, Elias returned carrying two bottles of water. He sat, and they ate. Partway through her meal, Bethany began thinking about the first time she'd met Elias, drinking a bubble tea right in this same place. She thought of that first night together and closed her teppanyaki container.

"I'll finish this later. Let's head over to your dorm."

Elias closed his container and stood. "Let's go. But I'm gonna make you play for me before anything else happens."

✷ ✷ ✷

Bethany readied her violin, then stood to play the first piece that came to mind: Elgar's *La Capricieuse*. Playing through its sparkling, romantically playful phrases, she smiled to herself. Then, as she reached the gentler, more expressive B section, her mind began to drift into images of soft golden locks framing a square jaw and perfectly cleft chin. She thought of gray sweatpants, soft lips, and strong glistening shoulders. Finally, moving on to the repeat of the lively A section, she fixed her eyes on her violin, refocusing on the warmth and charm of the piece's uninhibited wildness.

Upon reaching the graceful pizzicato ending, she quickly packed up. Feeling Elias watching her, she shyly climbed onto the bed beside him.

"Bethany…" Elias whispered, reaching for her.

Eighteen

Bethany lay breathless, her cheek pressed to Elias's chest as he stroked her hair. He kissed the top of her head, wrapping his arm tighter around her.

"I like you, Bethany Schechter."

She tilted her head up to face him, smiling. He tipped her chin back to kiss her lips.

"You should have me over to your place sometime."

"Oh, um…"

"You mentioned something about a roommate?"

"Yeah."

"Another psycho?"

"No."

He was quiet a moment. "It's not a guy, is it?"

When she didn't answer immediately, Elias sat up abruptly, pushing Bethany up with him.

"You live with a guy?"

"I… Yeah."

"Is he your boyfriend?"

"No, he's my roommate."

"Just a roommate?"

"Well…"

"Oh, shit," Elias said, rubbing his hands over his face.

"He's my best friend. He's my roommate, and he's my best friend."

"What kind of best friend?"

Bethany paused, thinking of how to answer that question.

"I'm asking if you're sleeping with him, Bethany."

"No," she answered. "I'm not."

He stared at her a moment, then relaxed back on his pillow, pulling her close again. "Okay," he said. "...but you can't have me over?"

"No. We don't have guests. It's just the way it is. House rule."

She noticed the hum of the mini refrigerator as she waited for him to speak again.

"It would be nice to have more time together. I'd like to actually spend the night with you."

"It's just easier to meet here," Bethany said. "Convenient. Right on campus."

"But I want to see more of you. I want this to be more than a sock on the doorknob."

"Elias…"

"What? I want to be with you. I want you to be my girl."

Bethany was quiet.

"Well?"

"You know you're getting the best of me already—all the benefits with none of the responsibility."

"I want the responsibility," he said, sitting up again.

Bethany sat up too, pulling the sheet over her breasts.

"That's truly sweet, Elias, and… well, it's actually incredibly sexy."

Elias stared at her, waiting for her to continue.

"I want you to know I think you're great," she said. "You're basically perfect."

"But you don't want to be my girl."

"It's not that. I just can't be."

"Because of your roommate?"

"No. Stop with that. It's…"

"What?"

"Well, I'm just not in a place in my life where I feel ready to have a serious relationship."

He blinked a few times. "Can I have a real answer now?"

"Elias—"

"No, I… I'm just trying to process this because I really thought we liked each other.

"We do like each other."

"Then help me understand. What is this? What exactly are we doing?"

"We're… enjoying each other's company."

"Wow," he said.

"Well, is that so bad? I think you're a great guy. I enjoy being with you. I look forward to it. It's all the good parts of a relationship."

"No, it's not… not for me."

"No?"

"No. I want an actual relationship. I'm ready to be called on for comfort and support. Bethany, I've thought about you a long time. I think you're a special girl. And I'm a solid guy. I'm hardworking, driven. I'm trustworthy…loyal. I can be somewhat flexible, but I'm—"

"Not Jewish," Bethany said flatly.

"What?"

She looked down at her lap. "You're not Jewish."

"Oh," he said, blinking a few times. "I didn't… I didn't realize…"

"That I was Jewish?" she asked, looking up.

"Well, I guess I knew that much. I just didn't understand that being Jewish was a prerequisite for dating you. Apparently, it isn't required for having sex with you."

"I'm sorry. I didn't realize… I mean, I'm sorry, you're right. I should have said something sooner."

"So, this is it? This is as far as it goes?"

"I really do like you, Elias. I like what we have. But I understand if it's not what you want," she said, looking back down.

Elias took a deep breath. "Shit."

"I'll go."

"No."

"No?"

"No, I don't want you to go."

"Are you sure?"

"Yeah, I'm sure," he said, lying back again and pulling Bethany with him. He ran his fingers over her hair a few times. "I'm sure."

Bethany could hear her phone buzzing in the back pocket of her jeans on the floor. She knew it was Klaus calling and wished she could answer, but she didn't dare pull away from Elias in that moment.

Nineteen

It was nearly 10:30 PM by the time Elias let her go. She'd missed three calls from Klaus. Bethany had thought a lot about what Cam had told her, that Klaus would never touch her. It was intriguing to her. Although the attraction was undeniable, she didn't necessarily want Klaus. Mostly, she found herself curious about just how far sexual tension could be pressed. What would happen if she lingered behind, alone with him in his dorm? What if she stood close and gazed into his eyes as he had done to her? What if she tried to touch him? What would happen next?

Elias insisted on walking her across campus to her car. The parking lot pavement was slick and shiny. The air was cool and misty. Bethany hoped the temperature was low enough to keep her curls from frizzing into oblivion. Her phone buzzed again as they approached her car.

"I'm just gonna get my violin into the car," she said, opening the driver side door and reaching over to lean her violin against the seat on the floor of the passenger side. She chucked her cell phone onto the seat, and closed the door.

"So, there's no wiggle room?" Elias asked.

"That's where you've been… in the wiggle room."

"Mmm. I like the wiggle room," he said, taking her into his arms. "It's nice in the wiggle room." He bent to kiss her, then looked into her eyes. "Can't you even imagine a real relationship with a..?"

"A gentile?"

"Is that what I am? Huh. Strangely, it's never before occurred to me that I was a gentile," he said with a shrug of his shoulders. He took a deep breath, examining Bethany's face. "So, you can't even imagine being my girl?"

"I imagine it all the time, Elias. But these are fantasies. It's not an actual option for me, for my life."

"Damn."

"I'm sorry."

"I don't want you to keep apologizing. Ya know… It is what it is."

"So… Best to cut our losses?"

Elias stared into her eyes silently for a moment. "Part of me thinks so."

"Well, I certainly understand."

"Another part of me thinks I ought to hold on to you tightly for as long as I can," he said, pressing her back against her car.

"I'm definitely game for that too. I just don't want to make it more painful."

"Is it painful for you?"

"Of course it is."

"I'd never know it," Elias said, watching her eyes. "I can hear your passion when you play the violin. I can feel it when I've got you in my bed, but otherwise, you just seem… You're just so…"

"Placid?"

"Yeah."

"Yeah. But I want to be with you as much as you want to be with me. I wish this never had to end. When it does, I'll be hurt. But I have to live my life and let you live yours."

"But why? How could this be so important? How can it be right to deny your own feelings?"

Bethany shrugged. "This is what's done."

Elias stared back quietly a moment before taking a deep breath.

"I've got you now though," he said, kissing her. "I've got you for the semester."

Bethany smiled. "It'll be a good semester."

* * *

As Elias turned to walk back to the dorms, Bethany got into her car. She drove out of the student parking lot. As she drove, her phone began to buzz. She saw it was Klaus calling once again. She wanted to answer, but as long as Elias was willing to hold onto her, she knew she'd have to forgo the temptation of flirting back with Klaus. And she certainly couldn't risk Elias catching her back at the dorms tonight and misunderstanding.

Twenty

Tuesday morning, Killian left early for the lab. Bethany took advantage of the morning privacy. She turned off her phone, which had already begun buzzing, went to the living room, and played a full hour's worth of scales and arpeggios before breaking into the Shostakovich. As she played through the *Prelude*, she could almost hear the velvety darkness of Klaus's notes playing along with her own. Closing her eyes as she played, she could almost see him, his sparkling blue eyes, his messy dirty blonde hair, his hands—manly and powerful, but still somehow delicate enough to create his exquisite sound.

Bethany carried her violin to her bedroom and hit play on the tape in her stereo. After listening to Klaus's intro, she began soloing over the 12-bar blues recordings. She played just for the fun of it, getting messy as Klaus had instructed, bending her notes, glissing into them, sometimes slamming into them, hammering her double stops. She let it all out.

Bethany still recognized the syrupy sweetness of her tone, but there was a new heat packed into it.

Hot honey.

She thought about Klaus. He had seen something in her and had forced her far outside her comfort zone in order to extract it. He had permanently changed the way she thought about music, about herself.

The tape ended. She was surprised to find her cheeks streaked with tears again. She set her violin on her desk, wiped her face with her hands, then rewound the tape. It was time to try moving out of Mixolydian. She reached into her back pocket and pulled out the folded sheet of paper Klaus had given her. Reading through the modes, she saw Ionian was a regular major scale, and realized Aeolian was a natural minor scale. Lydian looked less interesting but she tried it out a few times.

Bright… very bright.

She wasn't sure how or where she'd use Lydian, and decided to study Dorian next.

Dorian had a darker sound, but its raised 6 gave it something interesting, something mysterious, a bit brighter than Aeolian, a bit more hopeful. Bethany kept her phone turned off the rest of the day, playing Dorian in different keys, over and over again. In Dorian, she could see dark blue eyes surrounded by bright golden white lashes. As she played, she imagined a rhythm with a nice even tempo.

Bold. Vigorous. Resolute.

Dorian… the mode of Vikings.

She'd practiced until Killian returned from the lab. Then, she finished her reading for American Theater and wrote an essay based on her reading. When Killian left for work, she got out her violin again. Her body was tired, her fingers sore, but it felt good. By around 10 PM, she'd realized she should probably read over her physics notes, getting into bed with her notebook.

The next morning, she slept later than intended. She showered and dressed quickly in jeans and a white t-shirt, then went to the living room, slipped into her Keds, grabbed her backpack, and left for Physics.

In order to avoid walking past Presser, Bethany parked on the other end of campus. She knew she had over a dozen missed calls, and she'd have to come up with an explanation for ducking Klaus, but decided it would be best to wait until tomorrow, when she'd have time to jam.

As she strolled down Liacouras Walk, she saw Elias exiting his dorm building. She was about to call out to him but stopped herself when she noticed a small blonde girl walking out beside him. Bethany dropped back a few paces in order to widen the distance between them before continuing. She watched as the blonde frequently turned toward Elias, talking and laughing. At one point, she placed a hand on his arm for just a few seconds. Bethany felt her own arms growing prickly as she continued watching.

The pair approached Barton's side entrance, but didn't enter. Instead, Elias gestured, and they continued around to the front side of the building, where Bethany would normally be entering. Reluctantly, she continued following, hoping Klaus wouldn't happen to be standing outside Presser Hall where he might spot her across the street. She looked over. There was a small group of music majors out front, but no one she recognized.

Finally, Elias and the blonde girl stopped at the front entrance of Barton Hall. Bethany crossed W. Norris Street to stand behind one of the food trucks in front of Tomlinson Theater. From there, she studied the tiny girl's soft, delicate features. Given the distance, Bethany couldn't be sure, but she'd bet anything there was a pair of dreamy blue eyes to go with that long, silky flaxen hair. She felt the prickles climbing her shoulders.

She tried to reason through this, to think about it rationally. There was no call for envy. After all, she did not belong to Elias. He had wanted her to belong to him, had asked her to, and she had declined. Elias was certainly free to spend his time with another girl.

But the source of her discontent wasn't Elias with another girl. It was something else. Generally, men who admired Bethany seemed to favor her type in general. She was very grateful for these heroic men—men like Killian, who could have his pick, yet somehow maintained a strong proclivity for tall brunettes. But for these lionhearted paladins, the petite blonde would claim a fully uncontested victory.

Here, Bethany realized, she had made the grave mistake of carelessly mixing with a man who seemingly liked both types well enough. Elias had tapped into the latent heat, creating a stir. An angry undercurrent was forming. There was no stronger reactant, no worse torment than propinquity of the sundoll.

Bethany continued spying from across the street. She watched closely as Elias leaned a hand on the brick building, the tiny blonde quickly scooting in beneath his arm, reaching up to touch Elias's hair. Bethany felt a tightness in her chest as she imagined Elias kissing the tiny blonde, mounting her, making love to her in the bed where Bethany had lain little over a day ago. The prickles set in deep as she stared at the couple. She didn't want to continue watching, but found it impossible to look away.

In her mind, she could hear a frantic repetition of the Dorian mode along with the high-pitched screech of an engine, an explosive impact, screams of terror, structural elements raining down.

It wasn't until Bethany spotted Klaus exiting Presser Hall from the corner of her eye that she snapped back to her senses, summoning the strength to move on. She quickly ducked in front of the food truck, crossed back over W. Norris, and walked around to the side of the building to avoid both Klaus, and Elias with his blonde.

Blinking back a blinding jealous rage, Bethany approached the side entrance and pulled open the door.

"ID?"

There was a heavyset uniformed black woman perched on a stool behind a podium, holding a walkie talkie. A guard lady.

"What?"

"You need student ID to enter the building," the guard lady informed Bethany.

"Since when?"

"Since now," she responded contemptuously.

"Why?"

"Um...because our nation just experienced an apparent terrorist attack, and the university has wisely decided to beef up campus security," she said, rolling her neck as she spoke.

"Right," Bethany said, rolling her eyes and dropping her backpack to the floor to dig around for her student ID card. Other students stopped short behind her, stumbling around her, holding up their ID cards to enter the building as though it were perfectly routine. Bethany finally found her card, and held it up for the guard lady.

"Okay," the guard lady huffed. "You might want to invest in a lanyard so you don't keep holding everyone up at the door."

"Hmm," was all Bethany managed, continuing on her way.

Bethany didn't like the idea of wearing an ID card around her neck, deciding she'd probably rather hold up those who did. As she continued walking toward the classroom, she saw Elias approaching, sans blonde, from the front entrance.

"Hey!" he called to her. "Where are you coming from?"

"Parked on the other end of campus today."

"Why?"

Bethany shrugged. She didn't want to talk to Elias. She didn't want to be near him. Despite Elias standing at least 6 inches taller than her, all Bethany could think about now was how awkwardly large she must seem compared to his tiny blonde. She felt like an ogress. She needed to get far away from him.

With the start of class still a few minutes away, Bethany rushed ahead, swung open the classroom door, and jogged down the stairs to sit at the front of the classroom. She took a seat at the end of a row beside an older woman, greeting the older woman with a polite smile. The older woman politely smiled back.

Elias had followed her. He crouched down beside her in the aisle. Bethany shifted inward toward the older woman, then ducked down and began rummaging through her backpack on the floor.

"What are you doing?"

"Getting out my notes."

"Why are you sitting way up here?"

"I want to hear the lecture."

"Come back and sit with me. I'll behave myself."

Bethany flushed, knowing the older woman could hear him. She turned her face toward Elias.

"No," she spat.

Elias jerked his head back. "Why not?"

"Elias, I don't want to talk to you. I'm just here for Physics."

"Okay," he said, taking the seat directly behind her. He leaned forward, speaking quietly next to her ear. "I take it you saw Erika."

> *On the heath there blooms a little flower*
> *And it's called Erika!*
> *Eagerly a hundred thousand little bees*
> *Swarm around Erika!*

Bethany could feel the prickles creeping up the back of her neck. There was a swirling heat rising to the surface.

"Does it bother you to see me with another girl?" he asked, leaning closer to her ear. He was close enough that she could feel his breath.

Bethany swallowed hard.

"Does it, Bethany?"

Bethany kept still, feeling the burning heat on her face.

"I think it does."

She remained silent.

"Maybe that should tell you something."

Bethany dropped her notebook back into her backpack, stood, and began climbing back up the stairs. Elias followed. Bethany hurried, jogging her way back up to the top, Elias close behind her. Finally, she reached the door, pulled it open, and continued rushing through the empty hall toward the front entrance.

"Hey," Elias said, catching her in his arm. "Talk to me."

Bethany tried to pull away from him, but he held onto her, pulling her into a tight embrace. Being in his arms made her cringe. The screech and explosion repeated over the Dorian mode, growing so loud she couldn't tell if Elias had continued speaking. She couldn't see anything but the sundoll, her tiny delicate body, her shiny golden hair, her ethereal beauty. Bethany thought about what it must be like for a man to touch and to hold a girl like that. The prickles painfully edged up the back of her skull as she imagined Elias removing the girl's tiny clothing, parting her tiny thighs, wrapping his fingers around her silky blonde tresses.

"Bethany."

Bethany thought about how giant she must feel to him now, how dull she must look with her plain brown hair and plain brown eyes. She had to get away from him. She pushed and pulled as hard as she could, but he backed her into a wall and pressed against her.

"Stop it," he said.

"Elias, let me go!" she finally managed, her voice coming out a thin shriek.

"No. I want you to talk to me. Tell me why you're upset."

"Let me go."

"Just the other night, you told me you couldn't be my girl."

Bethany gave up fighting and stared downward silently, trying to control her erratic breathing.

"Remember?"

She closed her eyes, feeling the heat on her face.

"Look, there's nothing going on with Erika, okay? She's just some girl I know."

Bethany tried to pull away again.

"Stop it, goddamn it," Elias scolded, holding her tightly against the wall. "I just brought her to class to make a point. If it bothers you to see me with someone else, maybe you ought to reassess some things."

Bethany's face must've expressed the outrage she was feeling because Elias responded with, "Clearly, this wasn't a well thought out approach. Okay? I'm sorry. It was stupid. I just... I just want to be with you, Bethany."

"I can't be with you, Elias. I need you to let me go."

"I'll let you go if you hold my hand and walk with me, okay? Let's just walk."

Bethany reluctantly accepted his hand in order to free herself from his tight grasp.

"Come with me to my dorm."

"No," Bethany said. It was in that moment she remembered she'd parked on the other side of campus and was now headed out the wrong end of the building in full view of Presser Hall. She yanked her hand from Elias, pivoted, and rushed back toward the side entrance. Elias hurried alongside her.

"Bethany, stop. Stop. C'mon, I'm sorry. Can you at least talk to me? Tell me why you're so mad."

But Bethany wasn't mad. She was mostly just horribly embarrassed and desperate to get away from Elias. She needed to forget she'd ever met him. The world was full of beautiful men to admire. The world was full of women of all shapes and sizes. Bethany usually remembered she was one of the fortunate ones, that God had granted her many desirable traits. She liked knowing that much. But the idea of being compared to tiny sundolls made her forget it. It made her feel ugly, inadequate, inferior. There was nothing for her to do but run away from it and start over.

Elias grabbed Bethany around her waist from behind and swung her around.

"Fucking stop. Talk to me," he said, roughly turning her and pressing her back into the wall.

"There's nothing to talk about," she said, twisting against him, "This was over anyway."

"Stop," he repeated, pressing harder against her. "Look, if this can really only be a short-term relationship, a one-semester fling, then that's all it can be. I'm sorry about today. It was really stupid. Just forget it, will ya?"

Bethany craned her neck to see around Elias. Frantically, she scanned the hall, relieved to see that the scuffle had managed to catch the attention of the guard lady. Bethany held the guard lady's gaze until she stood from her stool and began ambling over, pulling out her walkie talkie.

"Excuse me," the guard lady said. Elias didn't seem to hear her.

"Bethany, come to my dorm," he continued. "We need to talk about this."

"Excuse me!" the guard lady repeated.

Elias looked over.

"I think you better let go of this young lady."

He paused, his lips tightening, his eyebrows drawing downward and pulling together as he glared at the guard lady then back at Bethany.

Frustration.

"Are you okay, miss? Do you know him?"

"I'm alright," Bethany said. "But… no, I don't really know him, and I'd like to be on my way."

"Sir, I'm gonna need you to let go of her immediately before I call campus security. And I'll need to see some ID."

Elias took a deep breath then finally released Bethany in order to deal with the guard lady. Bethany took off running. After a minute, her phone started buzzing. She continued running until she reached her car, then turned her phone off and drove until she got home.

Twenty-One

Once home, Bethany sat outside the apartment in her car. Killian's green Jeep Cherokee was parked on the cobblestone beside the church. More than ever, she wished she could go curl up in Killian's arms and forget everything else in the world. But the world would still be waiting for her, and she knew Killian was dangerous territory in her vulnerable state. So, she restarted her engine and drove.

Bethany thought about how irrationally she'd behaved. She was deeply ashamed, reflecting on how quickly she'd crumbled into a ridiculous, hyper-emotional wreck, and how horribly she'd lashed out at Elias. She knew she owed him an apology, but there was simply no way for her to explain herself, her intense phobia. She'd never discussed it with anyone. She simply managed to avoid it as best she could. And she knew she'd have to avoid Elias now too. Dropping Physics seemed a terrible waste, but she didn't want to face him again and was certainly not prepared to do it every week for the remainder of the semester.

As she continued driving aimlessly through the city, it occurred to Bethany that she was now free to play with Klaus in any way she wanted. She still wasn't sure about going to his dorm since it significantly increased the probability of running into Elias, but Klaus was officially fair game. Maybe he actually never would touch her. That would be just fine. The experiment itself would be more than enough. She smiled to herself, feeling a bit better.

After stopping for a slice at Lorenzo and Sons on South Street, Bethany made her way to Penn's Landing. She parked and began walking, staring up at the towering work of art sprawled across the second half of the pedestrian bridge: three steel and aluminum figures, holding hands, standing maybe 30 feet tall. Colloquially, the piece was known as "the Stickmen." From the start of the bridge, the figure closest appeared considerably larger than the other two. One day, Bethany had spent nearly an hour assessing the piece from all different angles until she finally realized it was an optical illusion, that the three figures were actually the exact same size. She continued gazing up at them. There was something about them that brought her comfort.

It was just after 8 PM when Bethany returned to the apartment. After showering, she dressed in an oversized purple t-shirt, combed Infusium through her hair and dried it. She wasn't sure if she was actually exhausted or just feeling drained from her wild outburst and scattered emotions, but either way, she was hoping to put the day behind her.

Lying in bed, she found herself unable to quiet her mind, turning from one side to the other, then back again. She couldn't seem to stop reliving the moments of her mortifying tantrum. Squeezing her eyes shut, she quietly sang to herself.

> *"Bei mir bist du schön, please let me explain*
> *Bei mir bist du schön means you're grand*
> *Bei mir bist du schön, again I'll explain*
> *It means you're the fairest in the land"*

Finally, she gave up, jolting upward and slipping out of bed, then wandering out to the kitchen. There, she pulled the bottle of Three Olives out of the freezer, opened it, took a swig, replaced the cap, and set the bottle back in the freezer. She moved into the living room and sat on the green recliner.

Settling back into it, her eyes landed on a book Killian had left on the small table beside it. Bethany knew it would be a chemistry book before picking it up. It was, but as she began skimming, she found several notes tucked in between pages. Some were printed, some handwritten on lined paper. There were directions on how to purify water with iodine, how to build and maintain emergency shelters, preventing oxidation of certain materials. There were also a few brief notes about long-term food storage, and a few she wasn't sure she understood about solubility and combustion. She neatly tucked the pages back into the book, and returned the book to the table.

Bethany stood, and wandered back toward Killian's bedroom. He had left his bedside table lamp on. She glanced at the clock beside the lamp. 10:17 PM. Killian wouldn't be home for hours. She entered and let her eyes gaze around his room. His olive green t-shirt was left hanging over his weight bench in the corner. She walked over to the weights and picked up the shirt, thinking about how perfectly it hugged his thick arms and bulky shoulders. She brought it to her face, breathing in deeply, then carried it to the side of his bed and sat.

His bed hadn't been made, so she pushed the light green quilt and white top sheet over a bit and rested back against his pillow, stretching her legs over his bed. The fabric was cold against her back and bare thighs, so she pulled the top sheet and quilt over her body, and soon warmed. She snuggled into Killian's bed, fantasizing about Killian returning home to find her there, and what she knew would happen next. Soon, she drifted off.

The clattering of keys on the kitchen counter woke Bethany with a start. She gasped, leaping from Killian's bed and scooted behind his bedroom door, holding her breath. She sighed with relief as she heard Killian turn into the bathroom. Bethany chucked his t-shirt back over the weights in the corner, then quickly and quietly slunk back down the hall to her own bedroom, and climbed into her own bed, pulling the covers up to her chin.

A minute later, she watched Killian pass her door on the way to his bedroom. Then, after a moment, she heard him coming back down the hall. Bethany held her breath. She closed her eyes, but could hear Killian stop in her doorway. She held her breath, her heart racing. She could feel him standing there.

Realizing he wouldn't be able to make out her face in the blackness of her room, she opened one eye just enough to see Killian's silhouette illuminated by the dim light in the hall. His arms were raised up, leaning against the top of her door frame, his head cocked to one side.

All she had to do was make a single movement, utter a single word. She knew he would come to her, and how she wished he would... But there would be no going back from it. With all the self-discipline she could muster, she silently locked her arms down over herself and pressed her lips together tightly. She squeezed both eyes shut and waited for him to leave. After another minute or so, he finally did.

Twenty-Two

During their Sunday call, Bubbie had informed Bethany that she'd arranged a date for her on Tuesday evening with Ruth's nephew. Naturally, Bethany protested, but Bubbie had insisted.

"This is what's done, bubeleh. No girl figures it all out on her own. Give in to the people who love you. Let them take the lead sometimes."

Bethany had spoken briefly over the phone with Ruth's nephew: Aaron Blumberg, 25, second-year UPenn medical student, originally from the Upper West Side. He'd made dinner reservations for tonight at Buddakan. Bethany wished they could just meet at a falafel cart or a water ice stand or something, take a walk together. She'd never quite understood the enjoyment people seemed to derive from fine dining at trendy restaurants. It certainly seemed like an awful lot of fluff to get through on a first date. But she'd promised Bubbie she would allow Aaron to set the date and make the plans.

The reservation was for 8:30, so she was able to wait for Killian to leave for work before getting herself ready. Bethany showered, took a bit more care than usual with styling her hair, dabbed on a bit of makeup, and slipped into her only formal dress: a slinky black cocktail that hugged her figure, showed off her legs, and served up just enough cleavage to be sexy but not sleazy. As she slipped into her only pair of kitten heels, she said a quick prayer that Aaron Blumberg was at least 6'2". This was the problem with blind dates.

She drove toward the restaurant, unable to fully rid herself of the feelings of dread but trying to keep focused on the purpose of the date: easing Bubbie's mind. By agreeing to meet Aaron, Bethany was showing Bubbie she was making an honest effort.

117

It was 8:18 when she parked as close as she could without paying for parking. She checked her reflection then began walking. As she reached the block, she noticed a man standing near the restaurant, slowly pacing back and forth a few feet in front of the entrance. Bethany knew right away he was her date and sighed in relief at his height. He was plenty tall, around Killian's height of 6-foot-4, but definitely on the more slender side. This was not a guy with a weight bench in his bedroom. He dressed in a pair of dark wash jeans and a fitted white polo shirt. He had dark wavy hair and a pleasant face that reminded her of home. Bethany watched as he pulled his hands from the pockets of his jeans then shoved them right back in, his shoulders slightly raised.

Anxiety.

With a heavy sigh, she continued toward him. As he turned back in her direction, Bethany caught his eye and smiled. He quickly stood at attention, pulling his hands from his pockets again and straightening his shoulders. As she moved closer, he finally smiled back, although she could see he was still uneasy.

"Bethany Schechter?"

"Yes."

"Wow," he said, looking her over, his eyebrows raised in appreciation. "It's very nice to see you—to meet you. I'm Aaron."

He held out his hand, and she took it.

"Very nice to meet you too," Bethany said.

Aaron gave her hand a somewhat rigid shake, releasing it quickly, then opened the door of the restaurant for her. Inside, they were greeted by a hostess.

"Blumberg," Aaron told the hostess before turning back toward Bethany. He was about to speak when the hostess told them to follow her. With his arm, he gestured for Bethany to walk ahead of him. At the table, he pulled out Bethany's chair before sitting across from her.

"So, you know my bubbie?" Bethany asked.

"We haven't actually met. My Aunt Ruth seems to be a close friend of hers though."

"Yes. I know Ruth well."

"Of course! You lived there, right? Brooklyn!" he said with just a little too much enthusiasm.

Bethany couldn't help rolling her eyes. Bethany's father had been from the Upper West Side. From the stories she'd been told, Bethany knew that, sometime after her father had moved to California, he'd tried to buy Bubbie and Zayde a home on Central Park West. Bubbie had described it as "fancy schmancy" and said it had been a very generous offer. But Bubbie and Zayde loved their home in Brooklyn, and refused to leave it. And now Bethany loved it too.

"Uh…" he began, noticing her eyeroll.

"And you're from the Upper West Side," she said with a tight smile.

"Uh… Right."

"Right."

"Yeah."

"Yeah."

There was an awkward silence.

"Sorry, did I say something wrong?" he asked.

"No, of course not."

"Okay."

"Okay."

Aaron blinked then began looking around the restaurant. "I wonder where our waiter is."

Bethany stared down at her menu.

"You said you've never been here?" Aaron asked.

"No, never been here. I'm not really an upscale restaurant person."

119

"Oh."

"Yeah. Ya know… pizza, deli, bagels… Brooklyn," she said.

Aaron's brow furrowed, but he quickly recovered. "Would you like to go somewhere else? Do something else?"

"Really?" Bethany asked suddenly hopeful. "Could we? Would that be okay?"

"Absolutely," he said, standing. "Let's get outta here."

He walked over to pull her chair out. Bethany stood, and they walked out together.

"So, what would you like to do?" Aaron asked.

Bethany stared blankly.

"I'd be happy to take you anywhere at all," Aaron said.

"Um… Ya know, you don't actually have to take me out. I know this wasn't your idea."

"Well… You're right, of course, but…"

"Let's not and say we did?"

"No."

"No?"

"No," Aaron said again. "I… I'm sorry, I'm getting the feeling I started off on the wrong foot somehow, but… Well, it's not irredeemable, is it?"

Bethany paused. She certainly didn't want to make Aaron feel bad. It's just that she could already tell she was going to have difficulty being nice to him.

"I don't take girls out very often. Maybe that's obvious, I don't know. I thought I was doing my aunt a favor here, but… Well, I can see that she's actually done me one," he said. "And I'd still really like to have this date… if you wouldn't mind."

Bethany examined his face, noticing a faint stubble along his nicely-defined jawline and above his full pink lips. His golden brown eyes were hopeful as he awaited her response.

"Of course," Bethany said quickly, taking a deep breath. "Why don't we skip the restaurant and just take a walk?"

"No dinner?" he asked.

Bethany shrugged.

"Okay… Sure," he said. "A walk. A walk here? …around Old City?"

"Um… We could go to Penn's Landing… walk along the water."

"Sounds great. Weeknight… easy parking. Let's take my car so we don't have as far of a walk to the river," he said, gesturing toward her shoes. "Unless…"

"Unless?"

"Unless… Well, of course, I'd completely understand if you felt unsafe about getting into my car."

Bethany nearly snorted. "I feel just fine about it, Aaron."

Aaron drove a white Volkswagen Passat. It looked like a brand new car. She smirked, thinking about the sort of man who buys a brand new white Passat. He parked at Front Street, and they got out and began their stroll across the South Street Pedestrian Bridge to Penn's Landing.

"So," Aaron began, "I'm told you're a theater major."

Bethany stared up at the Stickmen, trying not to look bored. "Right."

"And a violinist?"

"Right."

"That's fantastic. How long have you been playing?"

"Since I was 7."

"Wow. I'd love to hear you sometime."

"Mmm. And you're in med school?"

"Second year."

"Do you know what you plan to specialize in?"

"No, I haven't decided yet."

"So… Why medicine? You want to save lives?'

Aaron was quiet long enough that Bethany glanced over to make sure he'd heard her question.

"That would be the thing to say, wouldn't it?" he finally responded.

"What?"

"I want to save lives? That's the answer you'd want to hear, right?"

Bethany shrugged. "What's the real answer?"

"I… Well, the truth is, I never really thought about saving lives or about medicine at all until just a few years ago. I always thought it would be nice to own a store. I wanted to repair and sell old appliances."

"Like washers and dryers?"

"Washers and dryers, refrigerators, air conditioners, vacuum cleaners…"

"Do you know how to fix all of those things?"

"I'm very handy, yes."

"Really?"

"I am, yes," he said looking over at her. His lips curled in amusement. "This surprises you."

"Maybe a little."

"As a child, I enjoyed taking things apart and putting them back together. And actually, there are a limited number of things that generally go wrong with an old appliance. If you're familiar with the model, it's easy to diagnose, and usually easy enough to repair."

"Why not just sell new appliances?" she asked as they started down the stairs off the back of the pedestrian bridge.

Aaron looked at her as though she'd just said something blasphemous.

"Because the new ones are garbage. Sure, they're shiny and flashy, made to turn heads, but they're composed of fragile parts that break far too easily. Most are too flimsy to even bother with repairs." he said.

They reached the bottom of the stairs and he continued. "Old appliances aren't always pretty, but they're rugged machines that were designed to survive wear and tear. If you take care of them and repair the occasional problem, they'll last a lifetime," he said, sounding like a salesman. "If it was built to last, it's worth maintaining."

They reached Delaware Ave.

"May I?" Aaron asked, reaching out his hand.

Resisting an eyeroll, Bethany accepted it. He cupped her hand passively, palm across palm. It reminded Bethany of the way Zayde had held her hand to cross a street when she was a child. She couldn't help but wonder how Aaron would react if she lifted his hand to her face and sucked his thumb into her mouth. She pursed her lips to stifle a laugh.

Once they'd crossed, Bethany gently withdrew her hand.

"So... How did saving old washers and dryers turn into saving lives?"

"Well, my father is a doctor. Not a life-saving doctor exactly... a podiatrist, but he's got a well-respected practice, and it's what was expected of me. I suppose I could have strayed from the path, but... Well, I think ultimately, I want to be a strong provider... a husband and father. You know... someday. And I guess medicine seemed like the more reliable route for that."

"That seems sensible."

They reached the waterfront. Aaron turned to examine her face a moment. "Do you... Do you like sensible?"

Bethany smiled. "I come from a long line of sensible. I can certainly appreciate sensible."

Aaron returned her smile, and again held his hand out to her. She took his hand, and they continued their stroll along the Delaware River.

* * *

By the time they'd gotten back to Aaron's car, Bethany's mind had begun to wander. Aaron was tall, attractive, and of course polite. He asked all the right getting-to-know-you questions without ever delving into anything too personal, although Bethany of course knew that Aaron must know more about her than he was letting on. His Aunt Ruth was the biggest yenta in the building, and she'd known Bethany her entire life.

Ruth had been there for every single one of Bethany's recitals. She'd been there to help Bethany get dolled up for her first official date with Benjamin Abramowitz, captain of the chess club. She'd been there the time Bethany had come home drunk from a party at Stefania Esposito's apartment, and for the rumors that followed afterward about Bethany and Adrian Barragan, Stefania's older brother's friend from the Upper East Side. Ruth was there when, much to Bubbie's horror, Bethany had chemically straightened her hair. She'd attended Bethany's high school graduation ceremony where Bethany had been named valedictorian. And she'd been there for the shock Bethany delivered to Bubbie when she'd decided to major in theater at Temple instead of entering Julliard as expected.

"Should we go somewhere for a drink?" Aaron asked as they got into his car.

"I don't drink."

"Coffee?"

"I don't drink that either."

"Well, let's get you something to eat. Aunt Ruth would be appalled to hear I didn't at least buy you dinner. Something casual."

"I'm really ready to head back to my car, Aaron."

"Right," Aaron said curtly. "Where are you parked?"

"2nd and Walnut."

Aaron started the engine and began driving.

"So… Can I ask what I did wrong?"

"What? Oh, nothing. Nothing at all, Aaron. I'm just a bit tired."

"But you're not going to let me take you out again, are you?"

"Actually, I'd very much like to see you again."

Aaron eyed her suspiciously.

"This weekend?" she asked.

"Really?"

"Of course really."

"Alright," Aaron said brightly. "This weekend. Where? What do you like to eat?"

"Pizza?"

"Pizza. Great!"

"That's me," Bethany said, pointing to her car.

"Yellow," he noted, pulling in and parking behind her Neon.

"What's left of it," she said.

"I um… I don't want to push my luck, but… Well, would it be too forward to ask for a kiss?"

Bethany suppressed another eyeroll, instead smiling politely as she turned to him. Aaron leaned in, softly kissed her, then pulled back. On an impulse, Bethany leaped toward Aaron while reaching her hand around the back of his head to grab a fistful of his wavy hair. She thought about Jared in their first scene of the semester and mashed her lips against Aaron's, kissing him with a wildly undue passion. Aaron began kissing her back, reaching an arm around her. After a minute or so, Bethany finally released him, noting the look of wonder on his face.

"Don't ask permission next time, okay?" she asked.

He appeared to snap back into the moment. "Okay, I won't."

"Great," she said, turning and opening the passenger door. "This weekend. Pizza."

"Right. I uh… I'll call you to set that up."

She smiled again. "See ya."

"See ya," he said, still looking slightly bewildered.

After driving out of sight, she let out a laugh, thinking of Aaron's shocked expression. But soon, a sadness came over her as she realized her days of youthful indiscretion would soon be coming to an end.

Twenty-Three

By the time Bethany made it to her front door, she was aching to get out of the high heels. She kicked them off as soon as she got to the base of the stairs, then carried them up and to her bedroom closet where she slipped out of her dress. After a scalding hot shower, she dried her hair, dressed in an oversized white t-shirt, and walked to the kitchen.

Pulling the bottle of Three Olives from the freezer, she shivered, then opened it, took a swig, then another before putting it back. She rested a while in the green recliner, allowing the warmth of the booze to envelop her. Then, pulling herself back onto her feet, she wandered back through the kitchen and down the hall to Killian's room, turning on his bedside lamp. She sat at his desk. It was cluttered with stacks of books piled around his computer as usual.

Bethany was surprised to find several books that had nothing to do with chemistry. There was one providing first aid instruction, and two about hunting and foraging. She paged through one and found many more handwritten notes including some with detailed information about various types of firearms and ammunition. She wondered if Killian was dealing with a lot more anxiety than she'd realized. They had silently agreed to keep more of a physical distance from each other over the past few weeks, but Killian was still her best friend, and it seemed like he might be troubled. It was time to check in with him, to reconnect.

She moved over to his bed, lifting the light green quilt away from his plain white sheets, and climbed in. Knowing Killian wouldn't be home for another couple hours, she snuggled in and soon fell asleep.

It was 2:33 AM when Bethany woke. Killian would soon be home. She sat up in his bed, ready to rush to her own bedroom. But then, she lay back down. Maybe Killian needed her. Maybe she needed him. Pulling his covers up to her chin, she waited, squeezing her eyes shut.

2:34: Stay.

2:35: Yes. Stay.

2:36: Is this a mistake? No. Stay.

2:37: Just stay.

2:38: It's a mistake. You'll ruin everything, and there's no going back.

Bethany leaped out of Killian's bed. As she darted into the hall, she could hear Killian climbing the stairs and froze in a moment of panic. Her heart began to race. Trying to avoid creaking the floor, she crept down the hall toward her bedroom. She got about three quarters of the way to her door, and there he was, dressed in the very familiar olive green t-shirt that perfectly hugged his thick arms and bulky shoulders, and his worn, faded jeans. His wavy golden locks were tucked behind his ears. When he saw Bethany, he cocked his head, a few blonde strands falling loose over his face. His eyes were laser focused on her, and she found herself staring back at the tiny golden rings surrounded by the deep blue of his irises.

"I was just... Well... I um... I'm sorry," Bethany stammered. She hurried toward her bedroom door.

Killian stepped toward her, blocking her path, crowding her against the wall. Staring into her eyes, he placed a hand on her bare outer thigh. Slowly, he ran his hand upward beneath her oversized t-shirt, cupping her naked hip, pulling her close.

"I'm sorry," she repeated in a panicked whisper.

"Don't be sorry," he said quietly, lifting his other hand to the nape of her neck, then dragging his lips up and down the side of her face. "Get back in there."

Bethany felt a jolt and froze. Killian leaned in and began kissing her neck. Taking hold of her hair, he brushed his lips against hers. She stiffened, but he continued molding her lips with his. His hand tightened over her hip as he pulled her closer, pressing himself against her. Yanking away, she released a sharp gasp.

"Killian, stop."

He eased his grip. Bethany stared at him, trying to steady her breathing.

"Killian, stop?" he repeated, gazing at her.

She could feel her body trembling, her heart racing, and suddenly felt slightly dizzy, unable to respond. Again, he pulled her close against him and continued kissing her. Instinctively, she kissed him back, wanting him, desperately wishing she could forget herself, forget everything, and just let Killian take her back to bed, but another twinge of fear caused to to pull away again.

"No! Killian, stop."

Again, he eased his grip. With a sigh, he loosely wrapped his arms around her waist.

"Okay," he said, cocking his head. "Good night?"

She nodded.

"Alright." He leaned in and pressed his lips to her cheek. "Good night, Bethany."

He released her and stepped aside.

"Good night," she whispered, hurrying away.

Twenty-Four

There are relatively few practical applications of colorblind casting. The practice of disregarding visible and otherwise detectable traits of race and ethnicity is generally illegitimate as it is markedly detrimental to most productions. Obvious exceptions exist in some genres, including various forms of Comedy, Ancient Greek, and Ancient Roman Theater. Shakespearean or other Classical productions relying on stock characters to deliver lines in Elizabethan English can also be effectively cast with a disregard for the physical characteristics of race. However, some care must still be taken to avoid confusion. For the practice to be justifiable, it must be respectful of the text and non-disruptive to the storytelling. As theater is an art of communication, it's entirely appropriate for a production to advocate for social change and engage in political commentary; however, its top priority must be entertainment; otherwise it fails at its purpose as well as any tangential initiatives.

Bethany finished scribbling out the thesis paragraph for her American Theater paper then sat at her desk, staring at the pen hovering above the paper. All she could really think about was Killian. She knew he was likely sitting at the kitchen table. She'd seen him pass her door a few minutes ago, still wearing the olive green t-shirt. He'd traded the jeans for a pair of gray sweatpants. She listened for his spoon clanging against the cereal bowl, but couldn't hear anything above the street noise just outside her window.

She'd promised herself she was going to check in with Killian, and despite her embarrassing misbehavior last night, she knew she needed to face him today. She simply needed to exercise more self-control. The friendship had to take priority over her misty-eyed obsession and schoolgirl lust. Killian's mental wellness had to come first.

She nodded to herself and stood from the desk, nearly marching out of her room, then gasped as she remembered she was still only wearing her night shirt. She rushed over to the dresser, pulling out a pair of purple pajama pants, and slipped into them. Then she took a deep breath and headed out to the kitchen.

Killian sat at the table, reading. There was a nearly finished plate of scrambled eggs in front of him. She glanced at the book. It was a chemistry text she'd seen him with before.

"Good morning," he said, setting the book on the table.

"Morning, Pretty."

"Can I make you some eggs?"

"No, I'll eat a bit later," Bethany said. "Can we talk?"

"Absolutely," he said, holding his hand out to her.

She reached out, and he laced his fingers with hers, standing from his chair. Together, they walked to the living room. Killian sat in the green recliner, releasing Bethany's hand to ease her down onto his lap. She sat, and he pulled out the footrest. Bethany leaned back against him as he folded his arms over her. For a moment, she sat quietly, closing her eyes, enjoying the warmth of his body.

"Are you upset with me?" Killian asked softly.

"No, of course not. I... Well, I'm..." she paused, taking a deep breath. "I guess I'm kinda worried about you."

He waited for her to continue.

"I... Well, it's... It's just that I...." Struggling to find words, she took a deep breath. "Fuck."

"Easy," he said with a gentle laugh, running his hands up and down her upper arms. "Tell me why you're worried."

She took another deep breath. "I looked through some of your books," she spit out as fast as she could.

"Oh, yeah?"

"I'm really sorry."

Giving her a tight squeeze, he pecked the side of her face. "I don't really have any expectation of privacy living with you. You've always been kind of a snoop."

It was true. Bethany had always kept fairly close tabs on Killian. It never seemed to bother him any, but actively rummaging through his books and reading his notes felt more invasive than usual. Of course, she'd now also been caught sneaking from his bed on more than one occasion, and if he'd felt violated over it in any way, he certainly hadn't let on.

"Yeah," she admitted simply.

"So, you read through my notes, and now you're worried I'm becoming a deranged survivalist?"

"Well, no. Nothing I read seemed at all deranged, just, well… out of character mostly."

She could feel Killian nodding.

"Yeah, I suppose it is."

"Are you scared because of September 11th?"

"No. No, I'm not scared."

"Then..?"

"Bethany, I don't want you to worry. I'm really fine. I know I could tell you if I weren't, and that means a great deal to me."

Bethany was quiet. After a moment, she turned to look at him. His eyes met hers, and he puckered his lips out at her. She gave them a peck kiss before moving to stand up. He tightened his arms around her.

"Sit with me a while," he said.

Relieved to know he wasn't trying to dismiss her, she decided to try again.

"Well, if you're not scared because of September 11th, can you tell me what it is?"

Killian lifted a hand and began playing with her hair, gently tugging on curls, pulling them straight, and twisting them around his finger before releasing them.

"It's not fear," he said. "It's more like… wishful thinking in a way."

Bethany paused. "You want more outdoorsy activities in your life?"

Killian was quiet. Bethany turned to face him again, but he kept his eyes focused on her hair as he continued tugging curls straight and twisting them around his finger.

"Well, I like my life as it is right now," he said. "And I've always loved chemistry. Spending hours upon hours in a lab, analyzing and manipulating chemicals, would probably feel like a pointless, claustrophobic nightmare to many men, but I've always been drawn to it. I guess I just worry some about where it's leading me."

"You're worried about your future?"

"Somewhat, I guess. I mean, college is sort of bullshit, right? You go because… well, because you're supposed to. Get a degree so you can get a job and all that. But all the actual information has always been right there in the books, and now it's on the internet. The nice part about college for me is experimenting in the labs, playing around, trying to solve problems. But after graduation, it really won't be that way."

"How will it be?"

"I dunno, I'll probably be working some ordinary job, helping some corporation develop and monitor new plastics. My days will likely be very routine… dull and predictable," he said, taking a deep breath. "But that's where I'm headed. I guess I can't really complain. There's probably good reason for following the prescribed path and seeking security. That's why so many people do it, right?"

Bethany felt herself nodding.

"But sometimes, I guess it's… well, it's a little more exciting to think about what life would be like if everything we knew, everything that mattered to us, simply disappeared. If the whole goddamn world crumbled just like those towers, and all I had to do was survive and keep you safe…" he trailed off.

Bethany could feel her heart racing and was sure Killian could feel it. She felt him take a deep breath. He unraveled his finger from a lock of her hair then pulled her close and kissed the top of her head.

"Get up," he said. "I'm gonna make you some eggs. Then I need to shower and head to school."

Twenty-Five

For a few days, the weather had cooled down enough for Bethany to trade in her cutoffs and Keds for jeans and New Balance sneakers, but it was warm again today, and she opted to wear her blue and white sundress with a pair of sandals. Walking toward the computer lab, she enjoyed the sun and the cool breeze on her bare arms.

Her American Theater paper was due tomorrow, but Dr. Makena Ward-Washington had mentioned that students could drop their papers in her mailbox early for extra credit. Bethany was already getting an A in the class, but decided she might as well finish the paper and get it to Makena a day early.

She'd brought her violin to jam with Klaus and Cam afterward, then had plans to meet up with her new scene partner, Jelani, for a cold reading at 6 PM. She didn't know Jelani, but from watching his classroom performances, she knew he was talented. She'd also seen him in a Fringe Festival production that had required full frontal nudity of the entire all-male cast. It hadn't been an especially compelling story, but the spectacle had certainly managed to hold Bethany's attention. Jelani had given a strong, convincing performance. He was also nice to look at, and she looked forward to working with him.

There was a long line to enter the computer lab. As usual, Killian had offered Bethany use of his computer and printer, but she knew she'd never be able to concentrate in Killian's bedroom. Soon enough, she'd fold and get a computer of her own. She didn't like the idea of a home computer, worrying that the internet might end up absorbing too much of her attention. But now, here she was, wasting her time waiting in a line.

Finally, Bethany reached the front of the line and scanned her student ID. She sat at a computer and typed out the thesis paragraph she'd composed, then drafted and edited the remainder of the paper and read it back to herself. It was kind of a yawner, but seemed to be a clear and concise enough argument. She simply couldn't think of anything less obvious to say. So, she sent it to print, then collected her belongings, and went over to wait in line at the printers.

On her way to Presser Hall, she stopped at Tomlinson Theater, held up her ID, then climbed the stairs to the third floor, heading over to the faculty mailboxes.

"Hey, Bethany."

Without looking up, Bethany knew it was Quentin Baines. His office was directly across from the mailboxes, and Bethany was pretty sure she could already smell him.

"Hi, Quentin."

"Were you looking for me?"

"No, I just need to leave this paper in Makena's mailbox."

"Bottom row, on the right."

"Cool. Thanks."

"Can I buy you lunch?" he asked, standing up from his desk.

She could definitely smell him.

"I just ate. Thanks though."

"Walk with me anyway. I'll buy you a bubble tea."

She'd forgotten that Quentin had once bought her a bubble tea at the wall of food. Suddenly, the memory of sipping the honeydew flavored drink and chewing the tapioca pearls while listening to Quentin drone on and on about the heat in Tuscon, Arizona came rushing back to her. She remembered wondering how a person from such a hot climate hadn't learned to bathe on a daily basis.

"Sorry, I have to be somewhere."

"I see you've got your violin."

"Yeah."

"I'd love to hear you play again sometime."

"Of course… sometime. I have to get over to Presser now."

"Presser Hall? Across the street?"

"Yup."

"I'll walk you over. I'm heading out now."

"Great," she said.

Quentin insisted they take the elevator down, pointing to the brace on his knee. "Been acting up since last weekend's stage combat rehearsal."

He had some kind of long-term injury; the details of which Bethany couldn't recall, but Quentin had walked with a slight limp since before she'd met him.

Bethany followed Quentin into the elevator.

"I'd still like to get together with you again sometime," Quentin said once the elevator doors closed.

Bethany thought she might choke on his stench.

"Sorry," she said, staring at the floor. "I'm seeing someone."

"Not asking you to marry me."

She looked up at Quentin. His face broke into a wide, radiant smile. Bethany thought again about how handsome he must have been not so long ago. He seemed like a sweet enough guy, but taking their relationship off campus had been a mistake. She knew it was her hazy memories of Quentin panting and sweating on her more than his ghastly odor that was causing her stomach to lurch. She could kick herself.

"Sorry," she repeated, offering a gentle smile.

Quentin shrugged. "Can't blame a guy," he said.

The elevator doors opened. Bethany was grateful for the flow of fresh air. She stepped out, and they walked out to N. 13th Street.

"Well, I'll see ya."

"See ya, Quentin," she said, turning to cross the street. Klaus was already standing outside Presser, watching her.

"Hey, Bethany?" Quentin called out to her.

"Yeah?" she asked, turning back to Quentin.

He limped back over to her. "Maybe just drinks sometime, huh?"

"I really can't."

Quentin glanced across the street at Klaus.

"That the boyfriend?" he asked.

"Um, no… That's just a guy I'm playing with."

Quentin's heavy brow bone lifted, causing his hazel eyes to suddenly appear much wider. Bethany held up her violin to clarify.

"Right," he said with a chuckle and another warm smile. "Well, it was good to see you. Have fun."

"Enjoy your lunch," Bethany said, smiling back.

She turned again, crossing 13th Street to Klaus who had been inching closer to the curb. He was wearing the pale blue t-shirt that brought out his spectacular blue eyes. Bethany admired them as they sparkled in the sun.

"Who's the old guy?" Klaus asked, watching Quentin limp down the street.

"Theater prof."

"Ah," he said, turning back to Bethany, looking her over. "You wear that to distract me, warm honey?"

She smiled as they walked toward the building. Klaus pulled the door open for Bethany and entered the building behind her. The two of them held up their ID cards as they continued toward the practice rooms.

"Is Cam already in there?" she asked.

"Cam got called to do some studio work," Klaus said, opening a practice room door for her. "I've got you all to myself today."

"Um…"

"Um..? What, scared I might try to kiss you?" he asked, letting the door close behind himself.

"Scared *I* might try to kiss *you*," she said with a smile.

Klaus grinned back at her, sucking in his bottom lip.

"What are we gonna play without Cam?" she asked.

"Back to our roots today."

"Classical?"

"That okay?"

"Sure. I didn't bring any sheet music though."

Klaus lifted a folder. "Sometimes when I leave you alone to warm up, I actually just stand in the hall to listen, so I know you like this one."

He opened the folder and pulled out the Bach Double.

"Oooh! I do like that one."

"Say please, and I'll play second fiddle," he said, handing her the pages for first violin."

"Please," she said, accepting the sheets and placing them on the music stand.

Klaus picked up one of the collapsed music stands stacked in the corner, opened it up, then set up across from Bethany.

"Move that off to the side a little," Bethany said.

"My stand?"

"I wanna watch you during my rests."

Klaus winked at Bethany while setting the stand off to the side.

"Like uh…uh…uh…uh," he said.

Bethany nodded and watched as he lifted his arm and began the second violin part, savoring his round, crisp notes, relishing the determined movements of his strong, elegant hand, admiring his beautiful bow grip. The four measures passed far too quickly. She wished she could continue watching him, but she had to come in.

As soon as she did, there was a new fizzing intensity in the room. She felt the start of prickly tingles as their two sounds—his velvety forest green and her syrupy golden amber—mingled to create the energetic, vigorous interplay of Bach's first movement.

During Klaus's rest, she could feel him watching her. Her heart skipped as a bubbling heat moved throughout her body. She knew she was losing focus, her vision clouding, but the piece was familiar enough that she could allow intuition to take the place of conscious effort. She let her body take over the music as she breathed deeply, bringing the rolling boil down to a gentle simmer.

Klaus came back in, and again, the two of them moved together, building the interwoven puzzle of Bach's spellbinding fugue and counterpoint. The intimacy of their connection caused Bethany's pulse to quicken again. And again, she breathed in deeply, releasing the tension on an exhale, keeping her fingers strong and steady.

When at last they landed together on the final downbow, their eyes met. Bethany noticed a few strands of dampened dirty blond hair clinging to Klaus's forehead. He stood still, not turning the page to the second movement, so she dropped her arm and lowered her violin. Klaus did the same.

"Pack up," he instructed.

"What?"

"Pack up," he repeated, as he began putting his own instrument away.

Bethany removed her shoulder rest, secured her violin, and began loosening her bow.

"Is everything okay?" she asked once she'd locked her case.

"Golden," he said quietly, moving in close to her, backing her into the corner.

He held her gaze long enough that, this time, she was sure: Klaus was going to kiss her. Bethany stared back expectantly, waiting for him to lean in. But instead, he released a loud, forceful exhale, his eyebrows furrowing.

"We need to get out of here," he said, "Or I'm gonna do bad things to you."

Bethany felt her eyes widening in response to the sudden heat between her thighs.

"Do bad things to me," she wanted to say. But as she stared back at Klaus's face, she could see the panic, the helpless desperation, and she knew he needed her to be strong.

"Let's go," she said abruptly.

Her words seemed to jolt him a bit, but he continued blocking her path.

"C'mon," she said, roughly pushing him aside as she shoved past him. She snatched up her violin case and grabbed the doorknob. The flow of air outside the stuffy practice room seemed to resuscitate her senses. "Let's get bubble tea!"

"Get what?" he asked, lifting his violin case.

"Bubble tea. Boba. Sweet Taiwanese drink. You'll love it."

Twenty-Six

Bethany managed to get to the basement of Tomlinson Theater by a quarter to six. She was surprised to find Jelani already there. He was a tall, brawny, dark-skinned guy dressed in a long-sleeved white cotton shirt and relaxed fit jeans.

"Hey," he said, standing up from the stairs. "How ya doin'?"

"Hey. Good. How are you?"

"I'm just fine," he said, holding his hand out to her. "I know we're in class together, but I'm Jelani Green."

She gave his hand a shake. "Bethany Schechter."

"Nice to officially meet you. I always enjoy your work in class, and I saw you in a show a few months ago at The Adrienne."

"Oh, cool. Yeah, that was a fun play."

"You were great," he said. "Very impressive."

"Thank you!" she replied. "I saw you in a Fringe Fest production."

"Oh. ...Oh!" he said, his eyes widening.

"Haha… Yeah, that one. You were wonderful. I really enjoyed your performance."

"Well, thank you," he said with a shy smile. "So… Have you read the scene?"

"No. Have you?" she asked.

"I read it through once, so I can tell you this: there's dancing."

"What? Really?"

"Really. It's a kooky kind of modern social justice piece. We're a married couple… interracial obviously, and it seems to be about a power imbalance in the relationship based on ancestral power imbalances. It's actually fairly straightforward dialogue, but then, in this strange, dream-like fantasy section at the end of Act I, we waltz."

"Waltz."

"Yeah. So... I'm just gonna be upfront with you now and tell you I don't know how to waltz. I'm hoping maybe you have some experience there?"

"I do, yes."

"You can waltz?"

"Yup," Bethany said. "My grandmother had me take a few years of ballroom dance in my early teens. I think she hoped it would help me 'Meet a nice boy,'" Bethany said, doing her best Bubbie impression.

Jelani laughed. "Well, great. Is it something you think you'd be able to teach me without too much trouble?"

"Absolutely," she said. "It's easy."

"Sweet."

"You wanna knock out the dance lesson first?"

"Um... I guess... if you're up for it."

"Let's do it," Bethany said, moving toward the center of the basement floor. Jelani came over to stand with her. "Okay, first I'm gonna have you stand next to me and just do what I do. I'll show you the man's steps first, and then you can try leading me."

"Okay," Jelani said, standing beside her.

"Alright, so forward first with the left foot, then side with the right foot, and close left foot to right foot," Bethany instructed while demonstrating. Jelani followed her steps. "Then back with the right foot, to the side with the left, and close right foot to left foot."

Again Jelani followed her steps. Bethany turned toward him.

"That's it. Those are your steps," she said.

"Really?"

"Really," she said. "Simple box step. So let's do that a few times, and then we'll try it together."

Bethany said the steps aloud again as Jelani followed them, then again, and again.

"Excellent," she said, facing him. "So, now I'm going to have you put your right hand on my back," she said.

Jelani seemed to freeze up, so she took his hand, and placed it for him. "Just right here on my back, okay?"

"Okay."

"And I'm going to rest my arm over yours and place my hand here on your bicep."

"Okay."

"Now hold up your left hand for me, and take my hand in yours, almost so my fingers are perched atop your hand."

He held up his hand, but seemed reluctant to take hold of hers, so she dropped her left arm from his, and closed his hand over hers.

"Just like that. See how you're holding my hand?" she asked. "It's very m'lady."

Jelani smiled.

"Okay, so, back into position?" Bethany waited for Jelani to place his hand on her back again. "And we're going to keep our legs staggered… See?"

Jelani looked down at the position of their legs and nodded.

"And bend our knees," she continued. "Now, you're going to press your weight forward, leading me back in the first part of the box step, and then move back, bringing me back with you through the second part of the box step. And since we're married, I'm gonna have you hold me a little closer, okay? Diaphragm contact," she said, pressing her torso against him.

Jelani blinked several times, his jaw muscles twitching.

Apprehension.

"Don't worry. It's easy," Bethany said with a smile. "You're just going to lower your weight into your knees a bit, then push your spine forward so I can feel you leading me into the first part of the box step. And then I'll feel you when you use your entire frame to lead me back with you to complete the second part of the box step."

"I think my hand is sweaty. I'm sorry. Am I all sweaty?"

"You're fine," Bethany said. "Just relax. Try leading me, okay? Left foot forward?"

Bethany continued instructing as Jelani took the steps. After a few times, she began counting.

"One-two-three, one-two-three, one-two-three... How does it feel?"

"Okay," he said, releasing Bethany.

"Don't let me go yet," she said. "We need to add the technique now."

Jelani wiped his hands on his jeans before resuming the position.

"Okay, so, remember how we bend our knees?"

"Yes."

"Okay, so you're going to bend, and move into your first step, which is beat one with a slight heel lead," Bethany said, relaxing her arms a moment to demonstrate with her foot. "And then when you step to the side for beat two, you're going raise up onto the balls of your feet. Stay up there for feet together on beat three, then back to your heel, bending your knees again for that step back into beat one. And back onto the balls of your feet for beat two and three: the side step and feet together."

"I'm scared I'm gonna step on your toes."

"It happens," she said. "Don't worry about it."

Jelani froze up again, looking very nervous.

"Do you want to try it a few times by yourself?"

"Yeah," he said, releasing her again, looking relieved.

"Okay," she said. "Is it alright if I stand behind you and count?"

"Sure," he said.

Bethany moved in behind him, placing one hand on his hip and the other at the center of his back. Right away, she felt his body turn rigid, and tipped to the side to look up at his face.

"Would you rather not be touched?" she asked.

"I…"

"Oh, I'm sorry," she said, pulling her hands away. "Do you not like me touching you?"

"I like it just fine," he answered. "I tend to tense up a little bit when I'm trying something new. I'll be alright once I get the hang of this... and once we get comfortable with each other."

"Okay."

"Okay."

"Get comfortable with me, Jelani," she said, throwing her arms tightly around his middle and squeezing. "I'm friendly, and I've already seen you naked."

Jelani laughed. "Fair enough."

"Alright," she said, putting her hands back in place. "Let's try the steps."

Twenty-Seven

Jelani had warmed up to her quickly. They'd completed the dance lesson, a cold reading, and even managed to start on the blocking. Afterward, he joined Bethany for dinner at a small sandwich shop on campus, where they discussed the play.

"Seems like a common hitch in these social justice pieces," Jelani said, "...writers unable to keep themselves from hammering."

"Yeah," Bethany agreed.

"Bet you and I can still make it kind of great though," he said, holding out his fist.

"Let's do it," Bethany said, bumping her fist against his.

They made plans to meet up again on Friday after Theater 100, and possibly again over the weekend.

✷ ✷ ✷

That night, Bethany stayed up late, studying her lines, and had fallen asleep at her desk. When she woke up, it was nearly 3 AM. She wandered down the hall. Killian wasn't in his room. Some lucky girl had gotten him to follow her home. Bethany sighed wistfully, making her way back up the hall. After showering, she dressed in her oversized purple t-shirt, dried her hair, and went to bed.

It was a bit before 6:30 AM when she woke again. She crept down the hall to peer into Killian's room, smiling at the sight of him asleep on his stomach at the center of his bed before creeping back to her own room to sleep for another couple hours.

Class wasn't until 1, but she decided to drive to campus early for breakfast. After dressing in a white t-shirt and jeans, she carried her script out to the living room where she slipped on her Keds and grabbed her backpack.

She paused, staring longingly at her violin a moment before deciding to leave it behind.

✷ ✷ ✷

Bethany sat at the table in the cafeteria, studying her lines. Someone tapped her shoulder just after she shoveled the last forkful of scrambled eggs into her mouth. She turned to see Jared standing over her.

"Hey," she managed, covering her mouth with her hand and swallowing. "Have a seat."

"Thanks," he said, sitting beside her with his own tray of eggs. "How've you been?"

"Good. You?"

"Good. I miss working with you though."

"Aw… I miss working with you too, Jared."

"No, you don't. I know you got paired with Jelani Green."

"Lucked out again," Bethany said with a smile.

"I saw him do Moliere last year," Jared said. "I don't like Moliere, but his performance was stellar."

"You're with that Chris Benson guy, huh? How's that been?"

Jared pursed his lips, shaking his head. Bethany laughed.

"That's why you miss me," she said.

"Well, it doesn't help, but nah, you were always my favorite partner, even when you were mean to me. I uh… I actually used to have a bit of a crush on you, ya know."

"I *did* know," Bethany said, smiling at him. "So, how's Rachel?"

Jared's whole face lit up at the mention of her name.

"Great."

"Excellent," Bethany said, clapping her hands together.

"It's wild dating and already living together. Moves quickly."

"I can imagine."

"We've already met each other's parents. I'm planning to go home with her for Thanksgiving."

"Wow…" Bethany said. "Ya ready for all of that?"

Jared nodded, smiling, "Yeah, I think I am. Ya know… we're young, but uh… Both our families tend to start younger. I think this could be it. I think she's the one."

"That's really exciting, Jared. I'm happy for you."

"I owe it all to you," Jared said. "You just sailed in and… It's like you cast a magic spell. Presto! Suddenly, Rachel was mine."

"You just needed a little push," Bethany said. "Eat your eggs. They're getting cold."

Jared took a bite of his eggs.

"So, what about you? Seeing anyone?"

"Actually, I just met someone."

"Really? Temple student?"

"Med student at Penn actually."

"A med student…" he said with a smirk. "I won't say it."

"You don't know the half of it," Bethany said. "He's the nephew of my bubbie's best friend."

"Find me a find, catch me a catch, huh? Well…" Jared said, holding out his bottle of orange juice. "L'chaim!"

Bethany clinked his bottle with her own before taking a sip of juice.

"You like him though?"

"Only one date so far, but…" Bethany shrugged. "Feels like a good enough fit."

"Best we can hope for, right?" Jared said, turning back to his breakfast.

* * *

Bethany walked around campus a while, thinking through her lines. Around noon, her phone buzzed, and she saw it was Aaron calling.

"Hey."

"Hi. It's Aaron."

"I know."

"And you answered anyway. That's a good sign," he said. "I'm calling to schedule our pizza date this weekend."

"How would you feel about lunch on Saturday?" Bethany asked.

"Out for pizza on Shabbat, huh? Just don't tell my Aunt Ruth."

"Deal. Lorenzo and Son's, noon?"

"You got it. Sure I can't give you a lift this time?"

"Nah, easier to meet there."

"Alright. I'm looking forward to it," Aaron said.

Just before hanging up, Bethany spotted Elias crossing 12th Street at Cecil B. Moore Avenue. She froze, standing right out in the open, no place to hide, then sighed with relief when he continued on his way without turning his head. Elias still called her phone on occasion. He had filled up her voice mailbox after only a couple days. Bethany hadn't listened to any of his messages, simply leaving her mailbox full. It just seemed easier that way.

Twenty-Eight

She made it to American Theater about ten minutes early and sat in her usual seat in the back of the classroom. A short time later, Lisa Apgar entered and took a seat toward the front, by the windows. Lisa had never spoken to Bethany after that very first day. She no longer even looked like the same person Bethany had met. She now sported a buzz cut, a pierced eyebrow, and a labret spike. She was also rapidly packing on weight, and had begun dressing mostly in hoodies and jeans or baggy nylon joggers.

Although Bethany had found her exchange with Lisa no less discomforting than any other she'd ever experienced with a chatty blonde, she couldn't help but mourn the tragedy of the beautiful girl morphing into a person who now more closely resembled a chubby adolescent boy. Lisa's mannerisms had shifted along with her appearance. She'd gone from bright-eyed and wholesome-looking with a ladylike demeanor to seeming bored and sullen, slumping in her seat, frequently scoffing or loudly clucking her tongue to express disapproval whenever someone in class made a remark she didn't like—a true Shayla Colreavy convert.

Soon after the twenty seats had filled, Dr. Makena Ward-Washington could be heard clinking and clanking as she walked toward the classroom from the elevator in the hall. Makena wore her hair in micro braids heavily adorned with an assortment of beads, seashells, and silver pendants which clattered together with each of her movements. She was a small, dark-skinned woman with wildly long fingernails and multiple rings on each of her fingers.

Makena delivered every phrase she uttered with a dramatic flair. However, having taken Makena's Performance Poetry course first semester, Bethany knew that, despite her intensity, every lecture Makena gave was rehearsed, each remark scripted, her responses canned. Bethany had witnessed a number of occasions in which a student had made a thoughtful comment or asked an insightful question; Makena's quick retorts falling shamefully short of an actual response. Like most of the theater department faculty, and perhaps most professors in general, Makena was not a thinker, but a performer.

Upon entering the classroom, Makena scanned the room, her eyes landing directly on Bethany.

"Bethany Schechter!" She called to her. "May I see you a minute?"

Bethany stood and walked to meet Makena near the doorway.

"Hello," Makena said, eyeing Bethany.

"Hi," Bethany said.

"Miss Schechter, I've printed copies of your essay, and with your permission, I'd like to distribute them among your classmates."

"Oh... Okay," Bethany answered.

"Thank you," Makena said, "And just so you know, this is by no means intended as persecution. I gave you an A because you wrote a cohesive argument, and you'll receive the extra credit points for turning it in early. I simply find your perspective on colorblind casting... curious, and worthy of a class discussion."

Bethany paused, unsure of how to respond. Makena silently held her gaze, her eyes widening then narrowing. She seemed to be smiling, but then pursed her lips, her shoulders twitching a bit.

Exuberance? Conviction? Disdain?

Bethany stared back at Makena, trying to decipher, but before she could, Makena turned and began walking to the front desk in each row. "Take one and pass it back," she instructed.

"Today we're going to start with this opinion piece written by your fellow classmate, Miss Bethany Schechter," Makena announced as Bethany returned to her seat. "I will read the paper aloud, but I wanted to make sure you each had your own hard copy for reference. We'll be discussing Miss Schechter's notions of colorblind casting, and then we'll delve into last week's reading assignment: Amiri Baraka's *Dutchman*."

Several students turned to glance back at Bethany as Makena read her essay. Most of them simply looked curious, but she thought she might have detected a few scowls. She definitely heard a couple scoffs from Lisa.

Makena finished and stared back at Bethany a moment. Bethany wasn't sure if she was expected to speak or not, so she chose to sit quietly.

"Anything to add to that?" Makena finally asked, her eyebrows raised.

"Um… No," Bethany said.

Makena's eyes widened. "Okay!" she said, looking around the room. "Does anyone else have any thoughts to contribute?"

"I have a question," a girl in the front blurted, standing and turning toward Bethany.

Bethany recognized the girl as Patience Danquah. Bethany had watched Patience audition for Temple's production of *Lysistrata* earlier in the semester. She remembered it well because Patience had auditioned using Beneatha's monologue from *A Raisin in the Sun*, which had struck Bethany as an especially odd choice.

Patience was a slender girl with a very dark complexion, almond shaped eyes, and a slightly pointed chin that always seemed to tip upward. She wore her hair in neat cornrows down her back, and was dressed in a drapey button-down black and white geometric patterned blouse accessorized with unusually large bright yellow earrings that matched a chunky, bright yellow necklace, and a few bright yellow bracelets.

"So, you don't think African American actors can play roles that have traditionally gone to Caucasian actors?"

"Uh… no. They can and do," Bethany replied as it finally dawned on her what this was all about. "But that doesn't mean it makes sense to disregard race when casting a production."

"And why not?"

"Because the point of theater is storytelling."

Patience put her hands on her hips, opening her mouth to comment, but Bethany continued.

"Literature isn't like journalism. It meanders. Good literature does anyway. It's meant to entertain or engage people emotionally so they're able to let their guard down and receive a message they might not otherwise consider. It's the responsibility of the production to represent characters as they were written, to deliver the story in the most straightforward way possible."

"So, why would having people of color in a production make the story less straightforward?"

"In some cases, it wouldn't."

Bethany watched as Patience's nostrils flared and her lips tightened. Hoping to somehow ease the girl's frustration, Bethany made eye contact and held her open hands up in front of her. "I'm sorry," she said. "You seem to be taking this personally, and it truly isn't. This isn't about—"

"How can you tell me, an African American theater major, that this isn't personal?" Patience asked hotly. "Have you ever auditioned for a play, knowing you didn't get cast because of your race?"

"Are you sure it wasn't because you used a contemporary monologue to audition for an Ancient Greek production?"

"Excuse me?!" Patience growled, letting Bethany know it wasn't the first time she'd heard the critique.

Bethany knew immediately that mentioning Patience's *Lysistrata* audition had been as mistake, but there was no turning back from it.

"Well…" Bethany began delicately, "It would make sense to cast actors of any race in *Lysistrata*. If I'm not mistaken, that production did, in fact, end up with a mixed race cast." Bethany felt a few students nodding around her as she spoke. "It's just that a casting director would need to know the actor auditioning is capable of performing an Ancient Greek role."

Bethany could see from Patience's bulging eyes that she had again failed to improve relations. She wasn't sure how else to approach this. Was an apology necessary? Would it help? Before Patience could respond again, Makena interjected.

"Miss Schechter, since you've said this isn't personal, I would ask that you refrain from personal attacks."

"I apologize," Bethany said quickly, again looking back to Patience. "Sincerely. That wasn't intended as an attack."

"I just don't understand why you think it's okay for African Americans to get cast in *Lysistrata* but not in other plays," Patience said.

"My position on colorblind casting isn't specifically about any one race."

"Oh, so there are plays you think Caucasians shouldn't get cast in?"

"Of course," Bethany said. "Let's take *A Raisin in the Sun* for example."

"Are you serious?!" Patience shouted, staring daggers at Bethany. "Is she serious?!" she asked, turning to Makena.

"Miss Schechter—"

Bethany held up her hands for Makena. "I'm referencing a play I know she's familiar with that requires a nearly all-black cast."

"Did you just say 'black'?" Patience sneered. "Are you serious?! Is she serious?!" she repeated, again turning to Makena.

"Miss Schechter, you're free to say whatever you like, but you might have an easier time in my classroom if you would refer to 'African Americans' or 'people of color' instead of 'black' people," Makena interjected.

"Okay," Bethany said, turning back to Patience. "I'm referencing a play I know you're familiar with that requires a mostly African American cast."

"And why do you say that?" Patience demanded.

Bethany examined Patience's face, wondering if she'd somehow managed to trigger a strong enough nerve that Patience was no longer able to think clearly. She didn't want to continue upsetting her, but wasn't sure how to gracefully exit the conversation which now seemed to be heading toward the absurd.

"You're... I'm sorry, you're familiar with *A Raisin in the Sun*?" Bethany asked cautiously.

"Yes, I'm familiar with *A Raisin in the Sun*!" Patience seethed.

"I'm sorry," Bethany said, again holding her hands open in front of her. "Just double checking. So, you're asking why white actors shouldn't get cast as members of an African American family that moves into a white neighborhood and is made to feel unwelcome because of their race?"

"No, forget it. I'm done," Patience said, spinning around and sitting in her seat. Before anyone else could speak, Patience stood back up, spinning back toward Bethany. "I understand that Caucasians shouldn't play African American characters, okay? Colorblind casting was put in place to increase opportunities for people of color, to combat the underrepresentation of minority actors."

"Sure, I understand."

"But you don't support it."

"I don't," Bethany said simply.

"Well, there you have it," Patience said, again throwing her hands up and sitting.

Bethany noticed other students glancing around the room uncomfortably as they sat quietly a few moments.

"Okay," Makena said. "Does anyone else have anything to add?"

Lisa Apgar raised her hand.

"Miss Apgar?"

"Yes," Lisa said, turning in her seat to look at Bethany for the first time since the beginning of the semester. "I'm wondering what you think of women in theater."

Bethany stared back at her, unsure of what to say. "I… I'm sorry, how do you mean?"

"Do you think women have a rightful place in theater?"

"Of course," Bethany said, trying to offer a friendly smile. "I'm a woman in theater."

"Hm. But surely you know that women had to fight to work as actors?"

"Sure, I mean… centuries ago."

"All the roles were once played by men. So, why do you support women being given roles once only played by men, but not African Americans playing roles once only played by Caucasians?"

Patience stood and turned to Lisa, applauding, repeating "Mmm-hm" and "Thank you," a few times before sitting back down.

Bethany looked over at Patience, then back at Lisa, trying to figure out if these were questions they actually wanted her to answer. It seemed to Bethany that this was one of those situations where women were expressing emotion for reasons she couldn't understand. She could certainly tell they were unhappy with her, but she wasn't entirely sure why. Finally, she decided her best approach was to simply answer the direct questions.

"Okay," Bethany began. "Well, the roles were once only given to men, but many of the characters were written as female."

"Right?" Lisa said.

"So, you're asking if I think female characters should be played by female actors?" Bethany asked. She waited for Lisa to respond, but she didn't, so Bethany continued. "Yes, of course. Female characters were only played by male actors because it was illegal for women to participate."

"Right." Lisa said, looking back at Bethany.

Bethany noticed Lisa's pretty blue eyes and again thought of how sad Lisa's transformation was. She stared back at Lisa, waiting for her to continue.

"So, maybe that should teach us something," Lisa said.

"I'm not sure I understand," Bethany replied, still admiring Lisa's eyes.

"Women weren't allowed to participate in theater," Lisa said, now seeming exasperated. "Theater has improved since that's changed. Wouldn't you agree?"

"I do agree, absolutely. I'm just not sure I understand how that relates," Bethany said. Lisa's eyes narrowed as she stared back silently at Bethany. Bethany decided she'd better continue speaking. "There aren't any laws preventing black— Excuse me…. There aren't any laws preventing African Americans from participating in theater."

"So, African Americans should just be happy with whatever roles Caucasians think they can play?" Lisa asked with a scoff.

"I am also curious about that, Miss Schechter," Makena interjected. "Are you suggesting people of color should simply accept the fate we've been dealt by hundreds of years of oppression and underrepresentation?"

"I think if people of color feel underrepresented, it ought to be addressed by increasing the number of productions with African American characters, not by casting African American actors as white characters, which, in many productions, could lead to a muddying of the text, and a tremendous amount of confusion."

"A muddying!" Makena repeated loudly, her eyes popping as she stared back.

"And also the misrepresentation of history," Bethany finished, watching as Makena looked around the classroom at the other students, still wide-eyed. Bethany also took a moment to glance around the room, but wasn't able to detect anything unusual from her position.

"I take exception to your suggestion that underrepresentation is merely something people of color perceive and not the reality of modern-day theater," Makena said. "I'm also going to let you know that what you're saying is inherently racist. But now, we need to move on to our assigned reading."

Bethany felt a bit of a jolt. She'd never been accused of being racist before. Thinking back through her paper, she still wasn't sure how it could have possibly been interpreted that way.

Patience glared back at Bethany before turning back to face forward. Lisa glanced over at her with a smirk. Bethany noticed glances from many other students too, but was pretty sure most were still just curious or maybe even as confused as she was, and perhaps uncomfortable. She decided to open her notes on *Dutchman* and tune out the rest. This wasn't something she knew how to fix.

Twenty-Nine

Bethany was tired and relieved to be home. She climbed the stairs, put her backpack down, kicked off her Keds, then walked over and dropped into the green recliner. She closed her eyes and thought about Dr. Makena Ward-Washington.

She remembered Makena calling students "sheltered," "naive," or "rural," on a few occasions to insinuate they were unsophisticated and unfamiliar with black culture or the black struggle. Bethany had found Makena's conjecture somewhat unfair, but had never been interested enough to intervene in any way. She'd certainly never imagined she would end up the subject of Makena's ridicule.

She wondered about Patience and Lisa too. Although Lisa regularly seemed exasperated with someone on some level these days, today was the first time Bethany had seen any student become actively antagonistic during a class discussion. Of course, with Lisa being shepherded by Shayla Colreavey, there'd be no reasoning with her, but it bothered Bethany that she could never seem to decipher the intentions of other girls. It was incredibly frustrating that college hadn't improved her ability to read them at all. Were they genuinely thinking and feeling the words they were saying? Did they actually believe she was racist? It seemed almost impossible, but Bethany couldn't actually tell, and she certainly had no other explanation for why they'd be lashing out at her.

"Hey."

Bethany gasped, startling at the interruption of her thoughts.

"Sorry," Killian said with a wince.

She looked up at him, drinking in his beauty. He was dressed in an old white t-shirt, the thin fabric stretching over his thick arms and bulky shoulders, along with a pair of gray sweatpants. His hair hung in golden waves around his perfect face. He bent over, holding out his hands. Bethany took them, and he hoisted her out of the chair before sitting and pulling her onto his lap.

"You okay?"

"I'm okay."

"You seemed awfully deep in thought. You wanna talk about it?"

"Just… ya know… theater people."

"Jared Isaacs?"

"Makena Ward-Washington."

"Lady with the noisy braids?"

"Yup."

"What'd she do?" Killian asked, tugging one of Bethany's curls straight and twisting it around his finger.

"Called me a racist."

"Shit," Killian said, dropping his hand from her hair. "What the hell for?"

"I dunno. She didn't like a paper I wrote."

"Goddamn. What was the paper about?"

"Colorblind casting," Bethany said, sighing. "I should go study my lines.

Killian folded his arms over her.

"No. Stay," he said. "Sit with me a while."

Bethany rested her head back on his shoulder, and Killian pressed the side of his face to hers.

"Open the recliner," she said.

He pulled the lever, raising the leg rest, and eased back into the chair. Bethany eased back against Killian, pulling his arms tighter around her.

"I wouldn't take it too hard," Killian said, giving her a squeeze. "Seems to be a lot of that going on now. Everyone and everything is suddenly racist."

"Yeah."

"It'll blow over."

"Yeah," Bethany repeated, closing her eyes.

Killian went back to playing with her hair. Bethany focused on the warmth of Killian's body and the feel of his arm holding her snugly against him.

"I'm gonna fall asleep."

"Good," he said, kissing her cheek. "Fall asleep."

"Do you work tonight?"

"Nope. Off tonight," he said. "I'm all yours."

Bethany thought those might be the sweetest words she'd ever heard uttered.

"Mmmmm…" was all she managed as she drifted off to sleep.

*** * ***

Bethany woke but remained still. She could tell from Killian's breathing he was asleep. She tried to turn and look at him, but his arms reflexively locked tighter around her, preventing her from moving. She decided to wait for him to wake.

Just then, her phone started buzzing in her hoodie pocket. The vibration was enough to wake Killian.

"Mmmmm… Hey," he said, nuzzling against her hair.

He lifted his arms from her, running his hands over her shoulders and upper arms. Bethany pulled her phone from her pocket and saw it was Cam calling.

"Hello?"

"Hey. You gonna be on campus tomorrow?"

"Yup. Class at noon. Rehearsal after that."

"Stop by Presser beforehand. We'll jam."

"Yeah, okay. Like 10?"

"Make it 9."

"Okay. See ya then."

"Cool."

Bethany hung up, and tried to stand. Killian tugged her back, puckering his lips out at her. She peck kissed them, then stood.

"Eggs?" she asked, walking into the kitchen, and leaning back on the counter.

"Nah, let's order Chinese," he said, reaching around behind her, pulling a menu out of an overhead cabinet.

"Okay, but I need to study my lines after."

"Let me run them with you," he said, placing a hand on either side of her, leaning against the counter.

The last time Killian had run lines with Bethany had been just a couple weeks after that night. She had managed to avoid any lengthy or meaningful conversations with him after that night until one evening at the start of the new semester, when he'd stopped at her bedroom door while she was sitting at her desk, studying her lines. He'd asked what she was reading. She'd told him, and he'd walked over, sat on her desk, and asked if he could help. That was what had reignited their friendship, allowing them to push past what had happened.

"Really?" she asked.

"I've done it with you before."

"I know. I didn't think you'd want to do it again."

"I wanna do it again," he said softly.

Bethany felt her heart rate increase as Killian leaned in closer. Before she could say anything, he swept his lips across hers.

"No kissing," she said.

"No?" he asked, gazing into her eyes.

"Nope, not in this one. There's waltzing though."

"Waltzing?"

"Yeah. Toward the end of Act I."

"Sweet," he said with a grin.

"I can teach you."

"I know how to waltz."

"You do?" she asked.

"You're surprised," he said. "I don't seem like a man who can dance?"

"Well, I guess I never really thought about it."

"Give me your phone. I'll call in our order. Chicken lo mein?"

"Sounds good," she said handing Killian her phone.

He called and ordered their dinner from Golden Chopsticks, then handed the phone back to Bethany.

"Go get your script. I wanna dance with you."

Bethany smiled and turned toward the top of the stairs where she'd dropped her backpack. She fished out the scene, bringing it back into the kitchen.

"I only have one copy. We'll have to share."

"Okay."

"We'll be sitting at a table for a lot of the scene anyway, so let's just sit at the kitchen table."

Killian pushed his chair close to Bethany's, and they read up to the dream sequence with the waltz. Killian stood and held his arms in position. Bethany joined him, and Killian immediately began leading her in a graceful waltz around the kitchen.

One-two-three, one-two-three, one-two-three…

"I'm impressed," she said.

"This is nothing. You should see me tango."

"Where did you learn ballroom dancing?"

169

"My mother made me take lessons when I was a kid."

"Really?"

"Yup. Drove me to a studio in Montpelier once a week for a few years."

"Did you like it?"

"Hated it at first."

"Why'd she make you do it?"

"She worried I was too shy."

Bethany smiled, trying to imagine Killian as a shy little boy. "Did the dancing help you overcome your shyness?"

"Absolutely," Killian said, pausing and dipping her.

He brought her back up, and moved his arm down, tightening it around her. He leaned in and kissed her again. Bethany kissed him back. The knock at the door made her pull away.

"I'll get it," Killian said, turning toward the living room and disappearing down the stairs.

After a moment, he returned with a brown paper bag, and set it on the table. Bethany sat and opened the bag, pulling out her noodles, Killian's beef and broccoli, and his side of rice. Killian brought over plates and forks.

"Water?" he asked.

"Please."

"So, we'll eat and then run lines again," he said, carrying over two small bottles of Deer Park from the refrigerator.

"I think I might be better off studying them on my own, Pretty."

"You're saying I'm not helping?"

"Sorry."

"Let me try again. I'll be cool."

Bethany pursed her lips.

"C'mon," he said. "I promise."

"Alright," Bethany said, unable to keep herself from smiling. "Alright."

The two of them ate.

"Want some lo mein?" she asked.

"Yeah," he said, helping himself. "Want some beef?"

"Sure."

Killian served her some beef and broccoli.

"So, how bad is the situation with that professor?"

"I… Well, I don't actually know. She gave me an *A*, said I completed the assignment. She just didn't like what I had to say."

"Well, at least she's playing fair," he said. "Do you have any regrets about what you wrote?"

"No. I mean, now that I know it pisses people off, I wish it hadn't been read aloud to the class, but I stand by what I said."

"Whoa. It was read aloud in class?"

"Yeah. She actually printed copies for everyone."

Killian's head jutted back. "Did other people find it offensive?"

"Yeah, I think so. A couple girls seemed upset about it."

"Shit."

"It'll be okay," Bethany said. "Like you said, it'll blow over."

"Yeah," he said. "Well… Keep me posted, okay?"

"Okay."

They finished eating and stored the leftovers in the fridge.

"Let's go back to my room," Killian said.

Bethany raised an eyebrow at him.

"It's more comfortable," Killian said. "Don't worry. Keeping my hands, and lips, to myself."

Bethany stood, eyeing him.

"Promise," he said.

"Alright," she agreed, picking up the script, and turning toward the hall.

Killian followed.

"Wait," he said, as she passed her bedroom door. "Change out of your clothes."

Bethany spun back around.

"Killian…"

"C'mon. I promised, didn't I? Just get into some pajama pants so you're comfortable. You need to relax."

She stood, looking at him. He raised his eyebrows.

"Okay," she said, handing him the script. "Meet you back there."

In her room, she changed out of her jeans and hoodie, leaving her navy blue t-shirt on, and adding a pair of navy blue cotton pajama pants with a tiny white heart pattern. She could feel herself growing excited at the thought of going to Killian's bedroom and scolded herself for it.

Stick to the script.

Thirty

Killian was lying on his stomach, perched up on his elbows, looking at the script which was draped across his pillow. Bethany looked over the thin fabric of his white t-shirt, stretched across his thick arms, broad shoulders, and muscular back. Suddenly, she knew this was a bad idea.

"C'mon in," Killian said, turning onto his side.

"I um…" Bethany struggled for words.

Killian rolled off the bed, stepped over to her, and put his arm around her.

"C'mon," he said, pulling her toward his bed. "This dialogue is kinda bullshit by the way."

"Yeah," Bethany said.

She sat on his bed. Killian sat beside her. She could feel her heart begin to race.

"I just… I don't… I'm not..," she stammered.

"Relax," he said.

She turned toward him. He looked into her eyes.

"We're just running lines, Bethany. Okay? This is you and me, hangin' out. I'm sorry about earlier. No more kissing tonight. You have my word."

"Okay," she whispered.

"Okay," Killian said with a gentle smile.

He climbed to the far side of his bed, and lounged back, perching on an elbow.

"C'mon over," he said, patting his shoulder for her to come rest her head there. "Let's learn these ridiculous lines."

Bethany joined Killian, resting her head on his shoulder, and the two of them read through the script, passing over the waltz, and into Act II. Once they completed Act II, they repeated the entire scene from the beginning. Bethany tried to keep her eyes closed, attempting to deliver her lines from memory. Upon reaching the end a second time, Bethany rolled away, onto her side.

"Again?" he asked.

"Maybe later."

"Alright. So, what now?"

"I dunno."

"I could read to you."

"About chemistry?"

"Not unless you want me to read to you about chemistry."

"What else do you have?"

"Actually, I picked up this book called *The Unsettling of America*. It's by Wendell Berry. Ever hear of him?"

"Doesn't sound familiar."

"Well, he's a farmer and an environmental activist... not in the usual stupid sort of way; he actually makes a lot of sense. It's pretty great. I'm about halfway through. I can start over from the beginning if you want to hear it."

"Okay," she said with a shrug.

"Okay," Killian said, climbing over Bethany to rummage through the piles of books on his desk.

He returned with a book, climbing back over her and stretching out on his back to read. Bethany snuggled against him, resting her head on his shoulder again. He wrapped his arm around her.

"Okay?" he asked.

"Mm-hm."

"Alright."

Killian rested the book on his chest, opening to the beginning, reading through a preface, a second preface, and the acknowledgments. From this, Bethany could already tell Wendell Berry had some big things to say about agriculture, government policy, and human nature, and she already found herself liking him.

"Chapter One: The Unsettling of America

One of the peculiarities of the white race's presence in America is how little intention has been applied to it. As a people, wherever we have been, we have never really intended to be."

Bethany listened as Killian continued reading through the first two chapters: a hard-hitting indictment of modern "agribusiness," which removes farming from its cultural context, taking it away from families, while also causing destruction of the land. Bethany thought about that, wondering how on Earth she'd never thought about it at all before, when the realization hit her: She was just another American estranged from the land.

When he ended the second chapter, he rested the book over his chest.

"What do you think?" he asked.

"It's good. Strong. He seems to be leaving room for hope, but it's frightening and… well, kind of devastating."

"Yeah."

"What made you select this book?" she asked.

"Well, ya know… I was reading all that survivalist lit, and the book comes highly recommended on a lot of different websites about growing your own food. Figured I'd pick up a copy. It's certainly given me a lot more to think about."

"Are you… thinking of growing your own food?"

"I don't know," Killian said. "Growing up, my parents only had a couple acres, but we always did some kind of small-scale farming. Chickens... and we always grew a lot of our own fruits and vegetables. The neighbors did too."

Bethany imagined Killian surrounded by a flock of big yellow chickens, standing before an old red barn. She imagined him picking a ripe tomato from a sturdy vine. She imagined him waltzing her around an apple orchard. And she knew with absolute certainty there could be no other man in the world as perfectly beautiful as Killian.

"Adapting to the city has been easy," he continued. "...too easy."

"I've never known anything but city," Bethany said, thinking about how very different their lives had been.

"It would probably be hard to leave the city behind if it's all you knew," Killian said. "I've only lived in it a short time, and already... it'll be extremely difficult for me to give it up."

"You think you will?" Bethany asked.

"I always planned on returning to Vermont... or at least somewhere in rural New England. But it's not as easy for me to picture my future anymore."

Bethany understood what he meant, but it was, of course, very different for her. She'd always known exactly what her future would look like, and even as she felt it creeping closer, spent a lot of time trying not to think about it. But it was always there, waiting for her. At some point, in her teens, she'd become resentful of it, turning somewhat rebellious in response. And she still wasn't fully convinced she fit the mold. Nevertheless, she'd always known her wild, subversive days were numbered. It was only a matter of time before she would join the ranks of the established institution, a matter of time before she'd become Mrs. Someonestein, Mrs. Whateverberg, Mrs. Anonywitz.

Bethany looked over at Killian, propping herself on an elbow. She examined his broad forehead topped with thick, lustrous waves of beautiful blonde hair. She followed the golden locks down to his wide-set jaw, her eyes landing on his perfectly cleft chin. She gazed up at his deep blue eyes, into the bright golden rings, then down at his soft pink lips before moving in to kiss them. She barely managed to make contact when Killian turned his face away.

"Mmmm… not now. Not tonight, okay?"

"But I want you," she whispered.

Killian closed his eyes for a moment, inhaling sharply, then opened them, making eye contact.

"Not tonight," he repeated, smiling gently. "I gave you my word."

"But—"

"It's getting late," he said decidedly.

Bethany stared back at him a moment before relenting.

"Okay," she said, turning away to lift herself out of Killian's bed.

"No," he said, taking hold of her arm. "Stay."

He pulled Bethany back toward him, easing her head onto his pillow. Then, he climbed over her and turned off his bedside lamp before returning to lie beside her. He wrapped his arm around her, nuzzling the side of her face.

"Good night, Bethany."

Thirty-One

Bethany had once again fallen asleep in Killian's arms. And she woke in the morning, still in his arms.

"Good morning," he said as she opened her eyes and began to stretch.

"Morning, Pretty. What time is it?"

Killian lifted his head to look at the clock. "A bit after 7."

"You want first shower?" she asked.

"No, you go ahead," he said, kissing the top of her head, then rolling off the side of his bed. "I'm gonna make breakfast. Scrambled eggs?"

"Yes, please," she said, climbing out of Killian's bed.

She made her way down the hall, wondering what it would feel like now if Killian had made love to her last night. Would she still be floating in the afterglow of oxytocin release, or navigating waves of dysphoria and suffocating anxiety? In the moment, either seemed perfectly plausible. She shrugged to herself and got into the shower.

After drying her hair, she went to her bedroom, dressed in jeans and a black t-shirt, then walked to the kitchen.

"Right on time," Killian said, serving her eggs and toast. "Can I get you some orange juice?"

"Yes, please."

"So, listen," Killian said, pouring her orange juice. "I'm keeping my phone on me today. If you have any problems, I want you to get in touch right away. I'll be on campus most of the afternoon."

"Oh, okay." Bethany said. "I doubt I'll have any problems. I won't even have to think about American Theater until next Thursday."

179

"Good," he said. "Still… My ringer will be on just in case."

"Thanks, Pretty."

After eating, Killian brought his dish to the sink, kissed the top of Bethany's head, and went to get a shower. Bethany did the dishes, then went to retrieve her script from Killian's room. She looked over his bed, sighing, then carried her script to the living room, packed her backpack, slipped into her Keds, and grabbed her violin.

* * *

She parked in student parking on Diamond Street and carried her violin to Presser Hall. Cam was sitting on the bench out front. He was dressed in baggy jeans and a faded orange t-shirt. His hair looked even more out of control than usual. He stood when he noticed Bethany.

"Hey!"

"Hey!" she called back.

"Good to see you," he said as she approached. "Klaus is on his way. You wanna wait out here, or get set up?"

"I'm a bit early. Let's wait here," Bethany said, sitting and placing her violin on the ground in front of her.

Cam sat beside her.

"Klaus tells me you switched to classical while I was gone."

"Yup, we did."

"He mentioned things got a little… um…"

Bethany looked over at Cam.

"Well, he didn't say much actually; just that he shouldn't be left alone with you anymore."

Bethany laughed. She tried to stop, but only laughed harder.

"What exactly happened?" Cam asked, looking amused.

"Nothing at all happened," Bethany said with a shrug. "We got bubble tea."

"So, you're okay? He didn't..?"

"No, he didn't. Honestly, it wouldn't have bothered me if he had. He's the one with the hang-up."

"Heh heh… alright. But it's cool? No weirdness?"

"No weirdness."

"Cool." Cam said. "He did tell me about the bubble tea. I might need to try one of those."

"We'll go after if there's time. It's good stuff."

Bethany found herself watching a pair of squirrels chasing each other nearby. She remembered once buying a soft pretzel to feed squirrels for entertainment in between classes, and made a mental note to pick up a pretzel for them again soon.

"Mornin', warm honey!"

Bethany looked up to see Klaus walking over, holding a cup carrier containing three small bubble teas: a green, which she already knew was for her, a pink, and a purple.

"Let me guess," Cam said.

"Yup," Klaus replied. "Honeydew for my honey. You get strawberry or taro."

Klaus stepped up and handed Bethany the honeydew bubble tea.

"Good morning, Klaus. Thank you."

Bubble tea seemed awfully sweet for 9 AM, but Bethany appreciated the kind gesture.

"I'll go with strawberry," Cam said.

Klaus sat beside her on the bench, the three of them sipping and chewing tapioca pearls quietly.

"Huh," Cam finally said, blocking the top of the straw with his thumb and eyeing the few pearls of tapioca held hostage in the translucent yellow plastic tube. "This is so weird. I can't decide if I like it or not. Is it chewy and delicious, or slimy and disgusting? Could it be both?"

Bethany felt Klaus's eyes on her. She turned and looked at him, noticing his blue eyes sparkling in the sunlight.

"We cool?" he asked quietly.

"Of course," Bethany said, smiling at him.

He smiled back and stretched his arm out over the back of the bench behind her.

"Thinkin' we need bass today," Klaus said, arching his neck to look at Cam. "Got your bass?"

"Yup."

"Is Lonnie around?"

"Nah, he's with his girl."

"What about Bishop?"

"He played at Ortlieb's last night. Probably won't be here til around 10."

Ortlieb's.

Bethany had heard of the place before, or maybe she'd seen it. Yes, she realized. It was in Northern Liberties, near Jared's apartment. North 3rd Street. There was a saxophone on the sign on the door, which had caught her eye.

Someday...

"Any drummers?"

"Drew should be here soon."

"Alright," Klaus said, standing. "Let's see if we can get one of the bigger rooms. We'll mess around a while then check for Drew and Bishop in like an hour."

"Sounds good," Cam said, standing.

Bethany stood too, and the three of them walked toward the building. Cam held the door, and they all entered, chucking their empty or nearly empty bubble tea cups in the trash can, then holding up their ID cards before walking back to the practice rooms. Instead of stopping at one of the doors to the regular tiny rooms, they continued to the end of the hall. Klaus cracked the door and peeked before opening it for Cam and Bethany.

It was a full-sized classroom. Inside were stacks of chairs and music stands by the windows, a drum set in the corner, and a shiny black grand piano at the front center.

"Is someone playing piano?" Bethany asked.

"Our boy, Bishop, if we can catch him when he comes in," Klaus said.

Bethany hadn't played with a pianist in years. The downstairs neighbors, the Abramowitzes, had a girl Bethany's age who played: Frances Abramowitz, younger sister of Benjamin, whom Bethany had dated for a short time. At Bubbie's and Mrs. Abramowitz's insistence, the girls had played Schubert and Mozart concertos in Frances's living room for one hour every Tuesday and Thursday afternoon from ages 11 through 16.

Several times, Bubbie had asked Bethany why the two of them never spent any additional time socializing; a question Bethany could only ever answer with "I don't know," to which Bubbie would simply scowl or roll her eyes while waving her hand in the air. It wasn't that Bethany had actively disliked Frances in any way. It's just that neither girl had ever seemed to have much to say to the other. Frances had been a technically sound musician who played very mechanically. This suited Bethany just fine, since mechanical meant reliable. After playing together only a few months, they were able to breeze through the hour without discussion, and almost without any thought at all.

Finally, when Bethany was 16, the Abramowitz family had moved out West to live closer to family, and closer to UC Berkeley, which Frances was expected to eventually attend with her cousins. It was only after Frances had been gone a few weeks that it occurred to Bethany what an enormous relief it was to have her gone. Somehow, she hadn't noticed exactly how much of a chore that hour every Tuesday and Thursday afternoon had been until she was finally free of the obligation.

Klaus, Cam, and Bethany set up and decided to start with Joe Henderson's *Inner Urge*. After playing twice through the head, Klaus nodded to Bethany. She took the first solo. Apropos of its name, the tune was dark and intense with a very certain sense of urgency.

She could feel Cam and Klaus watching her, but it felt different. She felt loose… free to play around. There was a joy in the music alone, in playing off Klaus's pizzicato comping.

She thought of Klaus… his desire… her own… the intimate connection they shared that he'd deemed so precious and yet so perturbing. Then suddenly, she found it.

Lydian.

Lifting up from the dark intensity, her solo began to take on an extra swingy, bouncy, and bright quality.

Bright. Very bright. A sparkling blue in the sun.

Lydian… a lifeline… a sense of hope… strength and perseverance, a spurning of the darkness, a rebuffing of inner urge.

When she finished, she looked up to Klaus, who was grinning. Bethany sat as she listened, closing her eyes, delighting in Klaus's velvety sound and the glissy double stops of his tight, impressive solo as she comped for him.

After they wrapped it up, Bethany found Klaus still beaming at her.

"Lydian," she said shyly. "I didn't know what to make of it at first. Wasn't sure I'd know where to use it."

"You found it a perfect home," he said.

There was a knock at the door.

"C'mon in!" Klaus shouted.

As the door opened, Bethany inhaled sharply. In the doorway stood the strangest looking person she'd ever seen. He was so tall, his head almost reached the top of the doorway. He was otherwise large too—broad and sinewy but also quite chubby, his gray short-sleeved button-down shirt showing off a pair of thick, solid arms, while the lower buttons of the shirt strained against his full belly. He had the distinct facial features of a black man—a wide nose with flared nostrils, and very full, prominent lips, but his complexion was as fair as Bethany's, and his eyes an abnormally pale blue. Like his body, his face was strong and wide, but softer and fuller around his chin. His head was topped with longish, thick tight curls which were positively yellow.

An albino, she realized, still astonished by his appearance.

"Bishop!" Klaus and Cam called out in unison.

"Hey. What's good, guys?" Bishop replied. "Y'all usin' the piano?"

His voice was unusually deep, his words rolling out in a slow Southern drawl.

"We were hoping you'd sit in with us," Klaus said.

"Mos' def," he replied. "Any drummers 'round?"

"We're hoping for that too," Cam said. "This is Bethany."

Bishop turned his head, his eyes landing on Bethany. "'Nother violin?"

"Yup," Klaus said.

"Dope," he said, nodding at Bethany. "Bishop Honeycutt."

Bethany nodded back, trying not to stare.

"Lemme see if I can find Drew," Bishop said, turning back out the door. "Oh, hol'on… Drew!" he bellowed down the hall.

"Yo!" Someone called back.

"You busy, man?"

"Nah," the voice called back. "Who ya got back there?"

"Klaus, Cam, 'nother violin,"

"Another violin? Really?"

"Yup."

"Cool."

Bishop turned back into the room and sat at the piano. Soon, an attractive guy with a shaven head and dark mustache and goatee walked in. He was dressed in jeans and a black v-neck shirt. Bethany admired his muscular arms and chest as he approached her, holding out his hand. Setting her bow on her chair, she shook his hand.

"I'm Drew," he said with a smile.

Bethany smiled back, noticing his shiny gray eyes.

"Bethany."

"Good to meet you."

"Same," she said, watching him as he turned to walk to the drum set.

Drew sat on the stool and opened the case he carried over his shoulder, taking out a pair of sticks. Cam set down his guitar and got out his upright bass.

"What are we playing?" Drew asked.

"*In a Sentimental Mood*. You guys up for it?" Cam asked.

"Always," Drew responded, pulling a pair of brushes and a pair of mallets from his case.

"Sure thing," Bishop replied.

"We do it in F Major," Klaus told Bethany. "You know that one?"

"I do, yeah." Bethany said, fondly remembering the tune from Zayde's Duke Ellington and John Coltrane record.

"Sweet," he said, turning to nod to Bishop, who counted off slowly:

"One," *snap*, "two," *snap*, "a-one-two-three-four."

Bishop started playing. Cam began walking a bassline. Drew started in delicately with his brushes. Klaus came in with the melody. Bethany stood still, only wanting to listen. The tune had always been one she adored, and it sounded so different with violin in place of the saxophone. Klaus provided the rich, expressive voice it called for, but suddenly, it dawned on Bethany how very much she'd love to play along with a saxophone.

Someday…

Throughout the remainder of the melody, Bethany's eyes were drawn to Drew. She enjoyed watching the gentle flexing of his arm muscles as he played. But as soon as Bishop went into his solo, she turned to watch him. The piano was tilted outward, so she was able to see the movement of his arms. As he continued playing, she found herself stepping around her music stand and a bit to the side in order to watch his hands.

Like the rest of him, his hands were humongous. They looked monstrous over the keyboard. She wondered how he was doing what he was doing. He played so elegantly, his long, very thick fingers somehow gracefully dancing over the keys. She crept back to rest her violin in its case, then, almost involuntarily, eased up toward the piano.

She stood just behind Bishop, watching over his giant shoulder as he continued his solo.

Airy, feathery violet…

Then, it deepened a bit. Bethany closed her eyes, a tingle running up her spine.

Mellow lavender with tender but gloomy indigo undertones…

Soon, he shifted into something different.

Sweetness and longing… soft, translucent shades of periwinkle and rose vacillating back and forth into something much darker…. Heavy purples and deep reds… an intense but somehow still breezy sort of melancholy…

Bethany's eyes began to burn. Her throat began to tighten. Her lips quivered a bit. She opened her eyes, blinking several times, and continued watching Bishop's giant hands doing things hands so vulgarly large seemed to have no business doing. As the tingles moving up her spine turned prickly, her heart rate increased, and her breathing turned shallow.

Mystified, she was unable to pull her eyes away, her ears clinging to each and every note as he continued building into something wild and unpredictable, but somehow also oddly and intimately familiar. It was euphoric while also agonizing.

Bethany began to feel overwhelmed, wishing he would finish. But he pressed onward, plunging into even deeper, darker places, all the while continuing a delicate smattering of rosy sweetness. She struggled to control her breathing, unable to decide if this man was restoring something deep inside her, or shattering it further. She only knew she'd been overtaken completely.

At last, he played through the final measure, turning his strange pale eyes up to Klaus, giving his head a slight nod. Bethany gulped for air.

As Klaus began his solo, Bishop looked over his shoulder, noticing Bethany. As his eyes met hers, she felt a rush of color to her face. Abruptly, she turned around and walked back to her seat. She sat, still trying to steady her breathing, straining to listen to Klaus's solo as her heart continued pounding in her ears. After a few minutes, Klaus drew toward a close, turning toward her. She shook her head no, and he turned toward Cam who took the next solo. Klaus set his violin in its case and quietly pulled a chair to sit beside Bethany.

"You okay?" he whispered.

Bethany nodded. He cocked his head and furrowed his brow.

"I'm okay," she whispered. "Just wanna listen."

Klaus nodded, then returned to his violin.

Cam kept his solo short and snazzy as usual. Then, Drew began his solo. He was a talented drummer and certainly easy on the eyes. Bethany wanted to watch him but was still distracted, her eyes and ears continuously pulling back toward Bishop. Even his delicate comping was fascinating to her. There was something so odd and entrancing about him.

Bishop lifted his head to wait for his cue, then began playing through the melody again. As he did, he again caught Bethany's gaze. She quickly jerked her eyes away, instantly scolding herself. He'd likely think she was some sort of freak the way she continued staring at him. But then, she reasoned, he was almost certainly accustomed to people gawking on account of his bizarre appearance.

"Damn, Bishop…" Cam said after they finished.

"Yeah, that was intense," Klaus said.

"Thanks, man," Bishop said, nodding at the guys before turning to Bethany. "Why didn't you play?"

Bethany swallowed, feeling her cheeks warming again. "Oh, I just wanted to listen to that one."

"Fair 'nuff," he said. "But you're playin' the nex' one."

Bethany nodded, wanting to look away, but finding it difficult to pull her eyes off of his.

"You guys up for another ballad?" Klaus asked.

"Sure," Drew said.

Cam nodded.

"Let her call the tune," Bishop said, his eyes still locked on Bethany. "Whatchu thinkin' right now?"

Bethany stared back at him.

"*Ugly Beauty*," she finally breathed out.

She saw a flicker in Bishop's eyes. He tilted his head and raised an eyebrow, the corners of his plump lips curving upward a bit.

Amusement.

"Bethany, right?" he asked.

She nodded.

"*Ugly Beauty*…" Klaus said. "Let's do it."

"Let's do it," Bishop repeated, still looking at Bethany. "You take the first solo."

189

"Okay," she said, her voice coming out just above a whisper.

He held eye contact as he slowly counted off: "One," *snap snap*, "Two," *snap snap*, "a-one-two-three, a-one-two-three."

Bethany breathed deeply as she played through the melody with them. As they neared the close of it the second time through, Bishop looked up at her, his eyes catching hers again. Somehow, she felt relieved of her jitters.

Wanting to maintain her calm, Bethany closed her eyes and leaned into the music. She could feel herself breaking free, leaving the room behind. Only somewhere in the distance was a muffled piano accompaniment holding her steady as she waded past the breakers. Suddenly, she was immersed in the calming but powerful vastness of Thelonius Monk's only waltz, rising with its haunting beauty, crashing with its unsettling dissonance.

A delicate sea spray of water-colored greens and blues came at Bethany from the piano. She echoed the spray of notes back, swaying along in the smooth, serene tranquility. Suddenly, she was hit with something a bit choppy—a strange rhythmic pattern. She echoed it back, modulating into foamy waves of aquamarines and upward into the caps of white. Bishop continued tossing out lines, luring Bethany in again and again and again until finally, she knew it was time to rest. She opened her eyes, catching Bishop's gaze. His thick, heavy lips curled into a soft smile. She nodded and lowered her bow.

Bishop began his solo. Bethany generally preferred to leave most of the comping to others, but listening to Bishop, she couldn't help but want to contribute bits of texture to his solo. She closed her eyes again, and played along softly, offering him only the gentlest casts. Much to her surprise, he ardently received them, allowing her to lure him into greater and greater depths, and finally back around to the shallow. She opened her eyes just as Bishop looked up at her, again greeting her with a soft smile, then nodding to Klaus.

Klaus shook his head, and Cam took the next solo. Bethany sat and again closed her eyes. She listened to Cam's gently playful solo against the faint comping and Drew's soft drumming. Afterward, Drew took his solo. It was surprisingly structured and melodic along with the layering of chords from the piano. Bethany was amazed by Bishop's endurance as she sat listening to him. He was graciously minimalistic, but each and every note inspired, becoming an essential component to each solo.

Again, they played twice through the head, and sat quietly a moment after.

"Klaus not taking a solo…" Cam finally said, breaking the silence. "That's a first."

"She covered it," Klaus said, flashing his dazzling smile at Bethany. "Nothing more for a violin to say there."

"Definitely some magic between piano and violin," Cam said.

"Holy shit," Drew added. "Yeah, that was wild!"

Bethany looked up to find Bishop gazing at her, and began tugging her hair forward.

"You've played together before?" Drew asked.

"First time," Bishop replied.

"Damn," Drew said. "Well, let's keep it going. What are you guys up for next?"

"Actually," Bethany said, "I should get going."

There was still plenty of time before Theater 100, but she suddenly needed some fresh air.

"No way," Klaus said. "Stick around a while."

"I need to head out," Bethany told him, starting to pack up.

"Alright," he relented. "I'll walk you out."

"No, stay," Bethany said. "Gimme a call over the weekend. We'll meet up here again on Monday."

"What time on Monday?" Bishop interjected.

Bethany looked up, meeting his eyes.

"Um... 9 AM?" Bethany asked, pulling her hair closer around her face.

"9 AM," Bishop repeated. "I'll be right here."

Bethany nodded, quickly making her way to the door. She opened it just as two black guys were about to walk in; one short and heavyset carrying a trumpet, the other much taller with cornrows, holding a shiny gold lacquer tenor saxophone.

Someday...

"Hey, wait," Bishop said.

Bethany turned back.

"This is Jamal Martin and Eddie Evans... saxophone and trumpet respectively," he said. "Fellas, this is Bethany... Bethany..." He paused, waiting for her to fill in.

"Schechter."

"Bethany Schechter... violin. She's somethin' special. And she'll be back here on Monday at 9 AM."

"Excellent," Jamal said, tucking his saxophone under an arm to shake her hand. "Nice to meet you, Bethany Schechter. I have class Monday morning, but I look forward to jamming with you soon."

"Nice to meet you," Bethany repeated, suddenly feeling breathless. She thrust her hand at Eddie next. "Nice to meet you," she said again, shaking the trumpeter's hand.

She looked back at Bishop.

"Monday," he said.

"Monday," she repeated.

He gave her a nod, and she turned back out the door. She was feeling a bit dizzy, but couldn't help smiling to herself as she made her way down the hall, thinking of Bishop calling her "somethin' special."

"Hey!" she heard behind her.

Bethany turned to see Klaus hurrying down the hall after her.

"Y'alright?" he asked.

"Sure, I'm fine," she said. "Just wanted to get some fresh air before my next class."

"Mind if I tag along a minute?"

"No, of course not."

The two of them walked out the front doors. A fresh, cool breeze hit her face, and she dropped her head back a moment, breathing in deeply.

"Sure you're okay?" Klaus asked.

"Yeah. That was just… a little…"

"Intense?"

"Yeah."

"Yeah," he repeated. "You and Bishop gelled immediately. I mean, he gels with anyone who's good, but… That was something special."

"…somethin' special."

Klaus studied her face a moment.

"Don't you go falling in love with him, warm honey," Klaus warned with a smirk. "You'll break my heart."

Bethany reached up, tugging her curls forward again.

"Mmmm…" he continued, grinning at her. "Just keep the magic in the music. No fraternizing with other talent, okay?"

Bethany looked at Klaus. His eyes had turned serious, and she realized he was waiting for a response.

"Of course," she said quietly.

"Alright," he said. "So, where ya headed now?"

"Just gonna walk a bit before my class."

"Want me to hang?"

"No," she said. "Get back in there."

"Monday though, okay?" he asked. "9 AM sharp."

"Monday, 9 AM."

Thirty-Two

Bethany picked up her backpack from her car, then walked to the pretzel stand outside the library. She set her violin on the ground to pay for a soft pretzel then picked it back up, crossed 13th St, and continued onto Liacouras Walk. She wandered over to the wrought iron fence surrounding a small landscaped area filled with young trees and fresh shrubbery, setting her backpack and violin down beside her. Right away, she spotted several squirrels darting around on the other side of the fence. She tore a few pieces from the soft pretzel and chucked them toward the creatures. They rushed forward and began nibbling on the pretzel pieces. A couple more squirrels ran up, threatening to snatch the food away from their companions, so Bethany tore off a few more pieces.

It was then she detected someone approaching directly behind her. She figured it must be Klaus again and began to turn when the person's body pressed against her back, pinning her unevenly against the fence.

Definitely not Klaus.

She tried to turn but was being held too tightly. A strong hand moved upward on her outer thigh then clasped onto her hip.

Killian?

This would be an unusual approach for him, but if it wasn't Killian, she knew she was in for a difficult confrontation.

Bethany took a deep breath as a face pressed against her hair, nuzzling the back of her neck. Lifting her arm through the fence, she took her time tossing bits of pretzel in various directions in order to watch the squirrels scamper after them. Then, she tore up the remainder of the pretzel and continued chucking pieces one at a time, stifling a giggle when she accidentally pelted a chubby squirrel in the head with the twisty center part.

The hand released her hip and closed around a wrought iron spire, keeping her locked in while giving her a bit more space. Gazing downward at the hand, Bethany knew it was time to face the music.

"I just wanna talk," Elias finally said quietly next to her ear.

Bethany took another deep breath.

"I miss you, Bethany," he said, nuzzling his face against her neck again. "You won't even answer your phone."

"I'm sorry about that," she began. "I'm sorry for everything."

Elias took a step back, pulling his hands from the fence and turning her to face him. His thick coppery hair hung loose against his charcoal colored t-shirt. His dark blue eyes shone against his golden white lashes.

"Bethany..." he breathed out. His eyes scanned her face, dropped over her neck and chest, then lifted up to her eyes before falling on her lips. "I... I'm... Fuck."

He pressed himself to her, backing her into the fence. Without another word, he began kissing her fiercely, desperately, groaning against her mouth. Bethany finally managed to pull her face away.

"Let's talk, okay?" she asked.

He took hold of her chin, pulling her back to continue kissing her. She started to struggle a bit, and he finally released her.

"Okay, yeah," he breathed. "I'm sorry. I wanna talk."

Again he pressed his lips to hers, moaning.

"I'm sorry," he repeated against her lips, then took a step back. "I'm sorry. Let's talk."

He took hold of her hand, curling each of his fingers tightly around each of hers.

"Bench?" he asked, gesturing toward the one nearest them.

Bethany nodded. She picked up her backpack and violin and walked with him. Together, they sat, and she set her belongings back at her feet. Elias turned inward, sandwiching her hand between both of his.

"I'm sorry I upset you that day," Elias began. "I was trying to make a point. I didn't know it was gonna make you so angry."

"Elias—"

"I don't even like that girl, okay? I never wanted anything to do with her."

"Okay."

"You have to believe me."

"I do."

"It was so stupid."

"Elias—"

"I just want to be with you."

Bethany slumped forward, pressing her forehead into the palm of her free hand.

"I'm sorry," he said, holding his hand up. "Go ahead."

Bethany tilted her face toward him, then sat back, took a deep breath, and turned inward to face Elias.

"Elias, this was my fault," she said, resting her hand atop his. "You were making a fair point. I just overreacted."

"I'm so sorry, Bethany."

"Shhhh… Elias. Really. This was not your fault. Okay?"

She raised her eyebrows, waiting for confirmation.

"Okay," he said, pulling her hand to his lips. "I missed you."

"I've missed you too, but it's a bad idea for us to get wrapped up in something—"

"No," Elias said, wrapping his arms around her, pulling her close. "Don't do that."

"As much as I like you, this isn't sustainable, Elias."

"Look, I get it, okay? I get that. I'm not trying to make you commit to anything serious. I'm not," he said, looking into her eyes. "I just like you. I just want to spend some more time with you."

He leaned in, brushing his lips against hers.

"I need to get to my class," Bethany said. "Let's talk about this a little later, okay?"

"Uh-uh," he said, tightening his grip. "No way I'm letting you go."

"Elias, we'll talk later. I promise."

"You won't even answer your phone."

"I will."

"You dropped Physics just to avoid me!"

"I'm sorry."

"Bethany—"

"Elias, listen to me. I promise I will answer my phone from now on. I really need to get going."

Elias held tight to her.

"Really. I have a class."

"What class?"

"Theater 100. Then, I have a rehearsal, but I'll be free to talk this afternoon."

"What time?"

"Probably by 3 or 3:30. I'll call you, okay? I promise, I will. … right after rehearsal."

Elias studied her face a moment.

"Well, I'm gonna walk you to class," he said.

"Good idea," Bethany said.

Again, he leaned in, sweeping his lips across hers, then pressing into her more forcefully, wrapping his hand around the nape of her neck, kissing her deeply. Bethany kissed him back, softening her lips in order to gently conclude the kiss, but he wouldn't relent. Finally, she pulled her face away abruptly.

"Elias, I'm going to be late."

"Okay," he said, lightly kissing her cheek, then her neck. "I'm sorry."

"Walk me, okay?"

"Okay," he said, reluctantly releasing her.

Bethany picked up her backpack and violin, offering a gentle smile as she stood. Elias stood too, immediately taking her into his arms.

"Don't disappear on me again."

"I won't."

"You'll answer when I call?"

"I will. I promise, I will."

He brought his hand up to the nape of her neck, kissing her again. Bethany kissed him back.

"I'm sorry," he said. "I know I'm suffocating you. I'm sorry."

"It's fine," she said. "But I really do need to get to Theater 100."

"Okay," he said, releasing her from his arms and taking her hand.

They started toward Tomlinson. Bethany realized they were walking the same route as when she had tailed him and the blonde, and winced with guilt at the memory. She'd been so blinded by her own insecurity, she had overlooked the pain she was inflicting. She had doubted God's love for her and would undoubtedly have to suffer for it.

She could have enjoyed weeks of a good thing with this strong, sweet, sexy Viking. She could have allowed their fling to fizzle out naturally while also fulfilling her science credits. Instead, she'd dropped Physics and rejected Elias, wasting time, and causing an artificial spike in his admiration. She would now have to navigate through this intense infatuation she'd created without causing Elias any more undue heartache. Bethany could feel her life taking shape before her and knew time was running out. This would need to be managed and resolved quickly.

They reached the back door of Tomlinson. Elias had his fingers curled tightly around hers, holding her palm snugly against his. He pressed her against the brick building. Bethany squirmed uncomfortably as other students trickling past turned to gawk.

"You'll call this afternoon?"

"I will. I'll call as soon as rehearsal ends."

"Where's your rehearsal?"

"Here. In the basement."

"I want to see you tonight."

"I really need to study my script."

"Bring it with you."

"Where?"

"To my dorm."

"Elias—"

"To dinner then. I just want to spend some time with you, okay?"

"I don't think—"

"I'm not gonna let you go unless you promise," he said, pressing against her harder, leaning in to lightly kiss her lips, then again, and again.

Bethany flinched as she recognized Patience Danquah passing by, glaring at her.

"Okay," Bethany relented.

"Okay?"

"Okay. Let me go to class. I'll call you after my rehearsal ends."

"3'o'clock? I'll meet you here."

"Let's make it 3:30 to be safe."

"3:30, right here."

"3:30, right here," she agreed.

"Okay."

"See you soon," she said, offering a smile.

Elias smiled back at her. He leaned in to kiss her cheek, then again, and once again to softly kiss her lips before finally releasing her.

Thirty-Three

Bethany made her way into the theater with a few minutes to spare.

"There you are!" Jelani said, taking hold of her arm.

"Hey. How ya doin'?" Bethany asked.

"C'mon."

Jelani pulled her along, back out the side entrance of the theater, down the hall, and into one of the empty Movement classrooms.

"What's up?" she asked once inside the classroom.

Jelani closed the door.

"You know a paper of yours was published over the Listserv, right?"

"Shit," Bethany said.

"I'll take that as a no."

"I don't really bother with email," she said. "Colorblind casting?"

"That's the one," Jelani said. "People are upset about it. I'm pretty sure Quentin is planning to make an announcement about it today."

"In Theater 100?"

"Yeah."

"An announcement about my essay?"

"Mm-hm."

"What… Why? Is it..? Are you..? I mean… Jelani, I'm sorry to ask you like this, but… Do you find my position racist? Did you read the essay?"

"I read your essay, and I wholeheartedly agree with your position."

Bethany took a deep breath. "Okay, so... I don't know. I guess I just have to try explaining again."

"Well, I heard about your attempt to explain in Makena's class, and... I think you need to let me give it a shot."

"No."

"No what?"

"No, I'm not dragging you into this," Bethany said. "I'm actually kind of used to this happening."

"You're used to being called a racist?"

"Well, no... the racist part is new, but I'm used to... I don't know, upsetting women, for some reason. I just... piss them off... never on purpose, but they still turn awfully aggressive. Anyway, I'm mostly used to it, and, trust me, it'll only be worse if you get involved."

"Bethany, that essay reflects my own perspective. I might as well have written the thing myself," he said. "I'm not letting you take the heat for it alone."

"Shit. No. Seriously, Jelani—"

"Let's go," he said, giving her arm a gentle tug.

"I'm sitting alone in there."

"No, you're sitting with me."

Bethany glared at him. He stared back, eyes steady, mouth set in a neutral line, his chin pushed forward slightly.

Determination.

She took a deep breath and released it, feeling her shoulders slump.

"It's gonna be fine," Jelani said gently. Finally, his face broke into a smile. "C'mon, come sit with me. Stop being racist."

Bethany couldn't help laughing as he tugged her back out of the classroom. He gestured for Bethany to go ahead of him. Reluctantly, she started down the hallway, Jelani following close behind. By the time she reached the side entrance of the theater, the majority of students were already seated. Feeling their eyes on her, she began climbing the stairs, and took an aisle seat toward the back of house center, setting her backpack and violin at her feet. Jelani stepped over them and sat beside her. Bethany winced as other students already began turning to gawk at them.

"Jelani," she whined softly. "Please…"

"We're good," he said quietly, patting her knee. "We got this."

Bethany watched as Quentin entered from the side entrance and made his way up the stairs to the stage. He limped upstage, disappearing behind a leg drop into the wing, and returned carrying a stool, which he placed downstage right, and sat.

"May I have your attention?" he said, projecting his voice. "Let's quiet down, folks."

As latecomers scurried into seats, Bethany stared at Quentin, watching as he gazed around the room, waving at various students in the house. When his eyes landed on Bethany, he raised his heavy brow and nodded with a warm smile. Bethany realized he actually was going to make an announcement about her essay, and he was attempting to reassure her in advance. She only stared back blankly. Finally, he again lifted his eyes.

"Guys, I want to start today with an open discussion," he said, the house finally quieting. "It's been brought to my attention that a paper written by one of your peers has been making some waves. I have to admit I don't check the Listserv quite as frequently as I ought to, so while I've heard some soft rumblings over the past couple days, I only just read the essay myself this morning. I want to first express my sincerest apologies for not addressing this sooner. For those of you who were offended by the paper, I will make it a point to give you the floor, to let you say your piece today. But I want to first state my own belief that some of the points have been taken out of context and, from my perspective, grossly misinterpreted. I suspect that, like me, many of you read this essay after first hearing about it through gossip. I also suspect that some of you might have only heard about it. It's been cast in a very bad light, and when something is prefaced that way, deciphering its true intent can prove rather difficult. Can we all agree to that much?"

Quentin took a moment to gaze around the quiet house before continuing. Bethany pulled out her script and tried to study her lines as another Theater 100 went to waste. She wasn't sure how much time had passed when she heard her name shouted from across the theater.

"Bethany Schechter?! Wait. This is Bethany's essay?"

Bethany looked up to see Jared standing down front, house left.

Oh, shit… Jared, sit down.

"Sorry, I'm late to this," Jared continued. "I heard about the essay, but I haven't read it. Frankly, I don't need to read it to know how completely ludicrous this is. How many of you know Bethany?"

About half of the students partially raised a hand.

"Well, if you know her, you know this is total bullshit. Nearly all of you know me, and I can tell you, as someone who's consistently worked with her since the start of her freshman year, and as someone who calls her a friend, she is absolutely not a racist. And I think it's—"

"Can you define 'racist' for us?" another voice called out. Heads swiveled to the center of the front row to see Patience Danquah who was now standing, hands on her hips, facing Jared.

"Wait a minute, wait a minute," Quentin interjected, holding up his hand.

"A person who judges the value of others based on race," Jared answered, ignoring Quentin's objection. "That's how I would define a racist."

"So, what about a person who believes people of color shouldn't have the same opportunities as Caucasians?"

Jared scoffed. "Bethany doesn't believe that."

"Are you sure about that, Mr. Late-to-the-Party? You didn't even read her essay!" Patience shouted.

"I don't need to read it to know that much. I'm her friend!"

"Her *Caucasian* friend who really wouldn't understand the first thing about being discriminated against!" Patience shouted.

"I wouldn't understand *what* now?!" Jared shouted back. He continued shouting, but could no longer be heard above the roar of other hostile voices joining in.

Bethany dropped her head, pressing her palm to her forehead. Jelani placed a hand on her shoulder for a moment. She thought he leaned in and said something to her, but she couldn't make out what it was.

"YO!" she heard a voice call out above the rest.

She realized it was Jelani's voice, that he was now standing up beside her. The room suddenly fell to a hush. Bethany removed her hand from her face and stared blindly at her script as students turned to hear Jelani.

"Hey, everyone. Most of you know me. For anyone who doesn't: I'm Jelani Green. I'm a junior here. I'm currently working on a scene with Bethany Schechter, and I also count her as a friend."

"Of course you do!" Patience shouted.

"Miss Danquah, please," Quentin started.

"No," she continued. "Miss Thing, Miss Pretty White Girl goes and bats her eyelashes at him, and of course he's gonna defend her!"

Bethany felt her head jerk back as she stared at Patience.

Miss Thing? Miss Pretty White Girl?

Bethany pressed her lips firmly together to stifle a smile as Patience railed on.

"Miss Danquah…" Quentin repeated. "I'm going to ask that you yield the floor to Jelani. You will have a chance to speak again."

Patience crossed her arms and sullenly leaned back against the stage.

"That's fine," she said, turning to Jelani. "But you know, I've seen her big Norseman boyfriend. She's only working with you because you were assigned to her. She doesn't even think African Americans have a place on stage with Caucasians."

A few audible gasps came from around the house.

"That!" Jelani said, pointing at Patience. "Did everyone hear that? Patience just said that Bethany doesn't think African Americans have a place on stage with Caucasians."

Bethany scanned the room noticing every pair of eyes glued to Jelani, except for Patience's which were glaring directly at her. Bethany cast her eyes downward, not wanting to seem confrontational.

"The scene Bethany and I are in together is about a racially mixed marriage between a black man and a white woman. If you read Bethany's essay, you know that she would absolutely object to anyone other than a black man getting cast as the black male character, or anyone other than a white woman getting cast as the white female character. This has nothing to do with feelings about race, or opportunity, or anything else. This is about preserving the integrity of the story. There are lots of instances, many of which Bethany took the time to cite in her essay, where colorblind casting would cause confusion, where it would erode the story that the playwright is trying to tell. As people who participate in the productions of these stories, it's our responsibility to interpret them to the best of our ability, and to retell them in the most clear, honest, and meaningful way possible."

Bethany looked up to see students nodding in agreement. She noticed Quentin smiling brightly at Jelani, also nodding his head. Quentin noticed Bethany and smiled at her too. Bethany looked back at her lap. She hoped Jelani would sit down, but he wasn't finished.

"I want you all to consider something else. An important point was addressed in Bethany's essay, but for the sake of clarity, I'm going to add my own emphasis. For just a moment, I'm going to ask that you all think about Arthur Miller's *Death of a Salesman*. It's a play we've all read at least once, right?" he asked with a chuckle.

The other students responded, some cheering, a few booing, and some chuckling along.

"I like the play well enough, myself, but that's beside the point. I'm referencing a play we're all familiar with. On the off-chance someone here somehow missed it, I'll just quickly summarize: *Death of a Salesman* is about the Loman family. There's Willy Loman, his wife, Linda, and their two adult sons, Happy and Biff. Anyone who's read the play or who's seen it, knows the Lomans are white. And like Bethany, I believe the Lomans should only be portrayed by white actors... or at least by actors who look and can present as white."

"And why's that?" Patience shouted from the front row. "Why can't Linda Loman be played by an African American actress? You don't think an African American woman can handle the role? You're worried she'll impose her own 'colored girl' accent? Where exactly does it say Linda is white? Where? You do know there are Caucasian men who marry African American women, right?"

"Well, that's true, Patience, and I appreciate you making that point," Jelani said. "An important note, for anyone unfamiliar: *Death of a Salesman* takes place in New York during the 1940s. This is just about the time they'd integrated baseball. Interracial marriage was still explicitly illegal in many states. Very different time. In the 1940s, even in New York, white men did not marry black women... at least, not without a tremendous scandal at the very center of their lives. And *Death of a Salesman* isn't about the scandal of a mixed race marriage. It's about a whole set of other

209

very distinct troubles... troubles belonging to the common white man of the 1940s, and his family. To cast a black woman as Linda Loman asks the audience to pretend they don't recognize the race of the actress, or worse yet, asks the audience to pretend that a mixed race marriage would not have been a scandal in the 1940s —a complete misrepresentation of American history, which I think serves as an injustice to us all."

Bethany looked around as a large portion of the student body began cheering and applauding. Again, she wished Jelani would sit. But he waited for them to quiet, then continued speaking.

"To reiterate: This is theater. We are the storytellers. And it's our job to tell the story as it was written, to reflect the writer's perspective of a certain place and time, and its people. If we want to tell a different story, we need to produce a different play."

Bethany began to squirm as the cheering continued. She looked up to see Patience still scowling at her then continued scanning the room until she found Lisa Apgar. Lisa didn't look especially angry though. She sat, picking at a colorful sewn-on patch on the knee of her jeans, looking her normal level of bored and irritated.

Then, Bethany spotted Makena Ward-Washington, who stood just before the side entrance of the theater, arms folded across her chest. Like Patience, she too was scowling, but not at Bethany or even at Jelani. She was scowling at Quentin, who stood obliviously applauding along with the majority.

Bethany wished Quentin would move on already. Wasn't there a more productive way to spend Theater 100 than analyzing her essay? Jelani finally took his seat, lightly placing a hand on Bethany's knee. She glanced over at him.

"You okay?" he asked.

She nodded.

"You wanna get out of here?"

Bethany shook her head no. She actually very much wanted to get out of there, but she didn't want Jelani to be seen leaving early with her.

"Rehearsal afterward still though, right?"

She nodded again, and Jelani smiled.

Thirty-Four

Quentin had managed to wrap up the discussion of colorblind casting about three-quarters of the way through the normal class period, at which point, he'd decided to let them go early. Patience had stormed out soon after Jelani sat down. Makena had chased after her. Bethany knew there'd be hell to pay come Wednesday, but she was relieved to be away from it all for now.

After class, a group of students had gathered around Bethany and Jelani; many to thank Jelani for making some important points they'd managed to overlook, and several to apologize to Bethany for comments they'd apparently made about her over the Listserv. Bethany just kept flashing smiles and repeating, "It's totally fine. Don't worry about it," until she finally managed to slip away and out through the back exit. From there, she darted down the stairs to the basement where she'd agreed to meet Jelani for rehearsal.

Bethany set her backpack and violin down and sat beside them on the dark red carpeted floor. She pulled her script from her backpack and began reading through it again.

"Hey, Miss Pretty White Girl."

Bethany looked up to see Jared walking down the stairs.

"Hey, Jared."

"That was unbelievable," he said, sitting down in front of her. "Did you know that was coming?"

"Jelani warned me just before class."

"He was great," Jared said. "Much better than anything I said."

"You shouldn't have gotten involved at all, Jared."

Jared's head jut back as though he'd been slapped.

"Well, I wasn't going to just kick back and let them bash you," Jared said, sounding hurt.

213

Bethany bit down on her lip, resting a hand over his arm.

"You're a good friend," she said. "I just…"

"Just what?"

"I don't actually know what set them off, but I worry they could turn on you just as fast."

Jared sat quietly, looking confused.

"I'm saying I don't understand what causes this sort of thing to happen," Bethany explained. "And I certainly don't know how to resolve it. So, it worries me to see someone else getting sucked into it."

"I think they just misunderstood the paper you wrote. And it seems like Jelani resolved it. It's all good now, right?"

"Is it? I don't know. I never know," she said with a nervous laugh. "I can't even understand how my paper could have been misconstrued to that extent in the first place. It's kind of scary, because, I mean… I wasn't trying to be edgy or anything. I turned in what I imagined was a fairly benign argument against colorblind casting. It's just hard to believe all of this could really be about that essay."

"Well, so… What's the alternative? If it wasn't your paper that set them off, then… what?"

"I don't know. Maybe there's something about me that just makes some people angry, that makes them hate me."

"Nah. Who could hate you, Bethany? They just misunderstood."

Bethany tried to smile at Jared. "Thanks, Jared. Just… be careful, okay?"

"Hey, Miss Thing!"

Jared and Bethany looked up to see Jelani coming down the stairs. He walked over and sat on the floor with them.

"Hey," Jelani said to Jared, holding out his hand. "Jelani Green."

"Jared Isaacs," Jared said, shaking his hand.

"I know who you are. Big fan. Saw you in *The Rainmaker* over last break. You were fantastic."

"Wow, thanks, man! That's high praise coming from you. I saw you in *The Imaginary Invalid*. Very impressive performance."

"Thanks, man."

"So…" Jared said, nodding toward Bethany. "This was all just a misunderstanding, right? Bethany is concerned there might be something intrinsically loathsome about her."

"You don't understand. This just happens to me," Bethany said with a shrug. "Girls just… Well, they… kinda hate me. It's like they see something in me that makes them think I'm not one of them."

"Well…," Jelani began, "I don't think they necessarily hate you, but—"

"Did you see the way Patience was glaring at me?"

"Let her glare," Jelani said with a wave of his hand. "Patience glares at everyone who doesn't immediately fall in line with her moonbat ideology. You heard the way she came at me."

"She came at you for defending me."

"Yeah, this time. But that wasn't my first time going three rounds with Patience Danquah. She's just quick to make it personal."

"But this was just about the paper, right?" Jared asked again.

"I don't know," Jelani said with a shrug. "I mean, the paper definitely pissed people off, but I think a lot of the aggression we saw today was more about…"

"About what?" Bethany and Jared asked in unison.

"Well, I'm not sure how to explain it exactly, but… I think maybe some people just like to express outrage."

"Yes," Bethany said. "Yes! Like it's fun for them. Is that it? Is it fun for them?"

215

"I don't know that they necessarily enjoy it," Jelani began "But they're certainly rewarded for it. You notice how everyone and everything is suddenly racist? ...or sexist... homophobic... whatever. People in academia have a hard-on for that shit. Sorry," he said looking up at Bethany. "Ugly language. But you know what I'm saying, right?"

Bethany nodded, unsure.

"It's possible a girl like Patience has simply picked up on this and figured out how to exploit it to her advantage."

Jared nodded.

"I mean, I don't want to make Patience out to be some kind of egomaniacal villain, since I'm not convinced she's even fully aware of her own motivations," Jelani said. "But she's regularly rewarded for her emotional outbursts. And colorblind casting is very popular among academics, so this paper made you an easy target."

Bethany sat, gawking at Jelani—this man who'd stood up, not merely to protect her, but to communicate truth to people who had difficulty hearing it. She'd taught this man to waltz, and he'd revealed one of the universe's most vexing mysteries, casually delivering the answer she'd been pursuing for as long as she could remember. Women didn't hate her... not really. They were simply following the path that had been cleared for them.

"Oh, my God!" Bethany suddenly exclaimed.

Jared and Jelani looked at her, waiting for her to say more, but she suddenly felt very foolish.

"Um... It's um... already after 1. We should start our rehearsal, Jelani."

"Oh. Yeah, okay," he said, standing, and turning to Jared. "Very nice to officially make your acquaintance. Maybe we'll get to work together sometime."

"It would be an honor," Jared said, standing. "Great to meet you. Bethany, take it easy, alright?"

He gave Bethany's arm a squeeze.

"Thanks, Jared. I'll see ya Monday."

"Monday," he said. "And you guys better not laugh at my scene. I have a known handicap."

Bethany and Jelani both laughed.

Rehearsal had gone well. They were both fully memorized. The blocking was easy, and the waltzing was smooth. They'd agreed an additional over-the-weekend rehearsal would be unnecessary, which was great news for Bethany, who had a feeling she'd be in desperate need of a nice, boring Sunday.

Thirty-Five

It was only a few minutes after 3, but Elias was already waiting for Bethany outside, behind Tomlinson.

"Hey."

"Hey," he said, embracing her. "Buy you a bubble tea?"

"Sure," she said as he draped an arm over her shoulders and began walking.

"Got your violin again today," he noted. "Can I get you to play for me?"

"Um…"

"C'mon… Not like you haven't been to my dorm before."

"I know, but—"

"So, quit giving me such a hard time."

"Okay," Bethany said.

"Okay?"

"Okay."

"Alright," Elias said, giving her a squeeze.

They'd stopped at the wall of food where Elias bought her a bubble tea, instructing her to "drink it on the way." But somehow, the cup of tapioca pearls sitting in icy honeydew flavored, green sugar water seemed unappealing to her and remained nearly full by the time they'd reached his dorm.

Elias let her in, closing the door behind himself. Bethany wandered in, setting the bubble tea atop his microwave. Elias sat before her on his bed.

"So, you gonna play for me?"

"Oh, I dunno."

"Go on, play for me. I want you to."

"A little later maybe?" she asked, setting her backpack and violin on the floor.

"I bet you play for your roommate whenever he wants, don't you?"

"What?"

"Your roommate… the one you can't bring other guys around."

Bethany blinked. "Elias—"

"When you lived in the dorms, you invited me over the very day I met you, and you never had any objection to coming here. But for some reason, you can't have me to your apartment," Elias said, his eyes boring into hers. "So… that's it, isn't it? All along… He's the real reason you can't get involved in any real way."

"No," Bethany said. "Elias, I've explained why—"

"Sure, I heard your explanation."

Bethany stared at her feet.

"I said I want you to play for me," he said with a sudden edge to his voice.

"Alright," she relented quietly, dropping to open her violin case.

After putting on her shoulder rest, tightening her bow and quickly tuning, she stood before him and began Massenet's *Meditation* from *Thais*. Closing her eyes, she thought only of the notes, of her fingers on the strings and her bow drawing out the brief moments of tension and sadness inside the sweet introspective serenity of the piece.

By the time she finished, a soothing calm had washed over her. Quietly, she lowered herself to the floor to pack up her violin, and stood again, making eye contact with Elias.

"That was beautiful," he said, standing, taking her into his arms. "And maybe a little sad." He gently kissed her, stroking her hair. "What made you choose that piece?"

"I… I don't know."

"Sure you do."

"It's just what came to mind."

"Do I make you sad?"

"No, of course not," Bethany said.

"Good," he said, kissing her again. "I wouldn't want you to be sad."

She felt his fingers opening her jeans.

"Take these off," he said.

Bethany stepped out of her Keds and removed her pants.

"Get in," he said, gesturing toward his bed.

She climbed into Elias's bed as he turned and walked to the closet, pulling out a sock and carrying it to slip over the exterior knob of the door. When he returned, he stood at the side of the bed, gazing at her.

"I like seeing you here," he said, a warm smile spreading over his face.

For a moment, he seemed relaxed and content. It was how she remembered him. She smiled back, holding his gaze.

"I like being here," she said.

His smile faded.

"Take off the rest of your clothes," he said as he began undressing.

Bethany removed the remainder of her clothing, dropping it next to her jeans on the floor. Naked, Elias got into bed beside her and pulled her on top of him, plunging into her right away.

She gasped, squeezing her eyes shut as he continued thrusting aggressively, holding her tightly in his arms, grasping her hair in his fist.

"Look at me," he instructed.

Bethany opened her eyes.

"Keep looking at me. Keep your face right here next to mine."

His warm breath came in sharp pants against her lips. She tried to relax.

"Keep your eyes open," he ordered.

He held her tighter and tighter as he continued thrusting beneath her. Finally, he pulled out, groaning loudly, easing his grip. She felt his hot release on her backside. He held her another minute or so, then eased her over to lie beside him on her belly.

"Stay right there," he said, getting up and walking to the bathroom.

Soon, he returned with a half-dampened hand towel which he used to clean then dry her. He chucked the towel into the hamper and climbed back into bed, wrapping her in his arms.

After a few minutes, she tried to turn over, but he held her still, his chest pressed to her back.

"Stay," he said softly. "Stay with me."

"Okay," she said, lying still.

It wasn't until she felt him kissing across the top of her shoulder that she realized she'd fallen asleep. She didn't know how long, although she could see the light had changed.

"Hold still," Elias said in a low voice, entering her from behind with a grunt.

Bethany lay still, listening to his soft groaning as he slowly moved inside her, his strong hand clutching her hip.

As he began to speed up a bit, she closed her eyes and allowed her mind to drift, conjuring images of oddly pale eyes, tight yellow curls, and a pair of monstrously large hands gracefully moving over the keys of a piano. Bethany moaned softly, and Elias tenderly kissed her neck.

"I want to make you mine," he groaned. "I want to make you mine."

He continued speeding up, his hand gripping her tighter, his breathing growing more ragged. He groaned louder and louder, moving faster and faster. Bethany began to feel uneasy. As Elias roared in ecstasy, her mind flooded with an overwhelming sense of panic.

"Pull out!" she heard herself shriek.

"What?"

Elias slowed and then stopped. He withdrew from her, turning her onto her back.

"What's with you?" he asked, frowning at her, panting against her face.

"I… I'm sorry. I just thought…"

"Thought what?"

"I wasn't sure you were going to pull out."

"I always pull out."

"I know. It just… felt like you maybe weren't going to."

"I wasn't there yet."

"I'm sorry. You sounded close. It felt like you were."

"What, you think I'm trying to trap you into something?" he asked with a half smile.

"No, of course not."

She watched as his eyebrows shot up and his head jerked back.

"Oh, my God, you do!" he said, sounding amazed. "That's exactly what you think. You're too good for me, and I'm this needy, lovesick loser who's trying to trap you."

"No. Elias—"

"You don't think I'm smart enough to catch on to what you really think of me?!" he shouted. "You just got scared out of your wits, thinking the loser guy you're slumming it with in college was trying knock you up!"

Bethany began to sit up.

"I better go," she said.

Elias shoved her back down.

"No, you're not gonna go! You're not gonna fucking go!"

"Elias—" she began, trying again to lift herself up.

"Fuck you!" he shouted. "Fuck you. You're not gonna leave."

She twisted her body a bit, and he climbed on top of her, pinning her down.

"You're not gonna fucking leave," he said between clenched teeth, then forcefully kissed her while pushing back into her body. "You're not fucking leaving."

Thrusting hard, Elias stared down at her, eyes narrowed, brow furrowed, his lips pulled tight.

Rage.

"So, how's this work?" he panted. "If I impregnate you, I get to keep you? Huh? Is that it?!"

Bethany stared up into his angry eyes, gasping as he pounded her harder and harder. She could see the depths of his frustration, his jealousy, his insecurity, his tortured heartache, and in that moment, she felt a deep sense of love and empathy for him. Her eyes teared with both adoration and regret as he continued his thrashing. With each thrust, he released a loud, sharp grunt. She watched as his eyes twisted shut and he gnashed his teeth, veins bulging from his forehead. He released an angry growl as he finally pulled out and finished on her belly.

Hovering over her, he opened his eyes, and stared down at her, his face flushed, shoulders heaving.

"There. Now you can hate my guts anyway," he panted, pulling the top sheet loose from his bed and using it to sop the puddle from her abdomen before balling it up and throwing it toward the hamper.

"I couldn't hate you, Elias," she said.

"But I'm never going to see you again, am I?"

Bethany could only offer a gentle smile in response. And with that, Elias dropped onto his side, turning away from her. Sadly, she placed a penitent hand on his back. After a minute, she quietly stood to dress.

She picked up her backpack and violin, taking one last glance at Elias. He had come into her life, a strong and beautiful man, and he now held the posture of a sullen child. She wondered if God could possibly forgive her.

Thirty-Six

Bethany drove aimlessly around the city, Elias's face etched with pain continuously flashing in her mind. She had tried to make things right with him, but it had been too late. She had been careless, selfish, myopic. She had caused harm and was deeply ashamed.

Once again, she found herself parked at Penn's Landing. She got out and wandered to the pedestrian bridge. Gazing up at the Stickmen beneath the night sky, she took a deep breath and released it, then sat on the ground, staring upward at the three figures.

Thirty-Seven

Bethany had sat on the pedestrian bridge for a long time, maybe hours before wandering down by the river a while. It was close to midnight by the time she got home. She was cold and hungry, but chose to go without food. Instead, she showered, dried her hair, dressed in an oversized red t-shirt, and wandered down the hall to Killian's room. Killian had left his bedside lamp on. She spotted Wendell Berry's book on his desk and carried it to his bed, then climbed in and began reading.

Upon reaching the end of chapter 3, Bethany got up and set the book back on Killian's desk, then flopped backward on his bed and lay staring at the ceiling. She imagined herself living in a trailer on 30 acres in Vermont with Killian. Together, they'd work on the land, raising their own food. At the end of each day, they'd prepare a simple meal together, then make love and sleep in each other's arms. Eventually, she'd grow big with Killian's golden-haired, blue-eyed baby and would give birth right there on their own farm. Life would be hard but good because they'd always have each other, and there'd be nothing else to think about.

"Hey. Why aren't you under the covers?" Bethany heard Killian's voice asking.

She felt his hands pulling her in, his blanket covering her, then his strong arms holding her close. He was bare-chested and smelled of soap. Opening one eye, she lifted her head to look at his alarm clock. 5:03 AM. Killian pulled her closer and kissed her cheek. She could feel his freshly washed hair damp against her face and realized he'd just returned home from some lucky girl's bed.

"Come here," he said, pulling her closer. "Geez, you're really cold."

He began rubbing the palm of his hand up and down her arm.

"Oh, I'm alright," she said, trying to sit up.

"Stay," he said, pulling her back against him. "Stay with me. Go back to sleep. I'll keep you warm."

He nuzzled the side of her face, then softly kissed her neck.

"Next time, get under the blanket, okay?"

"I'm alright," she murmured, closing her eyes.

"I know," he said, continuing to kiss her neck. "You're the only girl I've ever wanted to coddle, and the only one who doesn't seem to need it."

Bethany began to drift back to sleep, feeling Killian press the side of his face to hers.

✷ ✷ ✷

She'd slept another hour in his arms before breaking away, explaining that she had homework to do. After studying her lines a while, she showered, dried her hair, and dressed in jeans and a violet blue sweater. Grabbing her purse, she walked to the living room, slipped into her Keds, and left. It would mean hours of aimlessly wandering the city, and Killian wouldn't likely be up much before noon anyway, but she didn't want to chance having to fib about where she was going.

Bethany started out toward Essene Market and Cafe on 4th Street. Hopefully, they'd have eggs available in their hot food bar. Luckily, there was still plenty of parking on Bainbridge. As she pulled into a spot, she noticed a meter maid approaching, then glanced up to notice the expired meter of the old maroon Pontiac 6000 parked beside her. Reaching into the center console, she grabbed a handful of quarters and hurried to feed the Pontiac's meter before feeding her own. The walkie-talkie-toting, heavyset black woman stuffed into a meter maid uniform rolled her neck while grimacing at Bethany. Bethany flashed a quick smile before looking away.

Grinning down at the bounty of prepared foods available in Essene's hot food bar, Bethany filled a container with an egg scramble and a side of roasted potatoes. After paying, she decided she'd rather eat outside than at a table in the cafe. She carried her food back to her car, and climbed onto the hood, enjoying the combination of the warm sun and cool breeze as she ate.

Pulling her cell phone out of her back pocket, she dialed home.

"It's your nickel."

"Hi, Bubbie."

"What's the matter? You're calling on Shabbos?"

"Nothing's the matter. You answered on Shabbos."

"What's happened?"

"Nothing's happened. I just had some time to kill, so I figured I'd call today."

"You're not calling tomorrow?"

"Well, I could hang up now and call tomorrow instead."

"Don't be absurd. We'll talk today."

"Great."

"How's Aaron?" she asked, singing his name.

"We're meeting for lunch."

"You're meeting for lunch on the Sabbath?"

"We are."

"I won't tell Ruth."

"I appreciate it."

"Where are you now? It sounds like you're outside."

"I'm in South Philly, near where we're going to meet."

"So early in the day?"

"No, we'll meet at lunchtime. I came out for breakfast."

"Oy, so much eating. How's your weight?"

"Hundred-and-forty-two."

"Good, good. You don't want to get buxom. You're so tall already."

"I won't, Bubbie."

"How's school?"

"Hmmm…"

"What? What's happened?"

"Nothing's happened. Just… Well, I think maybe I've learned what I came here to learn."

"You miss music. I knew you would. I told Ruth you would. She said, 'Bethany knows what's best.' 'Ech…' I said. 'Zi veyst vi a ku fun montik.'"

"Actually, I've been playing lately. I was thinking I might start playing out at some local clubs."

"Clubs? What clubs? They're playing Bach at the clubs in Philadelphia?"

"Not Bach. Coltrane maybe."

"Your zayde loved Coltrane."

"Yeah."

"So, what..? You're playing jazz now?"

"I've been learning, yeah."

"Learning from who?"

"Friends. Music majors."

"Shkotzim?"

"Just friends, Bubbie."

"You miss music. I knew you would. So, you're playing again. Gants gut! But what about school? You're dropping out?"

"I don't know yet."

"You can always come home. Maybe they'll still have you at Julliard."

"I don't know, Bubbie. I've got to think on it."

"Aaron's not so far either way. Not so much distance between here and there."

"Yeah. I've just got to think on it," Bethany repeated.

"So… You'll think. You'll think, and you'll let us know just as you always have. You know your father. Gelt is nisht kayn dayge. He'll support whatever decision you come to."

You know your father.

The statement sounded so odd. Bethany had grown up, sleeping in the same bedroom that had once belonged to her mother, in an apartment full of her mother's likeness. There were baby pictures, pictures of her as a child, running, playing, swinging on swings at the very same playground Zayde had brought her to. There were pictures of her teenage years, and several of her as a young adult. She'd been beautiful—slender and pale with long, curly dark hair just like Bethany's. Bethany's life had been enriched with countless stories of her mother, of *"our Aliza."* There was only one picture of her father, from her parents' wedding day. It was enough to let Bethany know it was her father's genes that were responsible for her height.

Little was ever said about him, other than him being successful and a good man who, in his grief, had done the right thing, leaving his daughter in the care of her grandparents while covering any and all expenses. Bethany had never met him, although she'd been told that he had once held her as a sleeping newborn baby.

"I know," Bethany said simply.

"Alright. You be good to Aaron. He's a nice one, from a nice family. Not so much distance from here to there," Bubbie said again. "Remember true happiness comes only from fulfilling our purpose."

"I know."

"No good can come of chasing fleeting pleasures."

"I know," Bethany said again.

"Alright, shefele. Ikh hob dikh lib. Zay gezunt."

"I love you too, Bubbie. Talk again soon."

Thirty-Eight

Bethany had taken a walk, then sat, listening to the radio a while in her car. Just before noon, she chucked her cell phone into the center console, topped up the meter, adding a quarter to the meter beside her own, where a turquoise Chevy Corsica was now parked, and walked to South Street.

Aaron stood just outside of Lorenzo and Son's. He was dressed in jeans and a bluish gray sweater. Again, his shoulders were hunched, his hands jammed into his front pockets. When he noticed Bethany approaching, he pulled his hands out, stood upright, and smiled.

"Hey, there," he said.

"Hi."

They turned to walk in, but just before entering, he turned and pulled Bethany toward him, kissing her gently and quickly releasing her. She smiled at him.

They sat on stools at a counter along the side of the narrow restaurant, facing a mirrored wall.

"Slices? Toppings?"

"Just one for me. Plain, please."

"You got it," he said, heading to the counter.

After a few minutes, he returned with a slice for her, and two for himself.

"What can I get you to drink?"

"Bottle of water would be great. Thanks."

He again turned back to the counter, and returned carrying two bottles of water.

"So," he said, sitting on the stool beside her. "How are things?"

"Things are just fine. How have you been?"

"Mostly great, although I have new downstairs neighbors I'm not terribly fond of."

"Nosy or noisy?"

"Noisy. Very."

"Rap music?"

"Rap music, late nights, parties… Couple bachelors."

"Sometimes, if you're sweet, people are sweet back."

"I'll bet people are much more receptive to sweetness coming from you."

"Well, I could come talk to them."

"I wouldn't actually let you take on my obnoxious neighbors for me," Aaron said. He took a bite of pizza and winced.

"Too hot?"

"No," he said, dabbing his lips with a napkin. "I… I'm sorry. I just realized you offered to come to my apartment, and I responded like… well, like the socially inept dolt that I am."

Bethany laughed. "I'll visit your apartment anyway."

"You will?"

"Of course, if you invite me," she said. "Only let's not rush it."

"Alright," Aaron said with a smile. He took another bite of pizza.

They finished their lunch and walked back out onto South Street.

"I don't have to return you to your car just yet, do I?" he asked.

"I'm in no hurry."

"Great! Where would you like to go? A museum? The movies? Ice cream?"

"We could just walk. I like to walk."

"Excellent," he said. He held out his hand to her. "May I?"

Bethany bit down on her lip, accepting his hand. He gripped her hand a bit more firmly than he had before, and she gave his hand a quick squeeze as they walked toward Front Street.

"So…" he began. "Would it be alright for me to ask about your family?"

"Of course," Bethany said. "I'm sure you've heard most of it, no?"

"Aunt Ruth…" Aaron said with a laugh. "The woman likes to talk."

"So, then… What questions do you have left?"

"Well, I suppose I'm wondering about the relationship with your father. She mentioned he lives out West."

"He does, yes," Bethany said. "He's always taken financial responsibility for me, but I don't actually know him."

"How? How—uh…"

"How does that make me feel?" she asked for him.

"I'm sorry. Would you rather not?"

"No, it's fine," Bethany said. "I appreciate the question. I don't know that I actually have any feelings about it though. I mean, it doesn't feel good or bad. I wonder what he's like sometimes, what it would be like to have had him in my life. But I've always known my bubbie and zayde loved me as much as they loved their own child."

"Your mother?"

"Right."

"And your zayde… He…"

"Died, yeah. …when I was 14. It was a sad time, although it wasn't unexpected. And Bubbie's always been braced for the worst anyway," Bethany said.

"Mm," Aaron responded with a nod.

"I don't mean to make her sound like a pessimist. She isn't one at all. Just a realist."

Aaron nodded again. Walking beside him, Bethany was unable to read his face.

"She's actually a deeply joyful person. It's just... well, it's... a different kind of joy."

"Sure, I get it," Aaron said. "Rejoice and laugh in the face of fate. Simcha. Grateful for the struggle. Never the pursuit of happiness."

"Exactly," Bethany said, sighing a breath of relief.

It had been a while.

"You miss home?" Aaron asked, eyeing her.

"Yeah."

"Yeah."

They walked quietly, finding themselves on Front Street, nearing the pedestrian bridge again.

"How's school?" Bethany finally asked.

"Oh... School's school," he replied. "Sometimes, it seems like that's all there is to life."

"Maybe I should pull you away from it more often."

"You definitely should," Aaron said, releasing her hand, stopping to turn toward her at the start of the bridge.

Bethany watched as his eyes dropped over her body, quickly moving back to her face. For a moment, he stared at her lips, then quickly looked up at her eyes, clearing his throat.

"How's uh... How's school been for you?"

"Kinda dull," Bethany said, leaning against the brick wall of the bridge.

"Sorry to hear. What sort of classes does a theater major take?"

"There's a lot of reading and analyzing of plays, acting, stagecraft, set design..."

"But nothing especially interesting this semester?"

"Well, I have a great scene partner. We'll perform for the class on Monday."

"That doesn't sound dull to me," he said. "Terrifying, maybe."

Bethany laughed. "Stage fright?"

"I've never tried acting, but having to perform on stage certainly sounds like the stuff of nightmares. I mean, I can give a PowerPoint presentation, but—"

"Well, that's a kind of performance."

"Sure, I suppose."

"If you can give a presentation, acting shouldn't be too frightening. It's just adapting the skill of public speaking for a different purpose."

"Huh," he said. "Doesn't it feel like someone else's purpose?"

"How do you mean?"

"I mean… When I give a presentation, it's generally to express ideas I have, concepts I've researched. It's usually something I'm invested in, so if I'm performing, it's to convey something that's meaningful to me."

"Gotcha. Yeah. Sometimes, I have to perform in plays I don't especially like."

"Seems like that would be sort of awful—studying a character, memorizing lines, rehearsing, performing all just to deliver someone else's message?"

"I guess it's the performance itself that I find meaningful. If I can convincingly deliver someone else's message, give life to what someone else finds meaningful, even if I might not fully embrace it myself… Well, that feels important," Bethany said. "Maybe that's enough meaning for me."

Aaron cocked his head. "That's… That's interesting," he said, studying her face. "Huh. I think I like that."

"Not sure about it, hmm?"

"No, I… I like that," he said definitively, a smile spreading over his face. "It's different from what I'm accustomed to hearing, but… it's admirable."

Bethany smiled.

"So, what's been dull about it lately then?" he asked.

"I guess it's all of the excess that's sort of tiresome… all the waste."

Aaron nodded, letting out a sigh. "Plenty of that for any major."

"Yeah. Well… I don't know, maybe there's some good in it… all the waiting, the wasting in between brief moments of magic," Bethany said. "Life in general is like that, but in school, it's somehow intensified. The days are full of static, but there's always this stored-up energy just waiting for the right force to act on it. Once it does, something new happens. But until it does… there's just a lot of waiting and wondering what will happen next. I don't know… Maybe that's the time to learn to embrace the static and just appreciate the potential."

Aaron studied her face again. His eyebrows raised a bit as his eyes widened, staring back at her. His lips softened into a slight smile as he gave a slight nod.

Reverence. Admiration. Connection.

Aaron took her hand again. This time, he laced his fingers with hers, holding her palm snugly against his. Bethany coiled her fingers around his, matching his grip.

"So, tell me about the scene you're performing Monday," he said as they continued onto the pedestrian bridge.

"Um… Well, it's not the best writing, but I have a strong partner. He had to learn to waltz for this scene. That was a bit outside his comfort zone, but once he learned and got comfortable, we were basically golden."

"Now, there's something I could handle," he said.

He released her hand and turned to face her, extending his left arm, holding his right open for her. Bethany smiled and slipped into his hold, taking his hand, and Aaron began leading her in a waltz across the pedestrian bridge. As they danced beneath the Stickmen, a cool breeze blew her hair away from her face, and she gazed up into Aaron's warm golden brown eyes. He paused a moment, pulling her closer against him. Reaching a hand to the nape of her neck, he kissed her, kneading her lips with his. Bethany held onto him, matching his intensity. After releasing her, he again studied her face a moment before taking her back into his hold to continue leading her over the bridge.

One-two-three, One-two-three, One-two-three…

Thirty-Nine

Bethany and Aaron spent a couple hours walking along the Delaware River before stopping to feed their parking meters. They walked along the bustling storefronts of South Street and through the quieter streets of the elegant gayborhood. Aaron spoke of his family, describing them as "close-knit." He was the oldest of four. His three younger sisters still lived in New York: Ruth was married to an estate planning attorney and newly pregnant with her first child. Hannah was pre-med at Columbia. Mayim, the youngest, was a pianist and an art major in her first semester at NYU.

Aaron told her he hoped to have a large family of his own, and asked Bethany how she felt about having children. She responded by saying she'd always known she would someday be a mother, unsure of what else she could say about it. Although she supposed the question was a common enough one to ask, it seemed an odd thing for her to be considering how she felt about having children. It was like trying to decide how she felt about being a woman or how she felt about being Jewish.

After splitting a falafel platter and an order of grape leaves at Alyan's on 4th Street, Aaron walked her back to her car. He held her gently in his arms and lightly kissed her goodnight.

"I'll give you a call later if you don't mind, just to make sure you got home safely."

"Of course," she said.

As she turned toward her car door, Aaron grabbed hold of her again, turning her back toward him. He held her firmly, pressing his hand against the nape of her neck, kissing her fervently. Again, Bethany was sure to match his intensity, and smiled warmly before getting into her car and driving away.

"Ion-Induced Dipole Interactions: attractions between an ion and a molecule where the molecule's electron distribution is distorted by the ion," she quoted aloud from a passage she'd memorized from one of Killian's texts. *"London Dispersion Forces: weak, temporary attractions that occur between all molecules due to instantaneous fluctuations in electronic distribution."*

Filled with a sudden deep sadness, she pulled over to the side of the road and sat quietly, waiting for it to pass.

Mesirus Nefesh. This is what's done. Simcha Shel Mitzvah.

Taking a deep breath, she pulled back onto the road, and continued on her way home. Once there, Bethany was relieved to find Killian's Jeep gone. She parked further down the block and went inside. In her bedroom, she stripped off her clothing and slipped into an oversized pale yellow t-shirt before wandering into the kitchen. She opened the freezer, pulled out the bottle of Three Olives and took a swig, then another, and another when she heard the door open and slam shut followed by footsteps rushing up the stairs.

"Where have you been?" Killian asked, wild-eyed. He took her into his arms, pressing his cheek to her forehead. "I was worried. I've been calling."

"Oh," Bethany said simply, remembering the phone still in her car's center console. "I must not have heard my phone. I'm so sorry."

She heard Killian suck in a deep breath.

"It's okay. I'm just really glad to see you," he said, kissing the top of her head. "You left so early this morning. You've been gone all day. I finally gave up trying to call and decided to go out looking a little while ago."

As he released her, he noticed the bottle in her hand. Taking it from her, he examined her face.

"What's going on?" he asked. "Why did you leave here so early? Are you upset with me?"

"No, of course not."

"Where were you?"

"I... I had a date," she said, casting her eyes downward.

"Oh," Killian said, placing the bottle back in the freezer. "Oh," he said again. "Oh, shit... It's happened, hasn't it?"

"What?"

"You've met him."

"Who?"

"You know who... the chosen one," he spat.

Bethany laughed, but it came out as a sob. She quickly buried her face in Killian's shoulder and wept silently. After a moment, she pulled back, wanting him to see her tears, to know her pain.

"You're crying," he said, sounding amazed. His eyebrows knit together as he ran his thumb over her cheek. "I didn't think you did that."

"I'm a woman," she said.

He released a heavy breath. "I know it."

Killian lowered his face to hers, softly dragging his lips back and forth across hers a few times before kissing her. Abruptly, he stopped, and pulled her tightly against him.

"Shit," he said. "Shit... I don't know why I assumed we'd have until graduation. Shit."

"I think I thought that too," she sighed.

He pulled back from her, making eye contact. A golden wave of hair fell partly over his face as he cocked his head. She heard him swallow hard.

"Do you love him?" he asked quietly.

Bethany shook her head.

"But he loves you," he said.

"No," she said.

"Of course he does," he scoffed, his eyes moving over her body, and back up to her face. "But I loved you first," he said gruffly, taking hold of her again.

He gripped her hair, pulling her face back, and began kissing her roughly. His other hand slid up her outer thigh, beneath her nightshirt, clutching her naked hip. Then, suddenly, he shifted, moving his hand between her legs, plunging two fingers inside her. Bethany gasped against Killian's mouth, her head swimming as the effects of the Three Olives took hold.

She heard muffled music—a short familiar melody in ¾. It repeated. She realized it was Killian's cell phone. He seldom kept it on him, and almost never had the ringer on. The ringtone was set to the *Nokia Tune*, same as her own, which she also rarely kept on.

Killian released her hair, and she tried to step away, but he pressed his body against her, pinning her tightly against the refrigerator, thrusting his fingers deeper inside her. Again, Bethany gasped. Killian reached into the back pocket of his jeans, retrieving the cell phone as it rang a third time.

"Hey, Audrey," he said, his voice calm. "No, it's alright. I found her. Yeah, I've got her here at home. I still need you to cover my shift though. I uh… I'm right in the middle of something."

Bethany tried to wiggle free, but Killian began moving his hand against her, causing her to freeze.

"Thanks, Audrey. I owe ya one," he said. "Have a good night."

He hung up and dropped the phone back into his pocket. Still manipulating her with his hand, he again took hold of her hair, pulling her head back to kiss her. Bethany moaned against his mouth. His hand moved steadily, never changing tempo or technique. As his lips moved down her neck, Bethany finally cried out, her body shuddering against him.

Killian released her and took a step back. He took her hand, lacing his fingers with hers, and gave it a gentle tug.

"C'mon," he said, turning.

She followed him a few steps toward the hall then stopped short. He turned back around to face her.

"I… I'm sorry for that," he said, glancing at the floor and giving his head a slight shake before raising his eyes back to her face. "Are you okay?"

She nodded. He nodded back.

"C'mon," he repeated, giving her hand another gentle tug. "Let me hold you a while."

She stood frozen.

"C'mon," he said again, releasing her hand and wrapping an arm around her. "I'll read to you."

Bethany began walking with him, and he dropped back a step to follow her down the hall. Reaching his bedroom, she saw his bedside lamp had been left on. She took a couple steps into the room, then spun back around. Killian quickly closed the door and leaned back against it.

"Get in," he said, tipping his chin toward the bed.

Bethany stared back at him a moment, then turned and moved to his unmade bed, slipping into it as modestly as she could manage in her nightshirt, pulling the covers over herself, and resting back on his pillow. Killian remained standing, gazing down at her for a few seconds, a gentle smile spreading over his face. Then, he took a deep breath, and lifted the Wendell Berry book from his desk.

He kicked off his sneakers, and climbed into bed beside her, still fully clothed in his jeans and white t-shirt. He rested his head back against the other pillow and patted his shoulder, gesturing for Bethany to rest her head there. She did, and he pulled his arm around her.

"Okay?" he asked.

"Mm-hm."

"Alright."

Killian rested the book on his chest, opening to Chapter 3. Bethany didn't bother to let him know she'd already read Chapter 3. She enjoyed hearing him read, enjoyed hearing about a trailer on 30 acres in Vermont in Killian's voice.

He read right through into Chapter 4. The longer he read, the more at peace Bethany felt. She brought her arm up to wrap around Killian's waist, snuggling into him.

"A culture is not a collection of relics or ornaments, but a practical necessity, and its corruption invokes calamity. A healthy culture is a communal order of memory, insight, value, work, conviviality, reverence, aspiration. It reveals the human necessities and the human limits. It clarifies our inescapable bonds to the earth and to each other. It assures that the necessary restraints are observed, that the necessary work is done, and that it is done well."

Although Bethany couldn't relate to the lifestyle Wendell Berry spoke of, he still made a great deal of sense to her. This was a deeply wise man giving an impassioned plea that somehow applied to her just as much as it applied to anyone else.

"It remains only to say what has often been said before—that the best human cultures also have this unity. Their concerns and enterprises are not fragmented, scattered out, at variance or in contention with one another. The people and their work and their country are members of each other and of the culture. If a culture is to hope for any considerable longevity, then the relationships within it must, in recognition of their interdependence, be predominantly cooperative rather than competitive."

Once Killian completed Chapter 4, he turned to her.

"Getting sleepy?"

Bethany shook her head.

"Should I keep reading?"

Hesitantly, she again shook her head.

Killian gently lifted her head from his shoulder, leaving her to rest on his pillow. He slipped out of bed to set the book on his desk, then turned back, staring down at Bethany. Bethany stared back, wide-eyed, feeling her breath catch as Killian pulled off his shirt and dropped it onto the bed, exposing his muscular torso. She watched as he removed his jeans, uncovering a pair of light green boxer briefs. Looking him over as he stood gazing down at her, she felt a sudden jolt, and quickly leaped from his bed, rushing around it toward the door. Killian caught her in his arms.

"Don't," he said. "Don't run away from me."

Bethany could hear his breath thicken as he held her and realized her own breathing sounded erratic. She tried to focus on taking deep, steady breaths. Killian held her close and began delicately kissing her. She kissed him back.

"Bethany…" he moaned against her lips.

Bethany felt herself losing her footing as Killian eased her backward onto his bed. He gently dragged her upward over his mattress, then pressed himself down against her. She tried to avoid thinking, to focus only on the warmth of his body, on his gentle kisses.

This was Killian, her best friend, the man she loved. Freeing a hand, she reached around to the nape of his neck, pressing her lips more firmly against his. Killian moaned again. After a moment, he lifted himself away in order to pull her nightshirt up over her head. He stared down at her naked body.

"Bethany…" he whispered before lowering himself back onto her.

She felt him removing his underwear as he continued kissing her. Once naked, he pressed his body to hers. Again, Bethany began to panic, unable to stop her mind from racing.

This was Killian, her best friend, the man she loved… a perfect person who had come into her life and loved her back, but who could never be hers… the gold standard male for whom she was not destined.

There's no going back from this.

"Killian, don't!" she cried.

"Let me," he said, staring down at her.

Bethany stared back, mesmerized as the light caught the tiny golden rings around his pupils. Finally, she closed her eyes, relenting. Killian thrust into her body. There was a bright flash, and a roaring sound in her ears. As her body rocked, she desperately tried again to steady her breathing.

Perched on his elbows, Killian maintained a perfect square frame of his thick, strong arms, housing Bethany in. He moved his hips in tight circles against her. His eyes remained open, staring down at her until finally, he lowered his face to drag his lips up and down the side of her face.

"Bethany…" he moaned in between soft kisses.

Before she could realize what was happening, she felt a boiling rush of pink, her face flushing as her body went rigid. She released a high pitched moan, followed by a soft grunt. As the waves of pleasure slowly began to subside, her body fell limp. Killian continued moving, still slowly dragging his lips up and down the side of her face.

"Bethany…"

As she began to catch her breath, she tried to focus on Killian. She wanted to be present with him, to match his movement. She desperately wanted him to know her love. Unexpectedly, he raised up onto his hands, locking his arms, still pressing his hips tightly against her, but applying more of a quick back and forth motion. Looking up at him, she noticed his thick glistening shoulders illuminated by the bedside lamp, his skin almost appearing to glow with a golden white light. She was caught off guard and her body began to respond before she could consciously react. Again, there was a sudden rush of heat followed by a powerful jolt prompting her body to seize. She could hear herself squealing as her pelvis began to quake. Once the pulsations began diminishing, she again lay languid beneath him as he lowered his face, brushing his lips against hers.

"Bethany…"

Killian maintained his pace, kissing her again and again and again. Suddenly, he climbed to his knees, pulling her hips up from the bed with him. He sped up then, reaching his hand to fondle her breast, then using both hands to pull her into an upright position over him, holding her tightly, moving her back and forth. Bethany had never had anyone take charge of her body this way before. She felt almost like a doll being jostled around helplessly. She tried to gain control of her senses, but suddenly, he plunged his tongue into her mouth, kissing her deeply. Then, without warning, he dropped her back onto his pillow, landing gently atop her. Once again, he began moving his hips tightly against hers.

Bethany began to feel overwhelmed, wishing he would finish. But he pressed onward, plunging deeper into her, all the while continuing a delicate smattering of sweet kisses all over her face and neck. She struggled to control her breathing, unable to decide if Killian was giving her something she desperately needed, or taking something she'd never reclaim. She only knew she'd been overtaken completely.

As she came a third time, Killian withdrew from her, replacing himself with his hand. He came with her, moaning her name one final time before dropping beside her. He reached his hand back and grabbed hold of his t-shirt which he used to wipe her belly clean.

Bethany kept still, listening as Killian's breathing softened. Keeping an arm draped over her, he perched himself on an elbow.

"Are you okay?" he asked quietly.

Bethany nodded.

"Can I get you anything? Some water?"

"Yes. Thank you."

"I'll be right back," he said, rolling out of bed onto his feet.

She watched him walk to his dresser, pull out a pair of yellow plaid boxers, and step into them. Soon, he disappeared into the hall. Bethany was sore. Her body was limp and weak, and she was grateful for it since it meant she was too tired to think.

Killian reappeared, carrying two small bottles of Deer Park. He stood on the side of the bed, handing her one before gulping down some water from the other and setting it on his nightstand. He waited as Bethany sipped from her bottle, then reached out to take it and set it on the nightstand beside his.

She watched as he climbed back into bed beside her. Turning onto his side, he stretched his arm over her.

"You'll stay, won't you?" he asked.

"Yes, of course," Bethany replied.

She thought of her phone still in her car's center console. She knew Aaron was likely to have called, and she wished she could go retrieve her phone and call him back, but she didn't dare pull away from Killian in that moment.

Forty

Bethany woke early in Killian's arms. She could tell from his breathing that he was still asleep and tried to slip away, but his arms reflexively locked over her, tightening his embrace. She decided to wait for him to wake, but after another hour or so, he loosened his grip and rolled partway onto his back. Quietly, she rolled in the other direction, grabbed her nightshirt, and climbed out of his bed.

Stopping in her bedroom, she dressed in a hoodie and her blue pajama pants, then went to the living room to slip into her Keds. She grabbed her keys, and went downstairs and out to her car. Upon retrieving her cell phone, she saw that she had three missed calls from Aaron last night. Wincing, she dialed his number. He answered on the first ring.

"Hey. Are you alright?"

"Yeah. Sorry for calling so early."

"I'm glad you did. I was worried when you didn't answer last night."

"Sorry about that too. I accidentally left my phone in the car and went to bed early."

"Get a good night sleep?"

"Pretty good. You?"

"Not too bad," he said. "So...uh… Where exactly do you live anyway?"

"Kensington, just outside of Fishtown."

"Huh. Aunt Ruth mentioned… Well, she said you're living with a guy?"

"Yeah," Bethany said. "He's a friend and an excellent roommate, but… Well, I've been thinking it might be time for me to have a place of my own."

"Glad to hear it," Aaron said. "I don't want to push, but… well… I like you, Bethany Schechter. Can't say I'm wild about the idea of you having a male roommate."

"Understandable," she said. "It won't be for too much longer."

"Well, alright," he said, sounding pleased. "Hey, so… no pressure, but I'd like to see you again soon. Would tonight be too soon?"

"I have my scene tomorrow, so I'll be studying my lines tonight. How about tomorrow?"

"Ugh. I have my last midterm on Tuesday. Molecular Epidemiology. But I'll be free after that."

"Okay. Tuesday night."

"Great! How about Chinese?" he asked. "Nothing fancy. I was thinking someplace in Chinatown maybe."

"I love Chinatown."

"I do too! Ever tried bubble tea?"

"Yeah," Bethany replied. "Bit too sweet for me."

"Okay, well… Maybe a noodle house."

"Perfect."

"Perfect," Aaron echoed. "I'll call you Tuesday afternoon, after the midterm, and we'll figure out where to meet."

"Sounds good. Talk to you then."

"Hey!"

"Yeah?"

"You think maybe I could get you to come over afterward and play some violin for me?"

"Yes."

"Yes?"

"Yes, of course."

"Wow. Well, that's great. I'll uh… I'll be looking forward to it."

"Alright. Tuesday."

"Tuesday."

Forty-One

Final

It was early, but the sun had risen enough that, upon waking, its golden white light blinded her, prompting her to squeeze her eyes shut again.

Killian…

He had tried again and again and again. First, he had come into her bedroom and asked if he could help run lines. When she declined, he had given her space until around dinnertime. Then, he asked if she'd like to order a pizza. When she said she wasn't hungry, he had again kept his distance. He'd left her alone through the night, and for over a week had managed to extract only basic polite conversation from her. Finally, one evening, he cornered her in the kitchen, nuzzling her face and petting her hair.

"Sit with me a while," he'd said, lacing his fingers with hers, gently tugging her toward the green recliner.

But she told him she was on her way out and already running late. He stepped aside, and she grabbed her violin and rushed out.

"Are you upset with me?" he had asked on three separate occasions.

"No, of course not," she'd replied each time.

And of course, she hadn't been. She had never been, could never be, upset with Killian. She loved him too much, almost worshiped him.

"Hey. Are you awake?"

"Mm-hm."

Bethany turned to see Aaron's golden brown eyes staring back at her from his side of the bed. He was naked beneath the white sheet and pale blue comforter, the small patch of brown hair on his chest shining in the streak of light from the window.

"Good morning," he said softly.

"Morning, ziskayt."

"Mmm... I really do like seeing you first thing. I wish you'd stay more often."

"I'm practically living here as it stands."

Bethany had been staying over Aaron's apartment several nights per week.

"Now, there's an idea," he said, smiling.

"I'll live with you eventually."

"You will?"

"Of course. If you ask me," she said. "Only let's not rush it."

Aaron nodded, smiling again. He reached over and kissed her forehead.

"So, when do I get to see your place?"

"Soon."

"Yeah?"

"Yeah. Soon."

"Alright," he said. "I better get in the shower. Can I see you tonight?"

"I'm performing."

"I wish you'd let me come listen."

"Soon," she said again. "I'm only starting to get comfortable playing out."

"Aunt Ruth says she's seen you perform many times."

"Yeah," Bethany smiled, thinking of Ruth sitting in the first row beside Bubbie at her recitals; both ladies in their fesht dresses, looking on proudly. "Ruth is definitely one of my most devoted fans," she said. "This is different though. I'm still new to jazz. I'm barely able to overcome my jitters just jamming with these guys."

"Alright," he said. "You'll let me know when you're ready."

Again, he kissed her forehead and got up to head to the shower. Bethany reached for her phone on the nightstand and saw she had a missed call from Klaus only about 20 minutes ago. She dialed his number.

"Hey, warm honey. It's early."

"You called me first."

"Wanted to make sure you'll be there tonight. Bishop's been asking."

Bethany swallowed.

"You're coming, right?" he asked.

"Of course."

"Great. Can you come jam at Presser this morning? Cam and I have a class, but we should be free by 10:30."

"Sure. Sounds good."

"Great! See ya soon."

It was a bit past 10:30. Bethany sat waiting on the floor outside the practice rooms.

"Bethany Schechter," she heard an unusually deep voice call out.

She turned to see Bishop strolling toward her. He was dressed in jeans and a green hoodie, his tight curls glowing even more yellow beneath the florescent hallway lights. She still hadn't quite grown accustomed to his strange appearance.

"Oh, hi."

"Whatchu doin' right now?"

"Just waiting for the guys to show up."

"C'mon back with me," he said, walking past her.

She thought to object and stood, lifting her violin and her black pea coat from the floor, nervously trying to think up an excuse. Once he reached the room at the end of the hall, he turned back around.

"C'mon," he called back.

"Um... Well, it's just that I told Klaus I'd be here."

Bishop walked back to her and placed a giant hand gently across her back, his touch bringing light prickles to the back of her neck.

"He'll hear us when he comes in," he said. "C'mon."

Bethany walked down the hall, Bishop dropping back a step to follow behind. She entered the classroom and turned to watch Bishop close the door behind him. She braced for his next move, but he remained standing in front of the door, his oddly pale eyes staring at her.

"Well?" he said.

Bethany only stared back.

"Get out'cha fiddle."

"Oh," she said. "Could I um... Would you mind if I just listen a while?"

She watched as Bishop's plump lips curled upward. He walked over and sat at the piano, playing a few scales, then patted the piano bench, gesturing for Bethany to come sit beside him. For a moment, she froze.

"Ain't gon' bite'chu."

Setting her coat and violin down, Bethany inched over to the bench and perched beside him. It was a full-sized bench, but his giant frame left little space for her. Sitting next to Bishop, Bethany felt tiny and fragile. As he began playing, his arm continuously brushed against hers. The friction caused by the sleeve of his green hoodie rubbing against her button-down blue and white flannel shirt started the prickly tingles climbing up her spine. She didn't recognize the slow-paced melody he played, but listened in awe, watching his enormous hands; the left thundering, the right fluttering.

Once he finished the dreamy sounding tune, he turned toward her. She watched his pale eyes drop over her chest, then move up to her neck, and finally stop to stare at her lips. His own thick pillowy lips pressed together a moment. Bethany felt her mouth run dry as a sudden heat expanded from her core, causing her cheeks to flush.

A knock at the door startled her. The door swung open as the two of them turned to face it.

"I knew it had to be you," Klaus said, sounding short of breath.

His hair was messier than usual. His black hoodie was open over a white t-shirt and falling off of one shoulder. He entered the room running his hand through his hair.

"That percussive attack with the airy pentatonic scales…" Klaus continued. "Sounds beautiful, man."

"Thanks, man," Bishop said.

"Sorry I'm late," Klaus said, turning to Bethany.

"She didn't miss you none," Bishop said.

"Good," Klaus said. "Well uh… You mind letting her go? Gotta practice room down the hall."

"She ain't tethered."

"I need coffee!" Bethany said, standing and grabbing her coat and violin.

"Great, I'll walk you," Klaus said, opening the door for her.

"Tonight," Bishop called after her.

"Yes, of course," Bethany said, turning back to smile at him. "Tonight."

Bethany turned and rushed down the hall toward the front door.

"Hey!" Klaus said, hurrying along behind her. "Where are we going? You don't drink coffee."

She kept moving until finally reaching the front door. A fresh, cold breeze hit her face as she pushed it open. Once outside, she stood still, dropping her head back, breathing in deeply.

"Hey," he said again. "Y'alright?"

"Mm-hm," she said, slipping into her coat. "Just needed some air."

"Mmmm…" Klaus said.

Feeling his eyes studying her, she began tugging her hair forward.

"You're not in love with him, are you?" he asked.

"What?" she asked, turning to face him. "Who?"

Klaus cocked his eyes and tipped his head to one side.

"No!" Bethany said. "No, I…"

She paused, still tugging at her hair.

"You what?"

"Well, I… I belong to someone now."

Klaus stared a moment. Then, his eyebrows shot up.

"Really?" he asked.

"Uh-huh."

"Is it serious?"

"Uh-huh."

Klaus's shoulders slumped forward as he sharply exhaled. His eyes raised up toward the sky, and a slow smile spread across his face.

Relief.

"That's wonderful, Bethany," he said.

It was the first time since the day she'd met him that he had addressed her with her proper name. Suddenly, he embraced her, pulling her close. It was the first time he'd ever made physical contact.

"I'm very happy for you," he said, kissing her cheek before releasing her. "So, who is he? When do we get to meet him? Bring him out tonight!"

"Oh, I don't know," Bethany said. "He's um... He's not a musician."

Klaus raised up his arms upward toward the sky, letting them drop back to his sides with a loud clap.

"Then he's perfect."

Forty-Two

Bethany, Cam, and Klaus had spent the rest of the morning jamming. They'd gone to lunch, splitting a pizza at Cartucci's on Liacourus Walk, then returned to Presser, where Lonnie and Drew had joined them. They moved into the room at the end of the hall and continued jamming late into the afternoon. When her fingertips had grown sore and her body tired, she excused herself, promising to meet them at Ortlieb's by 7 PM.

As Bethany headed to the parking lot, she heard a voice call out.

"Bethany Schechter!"

Bethany turned to see Quentin limping past Tomlinson. Taking a deep breath, she waited for him to catch up to her, noticing his worn, brown leather jacket was at least one size too small.

"Hey! I knew that had to be you. For a second, I thought I was seeing things. I tried calling."

Bethany had seen the missed calls, but hadn't been able to think of a reason to return them.

"Hey, Quentin. Sorry. Been busy."

"No worries. What uh… What are you doing here?"

"Just using the practice rooms at Presser," she said with a shrug. "My student ID is still good."

"Sure, yeah..." he said. "Hey, get what you can… all the money they charge. I uh… Well, I wish you had talked to me."

The corners of Quentin's mouthed pulled downward. He winced a bit as he met her eyes, then quickly glanced away.

Regret.

"That is," he continued, looking back at her, "I wish the whole crazy thing had never happened at all. I realize now how stressful it must've been for you. I just wish I could've helped. I'm sorry I didn't."

"You were plenty helpful."

"No. No, I wasn't," he said sharply, running his fingers through his sand-colored curly hair. "If I had been, I wouldn't have lost one of our most talented students," he said sadly. "I thought there could be an open, honest conversation, but somehow, I only managed to piss off the entire department. I just... I don't know, I wanted to make everyone feel safe, but I should have protected you first. The crazy part is, I thought it had been resolved, but—"

"I didn't drop out because of anything you did or didn't do, Quentin."

For a moment, Quentin looked like he was going to argue, but then he simply sighed, looking downward, shaking his head. He looked back up to meet her eyes.

"Any chance you'll reconsider? Start over next semester?"

"No," Bethany said. "Things are different now."

"C'mon, you can always go back!" Quentin insisted.

"No," she repeated. "I got what I came for."

Quentin sighed again. "Well... You'll let me know if there's anything I can do for you."

"Of course," Bethany said. "Thank you, Quentin."

Again, he winced a bit as his eyes met hers.

"Really, Bethany," he said, raising his heavy brow. "Anything. You've got my number. I hope to hear from you."

He stood waiting for her to speak again. Bethany offered a gentle smile. Finally, he nodded, then leaned in and kissed her cheek, giving her arm a light squeeze before turning and limping away.

Bethany turned back toward the parking lot. As she walked, she heard the voices of two black guys approaching behind her.

"How many female vocalists does it take to sing *My Funny Valentine*?"

"How many?"

"Every last fuckin' one of 'em."

There was some laughter, then one of them called to her.

"Hey, violin. Bethany, right?"

Bethany turned to see the two guys carrying their cased instruments.

"Hey!" she said. "Saxophone and trumpet. Jamal, and… Eddie?"

"You got it," said Jamal. "Heard you're playing with Bishop and them at Ortlieb's tonight."

"Yeah. Gotta be there by seven."

"I was thinkin' I might sit in for a tune."

"Oh! Really? Oh, I'd love that," Bethany said, excited. "I've never played with a saxophone before."

"Really?" Jamal said, smiling brightly. "Well, I'd be honored to be your first."

She returned his smile. "See you at seven then?"

"Seven."

Bethany glanced over at Eddie.

"I can't make it tonight," Eddie said, "But I'd love to jam with you sometime. Bishop talks about you a lot."

"I'd like that. I'll be back here later in the week. Maybe Thursday around 10?"

"Thursday," he said with a nod.

She nodded back.

"See ya tonight," Jamal said.

267

"Tonight," she repeated.

As she turned, Bethany's mind flashed to a pair of pale eyes and thick, pillowy lips. She reached for her cell phone and dialed Aaron, immediately reaching his voicemail.

"Hey, ziskayt. I'm ready after all. If you want to come out and hear us, we'll be starting at 8. Might even be a saxophone sitting in. Ortleib's on North 3rd. Hope to see you."

She continued walking toward her car. It was a cool, but sunny day. She lifted her hand to shield her eyes as she noticed another person approaching in the parking lot. Shayla Colreavey.

Despite the chill in the air, Shayla wore only a light denim jacket open over a tight-fitting faded black t-shirt with her large belly poking out of the bottom. The shirt read: *Silence is Violence.* Her hair was still short, spikey, and now a bright shade of fuchsia.

"Hey, Bethany."

"Hey, Shayla."

Shayla had stopped walking, but Bethany wasn't able to think of a reason to linger behind.

Forty- Three

With a little time to kill, Bethany drove to Front Street in South Philly, parking near the South Street Pedestrian Bridge. She got out and walked, wandering across the bridge, enjoying the cold, crisp breeze and golden light of the setting sun. Soon enough, it would be winter.

As she looked upward to the three figures, she thought of Bubbie, of Ruth. She thought of Brooklyn, her home... of the photograph of her mother on her wedding day, a soulful smile on her face.

Rejoice and laugh in the face of fate. Simcha. Grateful for the struggle. Never the pursuit of happiness.

Forty-Four

Ortlieb's was a small building with a blue facade. There was a blue and white sign on the door:

Ortlieb's Jazzhaus
847 N Third
922-1035

The *J* in *Jazz* was represented with a drawing of a saxophone. Bethany felt tingles as she reached for the door. Inside, it was dimly lit with strings of white lights over one of the dark ceiling beams. The place was packed with small tables covered in gray tablecloths across from and stretched alongside the narrow, gray-carpeted stage with a black grand piano in front of a PA system with wires running to various microphones. Currently, there were four older black men on the stage: trumpet, saxophone, bass, and drums. Bethany recognized the intense Afro-Cuban rhythm and distinct Middle Eastern sound.

Caravan.

The energy from the music filled the house. The audience seemed relaxed but fully engaged. Some were smoking, drinking, a few with eyes closed, bobbing their heads along, and many watching the musicians intently. Everyone was listening.

Bethany had heard stories from out of Ortlieb's, and knew it was a highly respected local jazz club. As she glanced around the tightly packed room, her nerves intensified. It was quite a crowd for a Tuesday night; not at all what she'd expected. She could feel herself inching back toward the door when she felt a giant hand press against her back.

She turned to face Bishop who tipped his head, gesturing for her to follow him. She did, sitting with him at a two-top table, setting her violin down beside her chair and removing her black pea coat to drape over the back of it. As the tune came to a close, she noticed Drew and Jamal at a nearby table, and Klaus and Cam at another.

Klaus approached, bending toward her.

"Ya ready?"

"I don't know."

"You'll be great."

"What are we playing first?" Bethany asked.

"I'm not playing."

"What?!"

"There's only room for one violin tonight. That's you."

"Klaus, I—"

"You're great. You'll be great," he said with a grin.

Bethany stared back in silence.

"Come outside," Bishop said abruptly.

"What?"

"Cain't talk over the music," he said, tipping his head toward the men on stage who were about to start back up. "Need to go over the setlist."

Bethany nodded, as the men began playing. Quietly, she stood with Bishop. He gestured for her to walk ahead. She began moving toward the door, Bishop following close behind. At the door, his giant arm stretched past and pushed it open for her.

Outside, Bishop leaned against the building. Bethany leaned beside him while buttoning her blue and white flannel over her t-shirt, wishing she'd brought her coat out with her. From his back pocket, Bishop pulled out a folded piece of lined paper, opening it.

"Gon' give you a few options. Whatchu feelin'?" he asked, looking over his setlist. "*Someday My Price Will Come, My Favorite Things,* or *Black Narcissus?*"

"I love all three," she said, moving closer to look over the rest of Bishop's setlist.

Without warning, Bishop placed his giant hand over the side of her face, and leaned in. His plump lips were even softer than she'd imagined. As they gently enveloped her own lips, she lingered a moment, feeling a rush of prickly tingles. It was a sharp gust of wind that shocked her back to her senses, prompting her to abruptly pull back from him.

Bishop opened his mouth to speak, then closed it and once again leaned in to kiss her. Bethany turned her face away.

"My apologies," he said, straightening. "I misread."

"No, you didn't," Bethany admitted.

"I'm real sorry, Bethany."

"Don't be sorry."

"I shouldn't'a done that. Crossin' a line. I'm—"

"Shhh…" Bethany said, placing a hand on his arm. "Really, Bishop. It's fine. It's just that I… Well, I'm in a relationship."

"Damn," he said, his pale eyes widening. "My bad. I didn't know."

"You couldn't have."

"Did I just make shit weird for us?" he asked.

"Nope. No weirdness," she said. "Let's just… keep the magic in the music."

Bethany watched as the corners of Bishop's lips slowly curved upward.

"A true Klaus Aufderheid convert," he said.

Bethany shrugged her shoulders.

"Ah'ight. Respect," he said with a nod. He took a deep breath, glancing back at his setlist. "Let's go with *Black Narcissus*."

"Alright," Bethany said.

Bishop stared back, his eyes exploring her face.

"You gon' make love back as usual though, right?" he asked, the corners of his lips curving upward again.

Tugging her curls closer around her face, Bethany pressed her lips together, managing only a nod as she cast her eyes downward.

"Ya' man comin' tonight?"

"I think so, yeah."

"Good. Let's make him jealous," he said. "We'll make 'em all jealous.

Bethany finally lifted her eyes back to meet his.

Bishop lingered a moment, gazing down at Bethany. She offered a gentle smile which he returned before pulling the door open for her.

Forty-Five

As Bethany, Bishop, Cam, and Drew were setting up on stage, Aaron entered, looking handsome in his black pea coat. His eyes lit up as they landed on Bethany. He waved to her and she waved back, catching the attention of Klaus who stood and quickly approached Aaron at the door. They shook hands, and Aaron soon followed Klaus back to his table. Bishop sat quietly at the piano, his pale eyes closely examining Aaron.

"We'll open with *Cherokee*," he announced after a moment.

Bethany felt her heart begin to race. She had tried playing *Cherokee* with the guys a few times, but had never really managed to keep up. They liked to play it at blazing fast tempos, and the changes gave her anxiety. Fearfully, she glanced around the crowded club, wishing she could object, but she didn't dare argue with Bishop in that moment. Instead, she quietly tightened her bow.

With the sudden feeling she was being watched, she looked up to find Cam studying her face.

"*Cherokee*?" Cam asked, turning his attention to Bishop. "C'mon, man."

Bishop looked up at him, blinking. Cam made a face at him.

"She can hang, man," Bishop said.

Bethany cast her eyes downward, pulling out her rosin, and began rosining her bow.

"I'm not in the mood," Cam said flatly.

"Oh, you ain't in the mood? I'm sorry, honey. You got a headache tonight?" Bishop jeered.

"Let's open with *Autumn Leaves*," Cam suggested.

There was a long moment of silence as Bethany continued rosining her thoroughly rosined bow.

"*Autumn Leaves*," Bishop finally responded simply.

Breathing a sigh of relief, Bethany put her rosin away and smiled gratefully at Cam.

Cam gave her a simple nod.

Autumn Leaves was one of the first tunes Klaus and Cam had gotten her to study. Its common chord progressions and simple harmonic structure had felt accessible to her early on. The ii-V-I sequences in both major and minor made it perfect for learning jazz harmony. And it was still one of her favorite tunes to play.

Bishop counted off a relaxed tempo. Bethany took the melody. Then, without looking up, she took the first solo. Closing her eyes, she found herself focused on the blue melancholic beauty... a wistful sense of love, of loss. But soon, she found that natural flow into the transitional yellows carrying her onward to a gentle landing in the peaceful golden browns... a place of warmth, comfort, and soulful contemplation.

✷ ✷ ✷

They next played Chick Corea's *La Fiesta*. Klaus had said it was one of the sexiest tunes Bethany played, that it brought out her fiery side. It was also the tune he'd recommended for studying the Phrygian mode. Because of this, Bethany had learned to think of Phrygian as the exotic flamenco-sounding mode.

La Fiesta was a crowd pleaser. Drew played his congas, enhancing the Phrygian bright blues, dark reds, and hot pinks, Cam working with him to create a solid, energetic groove, contributing to the samba-like rhythmic feel. The quick-tempo'd sizzling excitement brought the audience to their feet with enthusiastic applause. It was the first time Bethany noticed Aaron since they'd begun. He was standing and clapping, beaming at her. She returned his radiant smile, then noticed Klaus smiling beside Aaron. He gave her a thumbs-up before sitting again.

"Hey!" Bishop called to her.

She turned back to him.

"Whatchu feelin'?"

Bethany shrugged. "*Black Narcissus?*"

"I'm thinkin' *After the Rain*. You know it?"

"Coltrane. Yeah."

He nodded, opening his fake book to the page and handing it to her.

Bethany quickly looked it over. She'd heard the tune a number of times, but had never played it. Still, it didn't look especially complicated, and she was now feeling more confident. She looked back up at Bishop and gave him a shrug. He nodded again.

"*After the Rain*," Bishop called out to Cam and Drew.

Drew pulled out his brushes.

"Jamal, where you at?" Bishop called into the crowd.

Bethany looked over to where Jamal had been sitting, and saw he was already on his way up to the stage with his sax. She again saw Aaron smiling and smiled back. He winked at her. Bethany turned to stare at Jamal with his big shiny gold tenor saxophone, feeling the excitement stirring deep inside her.

Finally.

Bishop counted off a slow tempo and began, Jamal coming in on the melody with Cam and Drew after a few intro measures. Bethany turned toward Jamal and stood perfectly still, struck by the sexy wail of his saxophone; some notes sounding dark, fuzzy, and mellow, others bright and focused. As he began his solo, Bethany tried to contribute a bit of texture, but realized she wasn't able to hear herself against the saxophone. It was the strangest sensation. She desperately wanted play along with Jamal, but she couldn't seem to follow her own sound against his.

Bethany dropped her arm and continued listening. Jamal's solo ranged from soft and fluttery to deep and resonant. She closed her eyes, wanting to shut out everything but the picture Jamal created against the backdrop of Drew's soft brushes and thundering mallets, Bishop's gentle framework of chords along with his light dusting of sweet harmonics, and Cam's delicate ethereal rumbling. In a moment of sheer awe, Bethany felt her throat tighten and her eyes burn as she wondered how on Earth she'd managed to find herself sharing a stage with these majestic artists.

As Jamal's solo drew to a close, Bethany again lifted her arm. When Jamal's dark eyes lifted to meet hers, she began—softly, subtly, wanting to blend with the serene, misty atmosphere that had been created. She closed her eyes, listening to Bishop's soft harmonic plashes against the muffled roar of Drew's mallets, and Cam's easy consistent bassline. She could feel herself swaying along as she slowly began to build.

Just before the bridge, Jamal wove into her solo with a soft, woolly bit of texture, catching Bethany off guard. She opened her eyes just as the light hit Jamal's saxophone, creating a blinding golden white flash. Quickly, she squeezed her eyes shut again.

As she reached the bridge, she again found herself working into the Phrygian mode. It was unexpected, and for a moment, she worried it was out of place. But it wasn't. It was just different. This wasn't the exotic Latin sound she'd learned to associate with Phrygian. This was something more familiar, something far more intimate. This was the darkest purple, the deepest red, the blackest amber. It was desperate pining and somber, cavernous brooding. In the surrounding blue, she could see the glow of tiny golden rings.

"I miss you," he'd said. "Can't we just go back?"

He'd entered without knocking and stood over her where she sat at her desk, unwilling to be brushed aside any longer. She stood to face him, but only stared back blankly, unsure of what to say. Awaiting response, he cocked his head, a few golden strands of hair falling forward over his face.

"Friends, okay?" he asked. "Friends."

She nodded. He smiled, then puckered his lips out at her. She leaned in to give them a peck kiss, but he grabbed hold of her, reaching up to the nape of her neck, pressing against her. He ground his lips into hers as he pushed her backward onto her bed. She tried pulling away, but he held to her tightly, running his hand up her thigh, clutching her hip. Finally, he lifted his face from hers.

"Bethany…" he moaned.

"Killian, stop!"

He eased his grip, pulling back to stare down at her, examining her face.

"Killian, stop?" he repeated.

She nodded. He took a deep breath.

"Alright," he said, sitting up beside her.

She sat up too, reaching out to touch his arm. His eyes remained fixed directly ahead, his body rigid.

"I guess there is no going back," he said quietly.

"I'm sorry," she said in a whisper. "I'm so sorry, Killian."

He shook his head. "Don't be sorry."

He stood up, and began walking out, pausing at her bedroom door and turning back to face her.

"I guess… I guess I should move out?" he asked.

The jolt of pain to her chest left her breathless. Fearing she might topple over, she curled her toes tightly inward, holding firmly to her feet. Barely keeping steady, she found herself unable to utter a single word. In response, she managed only a gentle smile.

"I'll be gone by the end of the week," he said hoarsely.

She'd stayed at Aaron's over the next few days. When she returned, Killian was gone. He'd left his copy of Wendell Berry's *The Unsettling of America* on her bed with a note on a folded piece of lined paper:

> *My ringer will be on just in case.*
> *-Pretty*

Through the storm and after the rain, there is a place of peace and renewal. As Bethany moved off the bridge, her solo breathed into something fresh and viridian. Bishop followed closely behind, his gentle chords again accompanied by a delicate pitter-patter of soft harmonies.

As Bethany closed her solo, she realized her cheeks were streaked with tears. Embarrassed, she dropped her arm and wiped her face. The guys started back on the melody. No one else was taking a solo. She began to slowly pack. She wanted to be respectful and inconspicuous, but also desperately needed fresh air.

She was off the stage and partway to the door before they'd reached the final note.

"Bethany!"

As she reached for the door, she turned to see Klaus standing, calling out to her.

Forty-Six

Bethany shivered as the shock of cold air hit her face. Tossing her head back, she breathed in deeply.

"Hey!" Klaus said, stepping out behind her.

"I'm sorry," she said. "I just needed some air. I'm sorry."

"Don't be sorry," he said, reaching out to touch her arm. "Get back in there. Finish the set."

"Nah," she said. "Enough for me tonight."

"Bethany," he said, turning her to face him. His blue eyes sparkled in the light of the street lamp as he held her gaze. "That was glorious."

She smiled.

"It was magic," he said. "I don't know what it is that makes you run away like you do, but I want you to know you made magic in there tonight."

"Thanks, Klaus. That means a lot coming from you."

"Bethany!" Aaron said, pushing out the door. His arms were outstretched, and she saw he was holding her pea coat. "You left this. Put it on. It's freezing."

"Thanks," she said, setting her violin down to slip into her coat.

"Well, uh… It was good to meet you, Aaron." Klaus said. "I'll let you take it from here."

"Thanks, man," Aaron said, turning to shake Klaus's hand. "Good to meet you."

"I'm sure we'll be seeing more of each other," Klaus said.

"Sure thing," Aaron said with a nod.

As Klaus stepped back into Ortlieb's, Bethany turned and began walking down the block, breathing in deeply again.

"My place?" Aaron asked, following close behind.

"I think I need to sleep in my own bed tonight, Aaron."

"Alright, well, let me come with you," he said. "I'll follow you."

"Not tonight, okay?"

He was quiet a moment. "I thought he moved out," he said, speeding up to match her pace.

"He did, Aaron. I told you he did."

"Alright. So, what? Someone else?"

Bethany stopped short, turning to face him. "There is no one else, Aaron."

"Well, then, what?" he asked. "Why is there so much pushing and pulling with you?"

"What are you talking about?"

"You... You're... I... I don't know, it's like, one moment, I think we've got this very real connection. You'll stay at my place for days. You'll let me hold you for hours, and I'll feel so close to you, I think I could—" he broke off, swallowing, then taking a deep breath. He gave his head a quick shake. "But then... Then, there's this. You pull away from me. I won't see you for a couple days. Sometimes, you don't even answer your phone."

Bethany felt a sudden chill and pulled her coat tighter around herself.

"I'm sorry," she said, making eye contact with Aaron. "I'm sorry for that, Aaron. I tend to keep the ringer off, but I... I'll be sure to keep it on from now on. Alright?"

"Alright."

"Good," she said, offering a smile. "It's really cold. I'm gonna head home. We'll talk tomorrow, okay?"

Aaron stared back a moment. Bethany raised her eyebrows and brightened her smile.

"Okay," he answered simply.

"Okay," she repeated, leaning in to kiss him. He pulled her in close, raising his hand to hold the nape of her neck. Without intending to, she pulled back abruptly.

"Cold," she said.

"Right."

"Tomorrow?"

"Alright. Tomorrow."

Offering another gentle smile, she nodded and turned back to hurry to her car parked another block down. She reached into her pocket, fishing for her keys when she realized where she was. It was Jared's block. She was just half a block from Jared's apartment. Looking up, she saw Jared's door was wide open. Continuing toward it, she then saw Jared, backing out of his door, dragging something large and heavy. It was the yellow floral print wingback chair from his living room.

"Jared!" she called out.

Jared dropped the chair on its side and looked out.

"Hey! It's me!" Bethany called.

"Holy shit! Bethany?"

"Yeah. Whatcha doin'?"

"Moving."

"What? Where?" she asked, moving up to stand in front of his front stoop.

"Hey!" he said, turning to embrace her. "It's so good to see you. I've been calling. You never answer your phone." He pulled her back from him, looking over her face. "What are you doing here now?"

"Playing at the club up the street," she said, holding up her violin.

"Wow! Cool," he said, running his hand through his hair, which Bethany noticed was now cut much shorter and no longer falling into his eyes.

"So... Why are you moving?" she asked. "The semester's not even through."

Jared smiled brightly, throwing his arms up and letting them drop to his sides with a clap.

"Dropped out."

"What?!"

"Hey... you did it first," he said with a shrug.

"But..."

"I got a part. Lead role on a sitcom out of New York. NBC." he said. "I didn't think I'd get it, but... Well, I got it, so... I'm taking it."

"Oh, my God, Jared, that's wonderful!" Bethany exclaimed. "What about Rachel?"

"She's coming with me," he said with a wide smile and another shrug. "Dropped out. She realized she never really wanted to be a teacher anyway. Said I'm the better bet," he said, beaming.

"Well, I would have to agree with her," Bethany said, beaming back. "That's excellent, Jared. I'm very happy for you."

"Yeah... Who knows? Maybe I can parlay this role into an off-Broadway gig somehow."

"Don't sell yourself short. If anyone from our class is Broadway-bound, it's you."

Jared frowned at that. "Well, shit... Bethany... Let me toss your name to casting, give 'em your headshot. Seriously, I've been trying to reach you. I'd be happy to—"

"No," she said. "No, thank you, Jared."

"But why? Why not?"

"I got what I wanted from acting, from theater. I'm on my own path now," she said with a shrug.

"Music?" he asked, gesturing toward her violin. "You know you can do both, right?"

"Sure…"

"So, what then?" he asked. "This guy—the med student?"

She shrugged again. "He's a good fit."

He paused at that and smiled. "Well… Best we can hope for," he said, holding his arms open. "Good for you."

Bethany embraced Jared again. He gave her a tight squeeze.

"You changed my life, Bethany. I'll never forget it. You hold onto my number, okay?"

"I will," she said.

"And answer your damned phone once in a while, will ya?"

"Promise," she said.

Forty-Seven

She'd planned to drive to Penn's Landing to clear her mind, but after running into Jared, she felt calm again. It was cold and dark. Time to go home.

As she pulled onto her street, she couldn't help but allow her eyes to drift over the empty parking spot on the side of the church. Feeling her throat begin to tighten, she pressed her lips together, inhaling deeply. After parking, she sat in her car, the engine still running. She closed her eyes, enjoying the warm blast of air from the heat vents. Quietly, she sang to herself.

> *Meydl, meydl, kh'vil bay dir fregn,*
> *Vos ken vaksn, vaksn on regn?*
> *Vos ken brenen un nit oyfhern?*
> *Vos ken benken, veynen on trern?*
>
> *Tumbala, Tumbala, Tumbalalaika*
> *Tumbala, Tumbala, Tumbalalaika*
> *Tumbalalaika, shpil balalaika*
> *Tumbalalaika, freylekh zol zayn*

As she opened her eyes, the light caught something in her rearview mirror—a car parked illegally, slightly jutting out into the crosswalk. A white Passat. She'd been followed.

Shutting off the engine, she grabbed her violin from the passenger seat, and stepped out. Keeping her eyes straight ahead, she walked to her front door, intentionally taking her time unlocking the door, even waiting a moment after unlocking the door. But finally, she went inside and up the stairs. She hung her coat in the closet and kicked off her New Balance sneakers.

Walking into the kitchen, she pulled open the freezer door, and pulled out the bottle of Three Olives. Taking a deep breath, she carried it to the sink, opened the bottle, and dumped the remaining vodka down the drain, then dropped the empty bottle into the recycling bin in the cabinet below.

She sat at the kitchen table and waited. She waited nearly ten minutes before walking to the living room window and peering down at the street. The Passat still sat on the corner. She walked back to her bedroom and stripped off her clothing, changing into an oversized blue t-shirt, then returned to the living room window. The Passat was gone. From the corner of her eye, she noticed some movement.

Aaron had parked in a spot closer up by her car and was walking toward her apartment. He paused a moment in the middle of the sidewalk, looking like he might turn back. But then he continued toward her door.

Bethany started down the stairs and stood waiting for him to knock. Several minutes passed. She knew he was just standing out there, but she didn't want to startle or embarrass him. Finally, he knocked. She gave it a full thirty seconds before opening the door.

"Let me explain," Aaron began immediately.

His eyebrows were drawn together, eyes wide. His shoulders were raised, hands held out defensibly in front of him.

Panic.

She moved aside to let him pass.

"Come in," she said.

"Look, I'm really sorry," he continued without moving. "I swear, this isn't something I'd ordinarily do."

"Come in," she repeated, peeking back around the door.

Aaron stood, staring back, his eyes still full of anxiety.

"It's cold, Aaron. Please come inside."

"Sorry."

He followed her inside. She reached past him to close and lock the door, then began back up the stairs, Aaron following slowly behind. She reached the top of the stairs and turned, waiting for him.

"This is how you answer the door?" he asked, gesturing toward her bare legs.

"I saw it was you from my window."

"Oh," he said, reaching the top of the stairs.

His eyes darted around the living room and kitchen.

"Bethany, I'm really sorry," he blurted again. "I know I seem like a total stalker right now, but—"

"Aaron, don't be silly."

"This really isn't something I wanted to do," he said, his words spilling out at a rapid pace. "I just... Well, I just never felt so certain and also so uncertain about anything before in my life."

"I understand."

"And I don't know what happened. I started driving home, but then I saw you with that guy, and I decided to wait and see what happened. I know I shouldn't have. But then... Well, I don't know, I guess I just needed to see for myself."

"Of course," she said.

"I'm not usually like this, Bethany. I'm actually very—"

"Shhh," Bethany said, placing her hand over his arm. "This is my fault, Aaron," she continued, reaching to take his coat. He allowed her to pull his arms from the sleeves, and she hung the coat in the closet beside her own. "I should have invited you over sooner. That was Jared you saw... just a friend from school. I wasn't expecting to see him."

"I... I'm..." he paused, searching her eyes. "You forgive me?"

"If you forgive me," she said, leaning in to kiss him.

He kissed her back, lightly at first, then lifting his hand to pull her closer. She placed a hand gently on his face before pulling back. He released a heavy sigh, his inner eyebrows lifting. Bethany smiled at him, taking his hand.

"Come to bed?"

* * *

Bethany lay breathless, her cheek pressed to Aaron's chest as he stroked her hair. He kissed the top of her head, wrapping his arm tighter around her.

"I love you, Bethany Schechter."

She tilted her head up to face him, smiling.

"Well I love you, Aaron Blumberg."

"You do?"

"Uh-huh."

She kept her eyes on him, watching as his face began to change. His jaw tightened, his eyes began darting around, and she noticed him swallow hard. She lifted herself up, bringing her face close to his.

"What is it?" she asked.

"What?" he asked.

"You look nervous. What is it?"

"No, I'm fine," he said, smiling weakly.

"Okay," she said, kissing him and resting her head back on his chest.

Quietly, she waited. By the time he finally spoke again, she had begun drifting off.

"Bethany, I... I'd like you to move in with me," he said.

"Okay."

"Okay?" he asked. "You will?"

"Of course," she said.

Aaron gave her a squeeze. "When?"

"Well, it's awfully late," she said. "How about we wait until morning?"

"Tomorrow?" he asked sitting upright. She sat upright beside him. "You'll really move in with me tomorrow? Just like that?"

"Just like that," she said.

He grabbed her, and held her tightly to him, again resting back on her pillow. As she began to fall asleep, she felt him breathe out a heavy sigh. He gave her another tight squeeze and again kissed the top of her head.

Forty-Eight

It was the first day of Aaron's winter break. Tomorrow, they'd drive home to visit Bubbie and Ruth, and the rest of Aaron's family. But today, they slept in, then remained in bed to complete the *New York Time's* Sunday crossword puzzle together, which Aaron's mother went to the trouble of mailing to him every week. He'd explained to her that the *New York Times* was available in newsstands and retail outlets nationwide, and that it could even be accessed online, but she'd continued mailing the puzzles anyway.

"Can I take you to breakfast?" he asked.

"It's nearly time for lunch."

"Alright, lunch then," he said.

"Sure. Let me have the first shower so I can dry my hair while you're in there," she said, sitting up.

Aaron pulled her back down and lightly kissed her lips before letting her go.

After her shower, Bethany weighed herself.

One hundred and thirty-eight.

Good, good. Stay mindful. Stay trim.

She dressed in jeans and a white sweater, dried her hair, and waited in the living room for Aaron to emerge from the bedroom. He also wore jeans and a white sweater. Together, they bundled in their coats and scarves, then walked out to his car and sat shivering, waiting for it to warm up.

"Essene?" he asked.

"Perfect," she said.

The two of them sat in the cafe, finishing their egg scrambles and roasted potatoes.

293

"I started reading that book of yours," he said.

"Which book?" she asked.

"The one about agriculture and what's become of the farming business," he said.

"Ah."

"Have you read it?" he asked.

"Some of it."

"Really makes ya think," he said. "I mean, I know I'll never be a farmer or anything, but a lot of what he says made me think about my own life. It's a reminder to make solid choices, to live with intention."

Bethany nodded, pushing the remainder of her potatoes around with her fork.

"I'm following my father's path, and I'm good with that. I think he made wise choices."

Again Bethany nodded.

"And I've decided I'm going to specialize in podiatry as well."

"Really?" Bethany asked, looking up at him. "Feet?"

"Healthy feet are important to the quality of life," he said. "I don't want to be in the business of preventing death. I think I'd rather just work to preserve what is good."

Bethany smiled at him, taking his hand across the table.

"That sounds wise."

"Yeah?"

"Yeah."

He lifted her hand to his face, and kissed it.

"Take a walk?" he asked.

"I can stand the cold if you can," she said.

"We'll drive to Front Street, walk along the river."

"Perfect."

* * *

Although the air was still frigid, the sun was beating down as they left Aaron's car and started across the South Street Pedestrian Bridge. Breathing in the fresh air, Bethany paused and squinted up at the Stickmen. She thought of Bubbie and Ruth, of home. She was looking forward to their visit. Bubbie would be so glad and so proud to see her with Aaron.

"Beshert."

When she brought her face back down, Aaron was kneeling before her, holding out a small box. Inside was a band of gold bearing a glittering trilliant cut diamond. As she gazed down at the ring, the sunlight reflected off it, the blinding golden white light prompting her to wince. She squeezed her eyes shut as a deep sadness washed over her. Blinking back the burning tears, she opened her eyes again to stare down at Aaron, his warm golden brown eyes staring back at her, full of hope.

"Bethany Schechter, will you marry me?" he asked, firmly taking hold of her hand.

Bethany smiled down at him.

"Of course."

If you enjoyed this book, please consider leaving a review to help other readers find it. Your support is greatly appreciated.